BBC

DOCTOR WHO

I AM THE MASTER

BBC

DOCTOR WHO

I AM THE
MASTER

LEGENDS OF THE RENEGADE TIME LORD

Peter Anghelides, Mark Wright, Jacqueline Rayner,
Mike Tucker, Beverly Sanford and Matthew Sweet

BBC
BOOKS

BBC Books, an imprint of Ebury Publishing
20 Vauxhall Bridge Road,
London SW1V 2SA

BBC Books is part of the Penguin Random House group of companies
whose addresses can be found at global.penguinrandomhouse.com

Penguin
Random House
UK

First published by BBC Books in 2020

www.penguin.co.uk

A CIP catalogue record for this book is available from the British Library

ISBN 9781785946318

Editorial Director: Albert DePetrillo
Project Editor: Steve Cole
Cover design: Lee Binding © Woodland Books Ltd, 2020
Production: Sian Pratley

Typeset in 13.7/17.3 pt Albertina MT Std
by Integra Software Services Pvt. Ltd, Pondicherry

Printed and bound in Great Britain by Clays Ltd, Elcograf S.p.A.

Penguin Random House is committed to a sustainable future for
our business, our readers and our planet. This book is made from
Forest Stewardship Council® certified paper.

Contents

Anger Management

PETER ANGHELIDES

The colour of captivity is grey.

This was evident to him after only his first week's imprisonment. The concrete wall of the cell. The metal in the bedframe. The dead fireplace full of cold ashes beside an empty bookcase. Clouds scudding across a sunless sky were the only things visible from the single window high in the plain wall.

Even his prison uniform. Black was his personal preference for a collarless jacket, not the hooped greys of this itchy sackcloth.

The Master knew he'd have plenty of time here to contemplate the wisdom of his scheme to outwit the Hyrrokin dimension.

He stopped pacing around the space after the first three months. Beyond five months he gave up removing the stupid prison cap, because wherever he put it, the thing still somehow ended up back on his head.

By the first year, he had stopped trying to decipher what the murmur of distant voices might be saying behind the thick cell door. Its flyblown metal surface revealed the steel in his eyes and the grey in his beard.

One day, he felt a pressure at the back of his head, like a headache starting to build. And then the prison cell was gone.

* * *

His eyes adjusted slowly to the dappled light in the study. Across the heavy carpet from him the Hyrrokin biomechanoid stood by a wing-backed chair near the bookcase. Crackling coals spat and sparked in the adjacent fireplace.

'Here we are again, Loge,' said the Master.

Loge flexed its long, curling fingers around a silver-grey control device. 'How long was that? It was two or three minutes for me, I wasn't really counting, so for you that would be—'

'Three years,' snapped the Master.

'The blink of an eye,' it told him. Its own eyelids nictitated in a reptilian manner as though to emphasise the point.

The biomechanoid was an incongruous presence. In the dark, it might just pass for a man. Uncloaked in the soft light of the college rooms, it looked like a snub-nosed lizard, two metres tall, its pale flesh encased in a glittering skin of dull metallic scales.

'Now that you've released me ...' began the Master.

Loge waggled a twisted finger at him. 'I didn't say you'd been released. We have things to discuss.'

The Master barked a laugh. 'I have nothing to say. And I certainly don't have to listen.'

'You really do.' Loge raised the device again. 'Because I can do this.'

* * *

He was back in the grey cell. The shelves were still empty, the fire remained unlit, the inaccessible high window showed clouds again.

The muffled voices from beyond the door became no clearer over the following weeks. A bowl of gruel, with its pewter spoon, remained by the bed, untouched, for nearly a month. No point trying to eat it – he was never going to starve.

A Time Lord experiences Slow Captivity just like anyone else. This Time Lord could spend time planning for his eventual release. There was nothing else to learn from the experience. No rehabilitation. Just the anticipation of locating those who had caught, sentenced and imprisoned him. Plenty of time to think about revenge: to plan and literally execute – and he wouldn't even have to travel back in time to see things through.

The headache returned at the start of the second month, until—

* * *

'So …' Loge cocked its head sideways in an unexpectedly human gesture of curiosity. 'Are you ready to cooperate?'

* * *

Narvi stormed off the pitch towards the dressing rooms. The studs on his boots echoed on the concrete surface of the players' tunnel.

His teammates trudged ahead of him, their hot breath misting in the cold evening air. He eased past them, as effortlessly as he had eased past the opposition defence to slot in the equaliser just before the break. The home crowd had howled their protests, appealing in vain for an offside decision. Denied that, they had resorted to abuse – particularly vocal abuse of Narvi.

Maybe the referee had blown for half-time a little early. Narvi didn't care. He could still hear the home crowd's disgusting terrace chants filtering through as he turned off into the away team's dressing room. He perched on the bench, took some deep breaths, and looked around the room.

Defenders Olson and Brown were helping themselves to water and fruit, unable to meet his eye as usual when the crowd turned against him. A couple of bad haircuts further down the bench, the physio was talking to Bartolli, the goalkeeper. The team mascot, a preposterously tall raccoon figure with an enormous head, stood stock still by the far wall, like a huge stuffed toy.

Narvi had expected the usual combative speech from the manager to the whole team from the moment they came in. Juan Martino had been missing from the touchline for the final five minutes of the first half; the players assumed he had stalked off to prepare for the traditional torrent of curses, reproach and derision that their burly manager considered to be motivational.

But Juan Martino appeared unusually calm. The fat boss was sucking on an even fatter cigar as he talked to the referee, who had followed the team into the room. Above the hubbub, Narvi could just hear their conversation.

'If there is further violence or racist chanting on the terraces,' the ref was saying, 'I am minded to abandon the match.'

Martino guffawed a cloud of smoke. 'In a semi-final? That's hardly likely to happen, is it?' He looked around him as though soliciting a similarly incredulous response from everyone else. His gaze settled on the giant raccoon, which stood there as impassive as ever.

Uncowed by the glowing cigar, the referee leaned forward to get Martino's attention and emphasise his point. 'With respect, it's *me* who decides what will happen.'

Martino leaned in too. 'Calling off the game? That's *not* going to happen.'

It seemed as though the referee was unwilling to back away from Martino's intense stare. Or couldn't.

'That's not. Going. To happen.' Martino's tone was calm but emphatic. 'Do you understand?'

The referee frowned. Blinked. 'That's ... not ... going to happen.'

Martino nodded, apparently satisfied. 'Good. That will be all.'

The referee turned away from Martino, expressionless, and left the room without another word.

'The smartest people can be the easiest to influence,' said Martino to himself as he looked at the mascot.

Narvi unlaced his muddy boots and stripped off his sweaty kit. He could grab a quick shower. Wash away some of the grime from the first half, and his frustration along with it.

The shower hissed deafeningly as he plunged his head under it. He switched the water from hot to stingingly cold for the last thirty seconds.

The place was unexpectedly quiet when he stepped from the shower. He towelled vigorously before he walked back into an empty dressing room.

Olson, Brown, Bartolli, Walton … gone. No physio, no kit boy, no coaching staff. There was only Martino on the far side of the room, in his heavy coat and distinctive trilby hat. Beside him, incongruously, was the preposterous and immobile raccoon.

Narvi looked wildly around, momentarily panicked that somehow, impossibly, he had lost track of time while showering and that the manager was about to give him a rollicking. Or worse, substitute him for the second half.

'Sorry, Boss, I …'

The manager quashed his protest with a gesture of one gloved hand. 'I like Boss,' he said. 'Though I prefer Master.'

Narvi laughed insolently. 'Nice one, Boss.' He reached for his fresh kit, but Martino stepped between him and the clothes rack.

The manager removed his trilby and pushed his face close to Narvi's, uncomfortably intimate. Narvi rolled his eyes. He was familiar with this 'hairdryer technique' when the boss would bellow a demeaning stream of furious invective and inventively profane abuse directly into a player's face. He used to just let it wash over him, harsh words and flecks of spittle alike.

But this time, Martino spoke softly, seductively. 'Listen to me. I am the Master.' His eyes were much darker than Narvi remembered. 'I am the Master, and you will obey me. You will do exactly as I say.'

The nervous discomfort that Narvi had felt seemed to melt away, like the dirt and disgust had in the shower.

'Now is the time for you to return from hiding, Narvi.' The dark eyes burned. 'Time for the Hyrrokin in you to arise. Do you understand?'

The room swam around Narvi, until there was only the sound of this velvet voice in his ears and the deep, deep pools of his Master's eyes.

For the first time in thirty years, Narvi understood.

The Master beckoned to the raccoon mascot. 'Hurry up. He's surfacing, and we need to get out of here immediately.'

Narvi was looking around himself, as though seeing his surroundings for the first time. He stretched his limbs as his Hyrrokin personality reasserted itself after so many hidden years. It was, the Master thought, like seeing a butterfly stretch its wings experimentally. Narvi was finally breaking free from his invisible chrysalis. He looked the same, but his true self was emerging.

The Master shrugged off his heavy coat and fat suit, then began to peel away the mask he wore to disguise himself as Juan Martino. In due course, the club staff would find the shrunken corpse of the real Martino stuffed in the bottom of a dirty kitbag.

'Hurry up!' he snapped at the raccoon.

The mascot pulled off its furry head to reveal the pale reptilian features of Loge. The bio-mechanoid pushed itself off the wall on the far side of the dressing room and lurched across to where the Master was examining the dazed Narvi. It pried into the abdomen of its furry costume and removed a Hyrrokin scanning device.

'The psychic power is insufficient,' Loge declared.

'What?' The Master snatched the device from the biomechanoid and glared at the readings until he had to admit he couldn't work out what they meant. He thrust it back into Loge's gnarled hands. 'That crowd should be at fever pitch – certainly enough to power our escape.'

'That is not the case,' said Loge. 'The psychic energy is insufficient to project Narvi into collection orbit. There is barely enough to transmit him beyond the confines of this construction.'

'This construction? Oh, the football stadium.' The Master shook his head and glowered at Narvi. He considered the lengths he had gone to in order to bring this about: identifying hooligan ringleaders among the home supporters, hypnotising them to fuel their paranoia about the players in the visiting side, providing their crews with crude weaponry, enabling them to smuggle it past security and into the stadium.

The febrile atmosphere of the semi-final should have tipped the crowd into a full-scale riot. With tens of thousands of football fans in a state of heightened emotion in this confined space, the biomechanoid's device would channel the swirling psychic energy to transmit the liberated Narvi to safety far away.

Instead, in the players' absence during the interval, the crowd seemed to be simmering down.

From the distance, the Master could hear that crowd starting to cheer anew as the two teams began to run out onto the pitch for the continuation of the game. Now, there was an idea.

'Very well.' The Master reattached the mask, and retrieved his overcoat and gloves. He nodded decisively at the biomechanoid. 'Loge, put on that ludicrous disguise again.'

He snatched Narvi's football jersey from its hook, reflecting not for the first time how the hoops reminded him of his prison uniform. He threw it at his star striker.

Narvi pulled it on, gradually coming to recognise who and where he really was.

'Now you, young man …' The Master tried snapping his fingers imperiously, but it was tricky in these gloves. He settled for narrowing his dark eyes at Narvi.

'Lace up those boots. You're going on for the second half.'

Whilst enduring a period of comfortable confinement on Earth, the Master had recently seen a whole season of *Match of the Day*. It had made a change from watching repeats of *Hector's House* or *The Clangers*, at any rate, and Jimmy Hill's earnestness amused him.

The rules of the game seemed simple enough. The Master had mostly been fascinated by the simple, often blatant dishonesties perpetrated by even the most talented players.

Just as well, as it now turned out.

From the moment Narvi ran back onto the pitch and fell over his own untied bootlaces, it was evident that the slow reasserting of his Hyrrokin personality was catastrophically overwriting his previous skills as an international footballer.

As Narvi dithered on the ball, Bartolli bellowed at him from the 18-yard box. Olson and Brown quickly chose to punt the ball to Walton rather than their star striker.

The coaching staff in the dugout with the Master clasped their heads in silent disbelief. Ramón the raccoon remained, of course, unusually subdued.

The away crowd, the Master was pleased to see, were getting restless as this semi-final slipped away. The home fans sensed an opportunity, and the atmosphere in the stadium began to energise.

Two flares went off on the opposite side of the stadium, not quite reaching the pitch. The Master smiled approvingly; he recognised them as incendiary devices that he had furnished for the hooligan crew. A plume of greasy smoke drifted over the stand. Riot police ran to position themselves along the opposite touchline.

This was it.

The Master called Narvi across to the dugout, cupped his hand over one ear, and gave him instructions. Narvi nodded and stumbled gracelessly back across the pitch.

The opposition keeper was teeing up a goal kick. Narvi took a lumbering run half the length of the field. The other players looked on in astonishment as he threw himself into a sliding tackle through the mud that took the goalie's legs from under him. Narvi scrambled to his feet, hurled the ball into the net with both hands, and bowed sarcastically to the incredulous spectators.

The referee's whistle shrieked, but was lost in the roar of the erupting crowd.

The keeper angrily remonstrated with Narvi, who promptly punched him smack on the jaw. The ref was brandishing a red card in Narvi's face even as the goalie hit the turf.

By now six more flares had gone off, and a pall of dirty brown gas rolled over the increasingly frightened supporters in the three stands. Linesmen were rushing the outraged players off the pitch as riot police raised their shields. Narvi turned and stumbled towards the Master.

Futile and increasingly desperate calls for calm on the stadium tannoy changed into instructions for safe evacuation of the stadium, and the panicked crowds began to pour over the barriers and scatter onto the pitch, many of them making for Narvi.

The Master seized Narvi's arm and steered him towards the raccoon mascot. 'Now, Loge!' he hissed.

Loge had the Hyrrokin device in its malformed hands. The equipment glowed with a fierce, unearthly brilliance. Loge stabbed at one of the controls.

A swirling torrent of psychic energy spun like woollen threads from every part of the stadium, coalescing, plaiting together to channel into Loge's device.

Right next to the biomechanoid, Narvi was enveloped in a vortex of energy. When it abruptly dissipated, he had vanished completely.

Seconds later, Juan Martino's bulky overcoat lay where it had been tossed into the dugout, a crumpled face mask on top of it. The scattered remains of the mascot costume were kicked aside as the first of the fleeing spectators ran by.

The Master and Loge had already traversed the players' tunnel on their way out of the stadium.

* * *

'So …" Loge cocked its head sideways in an unexpectedly human gesture of curiosity. 'Are you ready to cooperate?'

The Master took three steps forward across the study's plush carpet, ready to confront the biomechanoid where it stood beside the bookcase. Loge raised its thin arm and waggled the silver-grey sentencing device.

The Master folded his arms and glared at Loge. 'Where is my TARDIS?'

'Concealed from you.'

'I've served my sentence,' growled the Master. 'You should let me go. Return my TARDIS. You can return to your psychic dimension, and I promise you will never see me there again.'

Loge's cold reptilian eyes stared at him. 'Where's the fairness in that?'

'I've had a sufficient taste of your justice.'

'Did you enjoy the setting?' Loge skirted the fireplace and settled clumsily into the wing-backed armchair. It pressed its body back against the antimacassar and studied the Master thoughtfully. 'I used the characteristics of a twentieth-century Earth prison to define your confinement. You're fond of this world, aren't you?'

'Fond?' The Master snorted a short laugh. 'I hold the primitives on this planet in the contempt they so richly deserve.'

'Familiar, then,' suggested Loge. 'You have spent a great deal of time here, and in this century. You know how humans behave and how to control them. That's why you are so useful to me now.'

The Master could feel his temper building once more. He couldn't afford to let it show. 'I've served my sentence,' he repeated coldly.

'You haven't given penance.' Loge's tone was admonishing. 'Think of it as restorative justice. I need your help. Sit down.'

The Master bristled.

Loge considered the sentencing device. 'Sit.'

The Master pulled a chair from the oak table beside them.

The biomechanoid gestured with its free hand, and the surface of the table shimmered and faded until the grain was replaced with a shivering picture.

Three furious reptilian faces scowled at the Master from within the image. 'Friends of yours?'

'Hardly. They are criminal fugitives, and I am a justice biomechanoid.' Loge stabilised the image and tapped each of the faces in turn. 'Narvi. Siarnaq. Karta. Three brutal warlords from Hyrrokin.'

The Master allowed himself a thin smile. 'My type of people.'

'If by that you mean they were caught,' said Loge, 'then yes. They were overthrown by their people. Unlike you, however, they escaped. Smuggled to safety from the Hyrrokin dimension by their supporters.'

'You're suggesting I should have tried harder?'

'I'm suggesting you assist me in recapturing them.'

The Master leaned forward to stare at the angry faces on the table between them. 'Where did they go?'

'Where do you think?' asked Loge. 'Here, to Earth. One of their supporters transferred their minds to three children in an Earth orphanage, hidden from reach of the Hyrrokin psyche. Far from home, awaiting a time when their supporters would take power again and rescue them. Now that I have discovered this, I am tasked with recapturing them so that they can face justice in the Hyrrokin dimension.'

The Master chuckled to himself and settled back in his chair. 'Tell me, Loge. Have you ever felt you were burning down a house to boil an egg?'

Loge's reptilian eyes flashed with indignation. 'A separate dimension. A different physical form. They did what they could in the little time they had.'

The Master felt himself relaxing now in the face of Loge's apparent discomfort. 'Just collect them, then. How difficult can it be to find three children?'

'They are no longer children. The rescue was long delayed.'

'Ah, well. Punctuality is the virtue of the bored.' The Master leaned forward and stared closely at Loge. 'You know me, Loge. And you will listen to me. Listen. To me.' His eyes locked with Loge's eyes, unintimidated, fierce and demanding. 'I am the Master, and you—'

'I'm a biomechanoid.' Loge's eyes blinked once in their side-to-side fashion. 'You're wasting your time.'

The Master snarled and slumped back into his chair.

'But hold that thought.' Loge tapped the screen, and the images morphed into human faces. 'Three decades have passed since the warlords arrived on this planet.'

'Come on,' said the Master in a weary tone. 'You have wasted plenty of time already. You've certainly wasted enough of mine. Return my TARDIS, and we can return your captives to Hyrrokin today.'

'The warlords' minds were hidden in the children, buried within their minds as they grew to adulthood.

They no longer know who they are, if they ever did.' Loge's reptilian face lifted to study the Master's, lit by the shimmering picture on the table. 'Your TARDIS cannot return them to Hyrrokin.'

'Why not?'

With an abrupt gesture, Loge scattered the image on the table top. It resettled to show a schematic of the solar system. The point of view swooped and refocused to reveal a space craft, an oblate spheroid in close orbit above the North Pole of the Sun.

'I can get them to this staging post with a suitable sustained burst of psychic energy. And then from the staging post I can transfer them to face justice back in the Hyrrokin dimension. But only once we have forced their true selves to resurface.'

The Master looked up from the image. 'We?'

'You may be unable to hypnotise a biomechanoid,' said Loge, 'but you have a unique ability with humans. Release the warlords from their fugue state, and I can transfer them to the staging post.'

'I'm no policeman.' The Master pushed his chair back and stood. His fists clenched, crinkling the palms of his black leather gloves and stretching the material taut across the backs of his hands. 'Why should I help you?'

Loge swivelled slightly in the chair and raised the sentencing device. 'Well, for one thing, perhaps you will no longer have to experience—'

* * *

The indistinct murmur of distant voices. Rainclouds visible through a high window. The Master was in the concrete cell again.

* * *

The farewell tour for Alienated Youth was not going well. Just three gigs in, thought Tania Siarnaq, and already the trio's long-nurtured mutual hostility was unbearable.

If it wasn't Chanelle whining about the venue amenities it was Bronwen demanding add-ons to the green-room riders. Earlier, Chanelle had berated their manager, Sam Quill, about the absence of specific tour merch. 'Where's my figurine?' she had demanded. 'You promised we could have five-inch versions before the tour started. Where are they, Sam?'

'I'll see what I can arrange,' Sam replied wearily, before excusing himself to make a phone call.

Just a few minutes later, Bronwen was quibbling about being allowed to take lead vocal on their biggest hit. 'Just once, babe ... just once, y'know ... is that too much to ask? Hmm? Babe?'

'Well, since you ask, babe, it *is* too much to ask,' Tania had told her in a rare but rash statement of the bald facts: (a) Bronwen hadn't sung lead when Alienated Youth were still actually youths, because (b) Bronwen was tone deaf.

Perhaps Bronwen would stop crying and emerge from the toilet in time for the opening number. She could mime in the background as usual, if necessary.

This latest row in the green room couldn't have had worse timing. Chanelle had arrived late on her return flight in from her overseas weekend with Waldo – or was it Warren? – so they were going to be late on stage tonight. A capacity crowd of fans, their loyalty etched in fading band tattoos, bayed impatiently for them to go on. And because Sam (the cheapskate) had refused to book a support act, it wasn't as though they could stall for much longer.

The thing about a sell-out tour, thought Tania, is that you can't sell out on the public.

Sam sidled back into the green room and stood in the doorway that led to the stage. He'd told Tania he would be calling his wife, concocting another excuse why he wouldn't make it home this evening. He'd given up trying to do that from Tania's hotel room since that time she had burst in from the shower half-naked and been unable to stop laughing at his furious shushing and the scared look in his gorgeous blue eyes.

In the doorway now, Sam looked a lot more calm and collected than Tania had expected. His traditional look was shabby casual mixed with nervous energy, but tonight there was none of the characteristic twitch in his facial expressions. His dress sense was … what was the word she was struggling for … sombre? Perhaps things were more serious than she thought.

Tania waggled her eyebrows encouragingly at him, and winked extravagantly. But Sam was apparently engrossed in a fresh argument that had erupted across the green room.

Bronwen had stumbled out of the toilet, even more panda-eyed than her usual stage makeup. Chanelle was giving Bronwen's latest plaintive whining the complete brush-off and affecting to show more interest in a tray of vol-au-vents (vegan and gluten-free, natch). She was banging on yet again about her stupid figurines, in a declamatory tone that implied she was making a public announcement and with a rising note that suggested she was summoning hounds.

Tania clapped her hands over her ears and looked at Sam, her eyes appealing with him to do something, anything.

Sam stalked into the centre of the green room, his face impassive. He studied the squabbling women on the other side of the room. 'Oh, shut up, the pair of you,' he snapped.

Then he took a weapon out of his jacket pocket and fired it at them. The shocked women barely had time to scream before they simply vanished, as if vaporised.

Tania blinked with disbelief. Blinked again. She shrieked.

Sam turned on his heel. His finger was on his lips as he walked swiftly towards her.

'No,' babbled Tania. 'Please.' She backed away from him until she bumped against the wall. 'Sam, don't … please … I thought I knew you.'

He stood right in front of her now and smiled. 'You knew me in that hotel room.'

When she looked into his eyes, they weren't blue any more. They were dark and cold and dangerous.

He stood close. How could this be the man who had touched her so tenderly earlier in the day? He wasn't holding her now, but it still felt like she was choking. She managed to croak: 'Who are you?'

'You may call me the Master.'

The thumping reverberation of thousands of stamping feet made it feel like the whole building was in danger of shaking to pieces. Howls and jeers from an audience of thousands filled the arena, a raw cacophony from exasperated fans already overheating in their studded leather jackets.

The Alienated Youth crowd was taking no prisoners tonight, thought the Master. He peered through the stage wings, judging the moment. He certainly wasn't going out there in front of them himself – especially not in the guise of the band's famous manager. He'd stoked passions earlier by ensuring the performance was delayed almost beyond endurance by misleading Chanelle about the time of her return flight from a visit to her latest paramour Warren – or had he told her he was called Waldo when he'd disguised himself?

To exacerbate things, he'd ensured that the touts outside the venue had many tickets for the event at extortionate prices. Only when audience members entered the main auditorium would they discover they had paid way over the odds for duplicate seats. Already he had spotted scuffles in the stalls and the upper balcony.

Tania Siarnaq stood beside him in the wings. She was still assimilating her renascent Hyrrokin memories, and simultaneously overawed by the sheer noise and heat emanating from the huge audience in the arena.

The Master pushed the singer in the small of her back, his hand pressing into the bare patch of skin that formed an oval at the rear of her absurdly short stage dress. He pressed his mouth close to her ear: 'Go on,' he urged. 'The biomechanoid is waiting for you stage centre.'

Glittering in the pre-show half-light, Loge was hidden in plain sight, for all the world like one of the set props in the performance backdrop.

As she hesitated just off-stage, it was clear that the rock star was gone and only the warlord remained – coming to terms with her unexpected new surroundings.

'I can't sing now,' protested Siarnaq.

The Master clucked his tongue irritably. 'When did that ever stop you before?'

He shoved her a little less gently. Siarnaq teetered forward in her thick boots, stumbling a little as she breached the curtain.

A distant, blinding spotlight picked her out at the edge of the stage. At once a guttural roar of delight rose from the audience as they recognised that one of the band had appeared at last.

She wobbled awkwardly as she approached the central microphone stand, just in front of Loge.

The crowd settled down as Siarnaq took her position, just a few shouts and whistles as the tension mounted. The house lights went down, the stage lights bloomed, and the backing track for the opening song swelled through the speakers.

Siarnaq seized the microphone and began to sing.

The Master winced as she missed the first four notes. But she ploughed on, hunting desperately for the right key.

Sections of the crowd began to boo. The whistles got louder.

Siarnaq's song screeched to an abrupt halt.

The Master saw the audience surge from their seats, a tsunami ready to dash against the beach of the stage.

'I'm sorry,' Siarnaq said, just as he'd instructed her. 'Bronwen and Chanelle can't be bothered to come out. The concert's off...'

'Go on, go on,' urged the Master under his breath.

Siarnaq stared out into the auditorium. 'No refunds,' she muttered and dropped the mike.

The crowd exploded with rage and disbelief, surging from their seats. Fights broke out across the arena, creating a wave of angry leather that crested forward. Glasses and bottles rained down on the stage.

They barely noticed when one of the stage props animated and stepped forward next to Siarnaq. Spirals of psychic energy lifted and coalesced in the air around the arena, snaking their way forward above the furious fans and zooming down into the device that Loge held in front of itself.

Interesting, thought the Master. It was the darker emotions that generated the most power – outrage, resentment, acrimony, hatred … anger.

A hurricane whipped up in a frenzy around Tania Siarnaq. When it dissipated after a few seconds, she had gone.

Back in the green room, the Master could still hear the furious reaction in the main arena. It grew louder as the biomechanoid opened the door to come in from the stage.

'Siarnaq has transported to the solar platform,' said Loge. It watched the Master remove his disguise. 'You do a very good impersonation of Sam Quill.'

'Well, when it comes to disguises, I'm something of a connoisseur.' He peeled off his mask. 'You should see my Hughie Green.'

Loge cocked its head on one side curiously.

'Never mind,' said Master. 'Still, just one more warlord to find and transport, eh?'

'Then I can return them to Hyrrokin to face justice,' acknowledged Loge, 'and you will be free.'

The Master cast Quill's jacket aside. It dislodged a pair of doll-sized effigies balanced on an adjacent table. They were the two band members whom he had killed earlier with his tissue compression eliminator, and he considered them with a smile. 'Well, I did promise the girls I'd sort out those five-inch action figures.'

Loge stared at him impassively. 'Don't even think of using that weapon on me, or you will never see your TARDIS again.'

'You can trust me.' The Master threw his face mask into the waste bin. 'I have nothing to hide.'

* * *

Loge swivelled slightly in the chair and raised the sentencing device. 'Well, for one thing, you will never have to experience—'

* * *

The indistinct murmur of distant voices. Rainclouds visible through a high window. The Master was back in the concrete cell again.

The metal door was firmly closed. The bed looked as hard as he remembered it, the bowl of gruel as unappetising.

The coarse material of the drab uniform irritated his skin, the edge scraping on his neck. He reached up to scratch below his beard, and found his hand was compressed so firmly into a fist that he could not unclench it. He tried to open it with the finger of his other hand, only to discover that had also spasmed into a tight ball.

He slammed his fists in vain against the unyielding door, on the empty bookshelf, and finally shook them impotently at the distant skylight window.

The days dragged on. By the end of the first week, the fingers of each hand had still not opened. He felt a knot of pressure in his shoulders, a hard tension in his jaw, and the fury building in him.

The Master knew he could not control the bio-mechanoid. Nor was he able to destroy it – certainly not while he was in Slow Captivity, and not when this latest sentence ended either, since only Loge knew the location of his hidden TARDIS.

What he could do, however, was help Loge find and recover the warlords. But once they were released from their own decades-long captivity on Earth, the Master had no intention of allowing Loge to repatriate them. He would ally with the warlords to overcome their captor, then exact his price from them for doing so.

He honed his plan as the days continued to pass. And after a week, he no longer noticed how tightly clenched his fists still were.

Shortly into the second week of his captivity, a headache started to build—

* * *

'— this again,' said Loge.

The Master rode the sensory overload of the panelled study as it washed over him. He stared at the biomechanoid. Its tall, thin frame was still positioned incongruously in the wing-backed chair beside the bookcase, just as he remembered it.

Loge tapped the middle face in the image on the illuminated table. 'Narvi is a sportsman. Shall we start with him?'

* * *

'OK, last question,' said O'Mahoney. He settled his camelhair coat more firmly on his shoulders, ready to leave.

Phoebe Karta glared at her campaign manager. 'I'm sure we can fit in a few more questions. We're on a roll here.' She surveyed the assembled hacks with a look of withering contempt.

The journalists all began to shout their questions at her together. Did her party really support her repatriation policy? How could she dismiss her opposition's campaign funding when she wouldn't reveal her own tax arrangements? Was it true she'd not read her own manifesto? Why was she charging an entrance fee to attend her political rallies?

She picked out a woman in the second row. Phoebe could ridicule her hairstyle, her dress sense, her lisp – that always went down well with the base, and no one could accuse Phoebe of sexism, because she was a woman herself, wasn't she? Self-made. No, she didn't think she was pulling the ladder up after herself, actually.

O'Mahoney seemed about to interrupt her when he got a call. Phoebe paid him no notice as he spoke quietly into his phone and slipped from the room,

More time to get her message across to the peasants in the press. No matter what the question, she would launch into her regular stump speech: God gave us hands to offer folk a friendly wave, not a cash handout. All social spending is communism. There is one true religion, and all others are atheist. For a strong defence you must banish undesirable aliens.

Phoebe did her 'wealth means health' mantra, then reprised her famously cruel impersonation of a blind activist. That had gone down well last week, causing snowflake outrage across the country: 'He literally cannot see what the truth is!'

Halfway through the impression her unfocused, rolling eyes spotted someone entering the room.

It wasn't O'Mahoney again, but she recognised him anyway. So did the press. Their cameras and faces refocused on him. Microphones and note-pads pointed in his direction.

'Father Wallingford! Are you endorsing Phoebe Karta ... ?'

'Can you confirm your church is funding ... ?'

'What's your response to accusations by parents about ... ?

Wallingford turned on his familiar evasive southern charm. His grin threatened to split his fat, ruddy face in half. He chewed a nonchalant wad of gum as he spoke. 'There'll be plenty of time for that later, friends! But right now, my candidate has to get ready for her rally.' He waved off any further eager questions. 'Bless your hearts, all of you! You can finish your interviews after the speech. Off you go now ... the press pit is ready for you.'

Phoebe glowered at him, the old fraud. All the energy in the room had switched from her to him in an instant. The moment was lost. She grudgingly allowed the fake Father to usher her away from the press room.

The lounge area had comfortable seating, a range of snacks and drinks, and a make-up mirror.

Phoebe tugged her elbow from Father Wallingford's grasp. 'Why have you dragged me out? I was killing them back there.'

'Yes.' Wallingford pulled out a chair for her. 'I know how satisfying that can be.'

Phoebe sat down, removed her spectacles, and peered short-sightedly into the mirror. She began to comb her hair. Wallingford stood behind her, smoothing down his cassock, so she was able to fix his reflection with a baleful look. 'And ... you said *my* candidate?'

His stupid grin hadn't dissipated. 'It's what they want to hear, Phoebe, and you know it.'

'I didn't ask for your endorsement.'

'You didn't reject it, either. You're happy enough for me to drum up support.'

Phoebe snorted. 'Stirring up, more like.'

He offered a mock bow. 'I am your humble servant.'

'Humble!' Phoebe put down the brush and looked for her lipstick. 'Did you fly here in your private jet, Father?'

He turned away from her. 'Well, it was too far to travel by donkey.'

Phoebe couldn't find her lipstick on the wooden dresser. She looked around the room and couldn't find her human dresser, either. The room was so empty and quiet that she could hear the distant chants and cheers from the waiting convention crowd.

'Where is everyone?'

Wallingford seemed preoccupied with something at the back of the room. Some sort of mannequin sat propped in a straight-backed chair against the wall. 'I sent them all away.'

'I need my make-up girl.' Phoebe scrabbled among the scattered accoutrements on her dressing table. 'And I need my campaign manager. Where's O'Mahoney?'

'He isn't here,' replied Wallingford. He popped a *Get Karta* campaign baseball cap on top of the mannequin's head.

Phoebe spun around in her chair and fixed Wallingford with a gimlet eye. 'I need him. Now.'

'No you don't.' Wallingford walked over to her and swivelled her chair back so that she faced the mirror. 'He'll be taking a much smaller role in today's proceedings.'

Phoebe started to protest, but stopped when she noticed the mannequin was somehow struggling to its feet.

Phoebe scrabbled for her spectacles and tried to turn around again, but Father Wallingford was holding the chair immobile in his iron grip.

'Just finish your make-up.'

'Who are you to tell me what to do?' She pushed her designer glasses onto her nose. 'Who do you think you are?'

'I am many things,' said Father Wallingford. He wasn't smiling any more. 'You may call me the Master.'

Phoebe choked back a scared laugh. 'Oh, come on! Who's going to call you that?'

'Practically everyone, my dear.'

She saw the mannequin had walked across the room to stand next to Wallingford. Beneath the *Get Karta* hat, reptilian eyes blinked at her.

Phoebe stared wildly at Wallingford. The reflection of his dark eyes locked her gaze, and she found it impossible to look away.

Phoebe Karta recovered her Hyrrokin memories faster than her two counterparts, the Master noted. She was talking surreptitiously to Loge over there, by her make-up table, as the Master checked the corridor outside was clear into the auditorium. Perhaps this extraction was going be easier than the others, once he got her and Loge in front of the crowd. Still, she would be in for a shock when Loge revealed its true reasons for transporting her.

Loge has its own surprise coming, he thought.

Once he was back in the lounge area, he had Karta help him dress the biomechanoid in

O'Mahoney's camelhair coat – he'd made sure he took it from the campaign manager before killing him. Loge's curled fingers dangled from the ends of each sleeve. The Master adjusted the baseball cap in an attempt to better conceal the reptilian eyes.

Karta wasn't convinced. 'It looks ridiculous.'

'When it comes to disguises, he's a bit of a connoisseur,' stated Loge reassuringly. 'You should see his Hughie Green.'

'Your audience awaits.' The Master nodded towards the auditorium exit, where the campaign music had started to swell in anticipation. 'Time to whip them up into a frenzy with your rhetoric.'

Karta's nasal whine became even more pronounced. 'I'm not sure you can expect me to remember what her campaign messages are.'

'Oh, come now.' The Master already had his hand on the door handle. 'Climate change is a hoax, deport all foreigners, eat the poor – how difficult can it be? Just read it off the idiot boards.'

He was struck by a sudden new thought. 'Or better still …' The Master sprang forward and pushed his thumb across Karta's astonished mouth, smearing her lipstick into her cheek. He ruffled her carefully combed hair. 'Now, follow me.'

The fanfare that welcomed Karta as she strode to the podium alerted the enormous crowd to her arrival at the podium. The packed conference centre reverberated to their full-throated roars of delight. A repeated chant of 'Wealth is health! Wealth is health!' echoed to the rafters.

Another big cheer echoed throughout the venue as a camera picked out the platform party. The crowd watched on the massive arena display behind the stage, and clearly recognised Wallingford as he grabbed the microphone.

Instead of calming them so he could be heard better, the Master rode the energy of their shouts and whoops and chanting. 'I came here to introduce Phoebe Karta to you,' he bellowed into the microphone in Father Wallington's affected southern drawl. 'But she needs no introduction from me. You know her better than anyone. Certainly better than the press. They attack her for anything she says …'

Howls of agreement and anger from the crowd resounded about the place.

The Master beckoned for Karta to join him in the spotlight.

'But in her press conference just a moment ago, *this* was how they attacked her!'

The camera zoomed in abruptly on Karta's face to reveal her dishevelled hair and smudged make-up. There was astonished uproar across the venue.

'Well, those fake news hacks are here tonight, my friends!' The Master pointed to the press pit at the rear of the conference centre. 'And they're no friends of ours. You know what to do.'

The crowd rippled and reformed, surging backwards like an ebbing tide. The mass of maddened supporters spilled over into the press pit. Arc lights tumbled and sparked. The camera feed to the main display cut out abruptly.

'Now!' he urged Loge. 'Do it now!'

The Master leaned back, laughing at the chaos he had created. He ripped off Wallingford's mask and hurled it aside. Time to make his escape with Loge, once Karta's transfer was complete, and then recover his TARDIS.

He peered around to see where Loge was. It wouldn't do to lose him in this pandemonium.

Something was different this time. The bio-mechanoid was not standing away from Karta; it had moved in close to hold her left hand as the familiar eddying effect of the psychic transfer enveloped them.

In a second, the Master knew that Loge was going to abandon him. Dumping him here, without his TARDIS, without a chance for revenge.

The Master's roar of fury was lost in the chaos around them. Loge was moving away now, tugging Karta behind it.

The Master hitched up his cassock and took two great steps towards the pair. He clutched frantically at Karta's trailing right hand.

A surge of energy snatched at him, pressing down in a deluge of power like a sudden tropical rainstorm. And then he couldn't see the auditorium any longer.

The howling deluge snapped off around him almost as abruptly as it had started. The sporadic blinding brilliance of the stadium lights was replaced with an unwavering brightness. The Master let go of Karta and stumbled backward into a wall. This could only be the Hyrrokin solar platform; the stark décor and bare furnishing reminded the Master strangely of his previous cell.

Karta barely acknowledged her abrupt and instantaneous transfer across 150,000 kilometres of space as she turned to Loge. 'Where are the others?' There was a new commanding tone in her voice. Not the nasal whining of the aspiring politician she had been, but the calm confidence of someone familiar with command and authority.

Loge was busy shedding his disguise with some difficulty. It indicated a way through an arched exit from their arrival space. 'They are waiting for you in the preparation room.' Then it spotted the

Master on the other side of Karta and did an absurd reptilian double-take of disbelief.

It fumbled to escape the heavy camelhair coat. Trying to find the sentencing device, perhaps.

The Master patted at a pocket in his cassock to locate the tissue compression eliminator. He was ready to exact immediate vengeance on the biomechanoid; that would be very satisfying after what he had endured. And it would immediately establish him as the warlords' saviour when he revealed that Loge's true intentions were to return them to justice.

But Loge was too fast. Its arm flashed out and the long, misshapen fingers closed around the Master's wrist like steel, twisting hard. The Master cried out as he was forced to his knees.

'Never mind him,' Karta snapped at Loge. 'Bring him through to the others, and maybe he can make himself useful before we leave.'

Before the Master could interject, she strode from the chamber. Loge jerked the Master to his feet, and then trailed after Karta.

'You're letting your own prisoner treat you in that way?' the Master hissed.

Loge made no reply.

The Master stalked after them, already re-hearsing in his mind the honeyed words and flattery he would employ to persuade the warlords to work with him.

The next chamber of the vessel was a curved space lined with buzzing equipment. Blast windows between the banks of machinery were firmly sealed, to prevent the devastating effects of the heat and light from the immediately adjacent star from overwhelming the occupants. Half of the far wall was filled with a display screen that showed an image of the distant Earth.

From their absurd haircuts, the Master recognised two figures crouched over a panel of instrumentation. Narvi was no longer in his football kit, though his face was still streaked with mud from the pitch. Siarnaq had also changed from her ridiculous stage outfit and, like Narvi, now wore practical coveralls that could have been the innards of a spacesuit. At the other side of the room, Karta was changing into similar clothes.

The Master pointed an accusing finger at Loge. 'This cyborg cheated me. And it's going to cheat you, too.'

The three warlords turned to look at him.

'Loge isn't freeing you. It's a judgment biomechanoid, and it's going to send you back to face justice in the Hyrrokin dimension. If you value your freedom, force it to reveal where my own ship is, so that I can help you. You can stay in this dimension with no consequences.' He pointed one gloved hand emphatically at the display screen. 'With me at your service, I can give you the Earth for yourselves.'

Narvi approached him, and that familiar insolent grin was plastered across his face again. 'We have no need for your service. That's why we have Loge.'

'Who do you think brought us to your primitive planet in the first place, all those years ago?' Siarnaq smiled. 'And who was ready to help us return when the time was most propitious?'

The Master stared disbelievingly at the bio-mechanoid.

'That time is now,' said Loge.

'Then you have what you want,' blustered the Master. He swallowed down the anger rising inside him, trying to keep the edge of desperation from his voice. 'Let me have my TARDIS, and I can be on my way.'

'The smartest people can be the easiest to influence,' said Loge. 'If you thought about it hard enough, you'd have realised how I had concealed your craft from your own perception.'

Loge tilted its head sideways in a sharp movement, and it was as though a window opened in the Master's mind. 'The bookcase!' he said. 'Back in the college rooms. Back on Earth.'

'We have no use for Earth,' said Siarnaq. She had returned to her ministrations at the far instrument panel. 'You're welcome to it.'

'Or to what will be left of it,' chuckled Narvi.

The heat drained from the Master now, and he felt a cold dread. 'What do you mean?'

Karta had joined the other two at the control panel. 'Getting to this station from Earth needed a lot of psychic energy. Thousands of angry, excited, anxious people was sufficient for each of us.'

'But returning us from here back to Hyrrokin,' said Narvi. 'That will require substantially more. Billions of people, I would say.'

The Master tried to understand. 'The whole planet?'

'We'll use this vessel to trigger your Sun into a supernova. That's not the kind of thing the Earth people will overlook.' Narvi was still grinning. 'Loge will make it plain to them with a planetary broadcast as the reaction starts to build. The subsequent terror and despair of billions will fuel our escape, and we will be home before your Sun devours itself.'

'And puts the humans out of their misery,' added Karta.

The Master looked wildly around himself. It was a futile attempt to take in all the equipment that surrounded him and identify something, anything, that could help.

Loge's grip on his arm had relaxed. The Master felt again for the tissue compression eliminator. Could he kill all of them before they set off the chain reaction?

He pulled away from Loge, and wheeled back around to face the warlords. Despair and anger washed over him in an unstoppable torrent. 'What do you expect me to do?'

'You will die here,' Loge told him.

'You can't do this!' bellowed the Master, and his hand gripped the handle of the tissue compression eliminator in his pocket.

Loge squared up to him, blocking his view of the warlords at their work. 'Come now. You know I can imprison or release you as easily—'

* * *

Grey, grey, grey. The cell stared back at him again, giving him nothing. The empty bookshelf beside the dead fire. The cold bed. The bowl of gruel.

He held his anger to himself, brighter than anything in the room. And in the pocket of his prison uniform he held the scratched pewter spoon. He knew he could not let go of it, even if he wanted to.

And he didn't want to. He could stay like this forever, if necessary.

He hoped it wouldn't be forever.

The Master stood there, unmoving, clasping the spoon in an unrelenting grip for five days before he felt the headache start to return.

* * *

'— as doing this.' Loge still had the sentencing device held up in his hand, with one curved thumb poised over the switch where it had just been clicked on and off.

The Master yanked the tissue compression eliminator from his pocket. With a savage laugh, he activated it.

Loge shimmered and seemed to vanish. A five-inch-sized biomechanoid dropped motionless onto the floor.

The commotion had drawn the attention of the warlords. The Master twisted to bring them into focus, but Narvi slid across the shiny floor surface and took his legs from under him.

The tissue compression eliminator jolted from the Master's grip and bounced across the floor to Karta's feet. She raised her foot and brought it down in a crushing blow on the device, which fizzed and sparked and died.

Narvi was up on his feet again, and kicked savagely at the Master's midriff. The Master curled up his body protectively, only for Narvi to launch another vicious kick at his head. The warlord had none of the power or finesse of his former footballing skills, but the strike was sufficient to send the Master rolling in agony across the room. He crumpled to a halt against the far wall – dazed, confused, and filled with boiling anger.

He could just make out the warlords' words as they discussed the final stages of their settings at the controls.

'Countdown is primed,' said Siarnaq. 'We should move to the transmission booth before the supernova injection takes place.'

The three warlords walked calmly through the archway that led into the space where, earlier, the Master had arrived. Narvi waved his fingers at him as he left. A transparent door slid sideways from the wall, like a reptilian eyelid, and sealed the archway.

The Master rolled onto his back with a groan, his whole body aching, his mind raging. His head knocked against something on the floor.

The miniaturised biomechanoid. Compression meant that the organic elements could not survive at that scale, but its mechanical components would be perfectly miniaturised … and perhaps still functioning.

He reached out and seized it. Forced himself to his feet with a savage yell. Dragged himself across the room with stumbling steps, grasping at the instrumentation desks to support his weight.

In the largest panel he saw the junction box he needed. But was there any way he could transmit himself back to Earth with this equipment?

No, he realised. There was barely enough psychic energy to transmit him to … of course! *Just beyond the confines of this construction.*

He dared a glance over his shoulder. Through the transparent door, Siarnaq was squinting in his direction. She nudged Karta and pointed at the Master.

They moved towards the door.

The Master ripped off his leather gloves and plunged the shrunken biomechanoid into the junction box. Sparks of raw energy crackled around him as he threw back his head and unleashed a howl of hatred and resentment for the creatures who would have let him die.

The anger mixed with the coursing energy and it felt to him like the uncontrolled, unstoppable power of a regeneration: a boosted psychic wave of his raw emotion.

In the transmission chamber, the warlords never made it to the door controls. A coruscating whorl of light seized them, spun them around, and transported them away.

The Master tore his hands off the sparking panel, staggering backward, his hands red and raw and shaking. The power subsided around him, and the fizzing controls faded and shut down.

The psychic boost could only have been enough, he knew, to transport the three warlords a short distance – just outside the exterior of the Hyrrokin ship.

The warlords had reappeared in open space, where the fierce heat of the adjacent Sun must have incinerated them in an instant.

The Master chuckled weakly. It was only a pity that they would not have suffered. But at least he could still picture the panicked look on the warlords' faces, staring at him through the transparent door in horror and disbelief as it dawned on them what he had done.

He surveyed the flight controls on the adjacent control panels. They seemed to be conventional enough. And if they needed an emotional boost to control them, well then the savage pleasure of knowing he had bested the Hyrrokin was sufficient to urge him Earth-wards to recover his TARDIS.

This ship would not remain his prison for long.

The Dead Travel Fast

MARK WRIGHT

Bram Stoker's Journal

30 July 1890. Whitby.

I must begin with facts. Stark, bare facts, which in the cold light of day could be mistaken for the ravings of a madman. The observations in this journal are as firm a recollection of my hellish experience as my nerve is able to conjure forth. You may believe what follows to be the product of a fevered imagination, but I assure you, this is no work of lurid fiction.

I arrived in Whitby at the height of summer on the recommendation of my employer. Henry Irving may be known as the greatest actor-manager in the history of the dramatic form, but at a certain juncture in his distinguished career he claimed to have overseen a circus entertainment in the Yorkshire town. This came as no surprise. In the years I had served Irving as manager and secretary of the Lyceum Theatre,

I never ceased to be amazed by his many and varied achievements.

In the summer of 1890, I found my spirit diminished by the theatrical tour of Scotland I had overseen for Irving. Perhaps sensing a waning resolve, Irving suggested a restorative holiday on the Yorkshire coast, where my wife and son could perhaps join me in due course. I took leave of my employer with his blessing, and duly found myself at the Whitby boarding house of Mrs Emma Veazey, situated at 6 Royal Crescent.

Mrs Veazey kept good house; I was satisfied it would provide fine lodgings when Florrie and Noel arrived a week hence. For now, I was happy to settle into a quiet routine, along with my fellow guests. I found particular enjoyment in mealtime conversation with a party of three delightful ladies: Isabel and Marjorie Smith, and their friend, a Miss Stokes, from Hertfordshire. I hoped they would not find my occasional company obtrusive to their stay in Whitby.

31 July.

Following breakfast, I was happy to leave Mrs Veazey's while the landlady set to cleaning my room. Although exhausted from the intensity of my recent travels, I found much cheer in the view to be taken from the Royal Crescent. It was at once imposing and comforting; the picturesque town with its red slate rooves nestling between the churning grey swell of the North Sea and the imposing skeletal remains of Whitby Abbey. It was to this structure on the opposite clifftop that my eye was frequently drawn: a decaying relic of history, still clinging to the edge of civilisation. Below it nestled St Mary's church.

It was with lighter heart that I took daily to wandering in the town below. Perhaps the restorative powers of sea air had not been overstated as I had previously assumed. I found the bustle and activity of fishermen, townsfolk and holidaymakers of all walks to be a refreshing change.

Free of the burden of employment, if only for a brief time, my mind was able to consider other matters. Alongside my commitment to Irving, I had experienced some little success as a writer of fiction. The notion of a new undertaking was beginning to suggest itself, and I hoped to give it some stronger form during this time away from the stifling confines of the Lyceum.

I was resolved to climb the 199 stone steps to the Abbey and St Mary's, to further investigate this magnificent ruin. But, however much I wandered those narrow streets in my daily sojourn, I somehow never contrived to be at their base. Still, there was much time ahead for investigation, the shadow of the Abbey ever present, standing sentinel.

1 August. Evening.

We dined well this evening. Mrs Veazey provided a fine dinner of dressed Whitby crab, and there was much merriment between our little party billeted here on the Royal Crescent. I retired early, feeling as much at peace as I had in some months.

I slept fitfully. Whether some subconscious worry had taken root, or merely the heaviness of last night's dinner, I woke suddenly in chill darkness. Curtains billowed in a brisk sea breeze flowing through the open window. I rose to close it. I sensed rather than heard the roiling of the waves on the beach below: a primal force. The full moon was bright, but obscured by driving black clouds. Even in the patchwork darkness, the skeleton of the Abbey stood dark and looming across the harbour, its remains hewn from something even darker than the night.

Feeling as unsettled as the waves below, I knew I would not sleep again that night. I dressed quickly, and crept from the house. I risked the wrath of my landlady, but the night air was preferable to the tortured journey until dawn trapped in my room.

The night was cold as I stepped through the light and shadow of moon and cloud. Not a soul did I see as I descended from the Royal Crescent into the town. I half-expected to be accosted by an early rising fisherman. How to explain being abroad at such an ungodly hour?

A salt tang touched my nostrils, leading me on towards the beach, where I had walked every day since my arrival. What stark contrast to walk a beach at night, bereft of the holidaymakers, children and bathers. Now there was a just a dark expanse stretching ahead, the sand giving beneath my shoes, waves breaking to the right; how close, I could not tell.

High above me, an uncanny sound carried over the sea; faint but distinct, a hollow booming.

Without warning, waves crashed, close and loud. The air was suddenly charged. Lightning forked across the sky, highlighting boiling clouds in myriad colour; purple, emerald green, yellow. Rain fell in a deluge, harsh on my face, joining this unnatural convulsion of the elements. Lightning forked once more, the shadow of the Abbey stark against the magnesium flare, the sky now a burning flame of angry red.

In that preternatural light, waves rose up as mountains, responding to whatever force was abroad. There! A shadow rose from the waves, a black angel suspended over heaving water, arms spread wide. I almost cried out in terror, but reason stayed me. What I had taken for a spectral apparition was just a man at the mercy of the ocean.

'Help there!' I called out in desperation, alerting anybody passing to the unfolding disaster. If a schooner or other vessel was in trouble, more help would be needed.

I plunged headlong into the swell, ignoring the biting cold, desperate to reach this poor wretch. I feared I had lost them, until that dark shape burst forth from the black water, arms raised to the sky as if beseeching the gods to intervene.

I was not heavenly, but I would not see a man die tonight. Not again.

I surged forward, arms pounding through the icy water that threatened to pull me under. But I was strong and sure. A wall of saltwater slammed across my chest, but then I was with him.

'I have you!' I cried, pulling him to me, shocked at how slight his frame was beneath a heavy, sodden cloak. He weighed barely more than my own son. I turned for shore, the rush of the waves pushing us on. My feet touched sand, allowing me to haul this unfortunate from the ocean that had so nearly claimed him.

Clear of the waves, I sank to my knees, laying the man on the sand. I was relieved to see a heaved breath, and I leant forward to loosen his travel cloak at the neck. Pulling the hood down, I recoiled at the visage beneath.

The poor, poor wretch. What manner of accident had befallen him?

The flesh was blackened and burned; what remained was cracked, stretched thinly across a hairless death's head skull. Wide, staring eyes turned to me, fixing me in an unblinking gaze. I looked back, fascinated, unable to pull away as burned talon fingers reached out to my face.

The mouth barely moved, a stench of rotting meat passing over me as he tried to speak. 'My ... ship ...' he croaked.

'Ship?' I said. 'There are others out there?'

Bony fingers grabbed at me, clawing painfully into my chest. 'My ship ... You must retrieve ... my ship!'

'I will fetch the harbour master!' I said in desperation. 'We must launch the lifeboat!' I feared we would be too late to rescue any others, but I knew we must try!

'No!' snarled the man, before his voice was stolen by a choking fit. 'You will retrieve my ship … or I will be lost.'

Yellow eyes wet with rheum locked with mine. The world receded into those sickly pools; I turned and plunged back into the ocean.

A rabid determination took me. Blinded by salt spray, breath sucked from me, I surged forward. My arms flailed into cold nothingness, but I would not fail him. Time held no meaning in those moments. I must keep searching!

My hand struck hard, sharp wood. A box! Cargo from the wreck that was surely out there? I gained as much purchase as I could and pulled it back to shore. Despite protesting muscles, I found the box moved easily, floating on the surface as I reached the beach. I dragged the box the last few feet and collapsed onto the wet sand. The sky was now free of clouds, the tempest abating as quickly as it had erupted.

'Good …'

I started in fear. The cloaked wretch I had pulled from the ocean slumped next to the box, his gnarled fingers stroking at the edge of the wood. It was only then that I thought to examine the cargo more closely.

I was perplexed to see a tall, slender grandfather clock lying on the wet sand. At this juncture, I considered that my reason had left me, or what I had experienced was a fevered nightmare brought about by indigestion of a crab.

'Good,' the man said. 'Good ...' He appeared to take some comfort from this out-of-place timepiece.

Practical concern asserted itself, whatever the bizarre circumstance I now found myself in. 'We must rouse the doctor, you need medical attention.'

The cowled head jerked. I could not see the face beneath the dark shadow, but sensed his distress. 'No!' He collapsed across the clock, coughing and wheezing. I reached forward, but could barely bring myself to touch his invalid form, whether out of disgust or fear.

The fit passed. '... regeneration failed ...' gasped the man. '... Artron deficiency ...' The words held no meaning for me, his delirium brought about by trauma. I was known as a practical, capable man, but this was outside my experience. What was I to do?

The man appeared to sniff the air, probing, his head twitching in all directions as some animal searching for prey. He exhaled a crackling, consumptive breath. 'There ...'

He rose on unsteady feet, pulling the blackened cloak about his frail form. A shaking hand pointed up into the night. 'Yes.' The word was a hiss. 'There ...'

I followed the line of his gesture, high up above Whitby to the East Cliff. He pointed straight at the ruin of the Abbey.

The man stumbled back. Instinctively I stepped forward, halting his fall. I felt his fingers pinching into my flesh. He clung to me.

'You shall help me …' he said. The face turned up to me, but those hellish features were wreathed in dark shadow. 'And you will call me … Master.'

2 August. 4 a.m.

Forgive the pause in this narrative. As I commit these events to the pages of my journal, they become immutable, inevitable. Not some fiction, or entertainment for the stage, but wholly real. To record them requires a gathering of spirit, for record them I must or forever would they remain a knot in my fevered subconscious.

The remainder of that night passed in something of a haze, the memories fading into snatched moments of clarity, contrasting with what I can only call a loss of reason. How else to explain these acts I committed of which I am forever ashamed?

I was dimly aware of the approaching dawn at the edge of perception, a mere suggestion of light in the now clear sky. The moon still hung bright as I dragged the grandfather clock across the sand, not pausing to consider the incongruity of such an action, nor the lightness of the object with which I laboured.

'Hurry …' urged my master – for that is what I now knew him to be – a wraith presence steeped in shadow despite the moonlight.

I feared the scrape of wood on winding town lanes would rouse the houses rising up on either side, but by good fortune – if it can be described so – we came to the base of the Abbey steps with no encumbrance.

For a brief moment, I thought my cadaverous new acquaintance had deserted me, or been overcome by what ailed him.

'Climb, fool …' He coalesced from the shadows at the base of the steps. 'There is … little time … Climb!'

I did as I was bid, much as I would in the coming days. I still find myself at a loss to adequately explain why.

I remember every one of those 199 steps. The clock scraped across each of them in turn, adding uncanny rhythm to our ascent. If anybody glanced up from the town below, what manner of tableaux would they have witnessed; a macabre cortège passing above the sleeping town.

At intervals, my master collapsed in a heaving, rasping fit. The very air around him shimmered in amber hue, glistening with a sickly opacity that quickly flickered and died as a lamp extinguished.

'The degeneration increases …' he croaked through another coughing fit. 'Hurry …'

Despite a powerful frame, my exertions this night were taking their toll on my body, yet I toiled on, heaving the clock the final few steps. The decayed frame of the Abbey rose above in the darkness, towering over St Mary's churchyard, but I had no pause to gaze on them. My master lurched forward amongst the gravestones dotted around the churchyard; an angel of death among the dead. He stopped.

'Here …' he commanded. 'Bring me my ship.'

I did as he bid. I deposited the clock with a reverence I cannot explain on to the grass. He fell on it with something approaching hunger, scrabbling at the edges, searching. That ethereal glow suffused his form, causing him to scream out in agony.

'I am dying …' he whispered. '… must metabolise … you will bring me sustenance.'

I stood, mute, looking upon this pathetic wretch who yet commanded me.

'Go!' he wheezed.

I have few words to describe the disgust at the act I perpetrated in the shadows of the churchyard that night, scrabbling among the gravestones like some scavenging dog. My master had given few words, but I understood implicitly what he required. After some minutes, I sensed movement near the corner of the church itself, a small shadow scurrying from me in fear. I fell on it with a rabid determination, barely sensing the warmth of fur or protesting rodent shriek.

I truly cannot describe these moments in more detail; I fear the naked truth would prevent you from reading further.

I returned to where I had left my master. With mounting relief – and not a little fear – I saw the clock, and with it my master, had gone. In its place was a gravestone that I knew had not been there before. It listed at a frightening angle on the uneven ground and though pocked and marked with age, the face was curiously blank, nothing to mark the life that slept beneath. I extended a shaking hand to touch the stone. The stone itself vibrated with some uncanny energy, my fingers tingling at the touch.

I stepped around the gravestone, perplexed at the shaft of light falling in a square behind it. This was no trick of the moonlight that still shone brightly in the face of encroaching dawn. I knew not how, but it came from within the stone itself, pouring from some aperture.

Peering closer, the gravestone appeared to loom over me, blotting out the surrounding graveyard, church and the Abbey. I was engulfed in all-consuming blackness, the air fizzing and humming around me, that vibration threatening to blot out all sense of self.

My feet touched solid ground, disorientation abating as I was assaulted by a rank, charnel house stench. Gagging, I tried to blink and realised my eyes were closed.

'Welcome ... to my domain ...'

I stood in a darkened sanctum. The stone slabs beneath my feet were cracked and broken, walls crumbling and blackened as if in some great conflagration. A cloistered walkway encircled this chamber, ornate stone columns rising up at intervals, ending suddenly as if their ends were roughly hewn away. It reminded me of the ornate burial markers I had seen at Highgate Cemetery, the columns' curtailed summits marking a life cut short.

This place of ruin and decay was as rotted and broken as the creature that awaited my arrival. My master lay at the very heart of this place, his withered form slumped weakly across a raised central dais. Dials and switches adorned this rusted construct, like something from the works of Mr Verne. At its centre was a tall glass valve, its surface blackened and blistered, again suggesting the application of some great heat.

My master barely moved, inclining his head to me. 'Bring the creature to me,' he commanded in barely audible fashion.

At first I knew not what he meant, until I looked to my hands. Bile rose in my throat.

I was clutching a live rat, squirming and screeching in my grip.

My master reached out with an eagerness bordering on desperation. 'Bring it!'

In disgust I held out the creature, which was snatched from me. My revulsion urged me to turn away, but I could not.

The rat gnawed at grey, dead fingers but my master seemed not to notice, gibbering as he turned dials on the charred surface of the dais with his free hand. A low, angry hum, not unlike that heard at the electric light demonstrations I had witnessed, filled the chamber. My master's breath came quick and hoarse, as if the act of pulling air into his lungs was painful. The electrical hum grew in intensity, air growing hot with an ozone tang.

Dirty yellow light illuminated a tall alcove set near the base of one of the broken pillars. My master lurched across to this, placing the still writhing rat onto a shelf set into this space. Caught in the light, the verminous creature became paralysed, joints freezing. A second alcove set against the opposite pillar lit up. My master turned swiftly to this, but the action appeared to exhaust him, his body stumbling to the cracked floor.

Without clear thought, I ran to him, lifting a broken form that seemed to become lighter with each passing moment. Instinctively, I guided him into the second alcove. His eyes stared glassily into mine and I realised in that moment that he could not close them. Whatever horrific accident had befallen this poor wretch had left him with no eyelids with which to block out this world.

'The lever,' he whispered. I looked to the side of the alcove and saw a wood-handled copper lever. Without hesitation I gripped the handle and pulled. It resisted, the action of its movement rusted and aged, but by degree it shifted.

A red maelstrom engulfed the paralysed rat, the only mark it was alive a final, terrified squeal. The dials and valves across the dais glowed and chirped briefly and a moment later, the same whorling vortex suffused the body of my master. His skull-like face dropped forward, the body heaving and bucking before his breathing calmed.

The scarlet light of the maelstrom faded into the ether. He exhaled, a moment of ecstasy.

In the opposite alcove, the rat's now-desiccated form cracked and crumbled away to fine dust.

My master's head rose. He took another breath then stepped from the alcove with a strength I had not perceived within him before. Had that vermin life restored his spirit in some manner? Despite myself, I could not draw away when he stood close to me, a clawed hand gripping my shoulder.

'You have served me well this night,' he said. 'But the respite will be brief. My Artron reserves are depleted beyond this frail body's ability to regenerate. It is by cursed fortune that my TARDIS came to earth here. I will die if I do not receive further transfusions. Do you understand me, human?'

I swallowed, my mouth dry, searching for the words to resist, to deny this disgusting creature. But I could not.

'I understand, Master,' I replied.

'Good. You will bring more creatures for me to … feed upon.'

'Yes, Master.'

I turned from him and the foul apparatus that had restored him, knowing what I must do, however much it disgusted me.

'Wait.'

I stopped at the square of darkness I knew led back to the churchyard and turned to face that decayed visage. 'Master?'

'You humans put much value in names. Tell me, what name do you go by?'

'Stoker. Bram Stoker.'

The taut, burned features barely moved, but I could sense amusement playing across them. A gurgling emanated from the rictus mouth. He was laughing. What possible amusement could my name bring to him?

'Then go, Bram Stoker. Go and bring your master life!'

I stepped into darkness, leaving that hellish domain, that screeching and cackling echoing after me.

Same day. Later.

I can only hope that I will be judged by the actions that were yet to come, and not by the heinous and despicable sequence of events that unfolded in the immediate aftermath of that night.

I look on these shocking acts as if they were perpetrated by another. That is the best explanation I have for the loss of reason that overtook me and led me to walk under that engulfing shadow.

It was light when I returned to Mrs Veazey's. I suppose I had dallied further in the churchyard as the silver dawn picked out the edges of clouds, returning to my master with what vermin I chanced to catch in the shadows.

I let myself into the boarding house finding it quiet and still. I reached the confines of my room with blessed relief and immediately fell into a fitful sleep; my mind was terrified to slip into darkness for fear of what I may find there, my body exhausted beyond all measure pulling me there. Sounds came and went, the odours of breakfast twitching at my nostrils serving only to make my stomach churn with nausea.

I heard a gentle tap at the door. 'Mr Stoker?' enquired Mrs Veazey softly. 'You have missed breakfast!' I gave no reply, unwilling and unable to face any company. I drifted into exhausted oblivion.

What I dreamt, I cannot say, but dreamt I must have. I woke, clutching tightly at tangled bed sheets damp with cold perspiration. How long had I slept? Limbs heavy with fatigue, I stumbled to the window and peered out onto the Royal Crescent. It was still light, early evening perhaps.

The North Sea churned grey and fast, but the falling sun hung in a clear blue sky.

I exhaled. Perhaps it had been some terrible nightmare. My eye was then drawn to the cliff across Whitby Harbour, up and to the ruin of the Abbey and the church. Even at this distance, I could see the dotted smudges marking the grave-stones, and I knew then with all certainty that I had experienced no nightmare.

But I was free of that nightmare now, was I not?

I bathed, washing away all thoughts of grand-father clocks and gravestones with my ablutions. Suitably refreshed, I dressed and resolved to join my fellow guests for the dinner our landlady would no doubt be providing for us.

Descending, I heard the pleasing lilt of female conversation. Much cheered by this, I entered the dining room, announcing my presence.

'Good evening, ladies,' I said, finding Mrs and Miss Smith, and Miss Stokes already seated. Their conversation ceased as I sat at table. A look passed between Miss Smith and Miss Stokes.

'Mr Stoker,' said Mrs Smith. 'We were worried, you have spent all day in your room. Are you ill?'

I smiled. 'I am quite well, Mrs Smith, thank you.'

'You have a paleness, Mr Stoker,' ventured Miss Stokes. 'Are you sure you should not return to bed?'

'Forgive me,' I said. 'The exertions of my recent tour with Mr Irving have overtaken me. Nothing that some sleep and one of Mrs Veazey's fine dinners will not cure.'

The three women exchanged further looks, but conversation was halted by the arrival of Mrs Veazey, carrying a large platter. She stopped when she saw me, almost dropping the platter in shock.

'Mr Stoker!' she exclaimed, placing the platter heavily on the table. But she said nothing further. Visibly flustered at my appearance, Mrs Veazey backed out of her dining room.

I attempted to break the silence. Mrs Smith, her daughter and Miss Stokes stared when I rose and lifted the silver cover from the platter. 'Shall I carve?' I said lightly.

I took up the carving knife, preparing to sharpen, but stopped at the sight of the joint of fatty beef, blood oozing from its underdone carcass. My stomach churned, and I stifled a gagging cough.

'Forgive me,' I spluttered, and staggered from the dining room.

Same day. 9 p.m.

The next thing I remember was a face staring at me. I realised with some surprise it was my own, reflected in my bedroom mirror. My fingers touched at the dark smudges encircling my eyes. I had a full, round, bearded face, but the skin had become grey, the cheeks sunken and gaunt. No wonder the ladies had reacted to my appearance in such fashion.

What had become of me?

I stared back into the mirror. Darkness encroached from all sides, my features blurring, fading, coalescing, reforming into a decayed skull.

'Stoker,' my master's voice echoed. 'Come to me.'

3 August.

And so my ordeal continued.

I spent my days locked away in my room at the boarding house, hiding from the light, slipping in and out of oblivion. It mattered not; the nightmare remained whether I woke or slept.

The light seeping through the curtains gave way to the darkness, and with it would come the summons. Each day I hoped beyond measure that the compulsion would not return, but every night after the house fell silent, I found myself walking the narrow, empty Whitby streets.

Searching, hunting for more prey to bring to my master.

3 August. Later.

The burning ozone tang dissipated along with the electric hum. The red, whirling haze faded from my master's form and he stepped from the alcove. Even seconds later I could not recall what manner of animal I had brought to the gravestone, but with each transfusion of life force, my master was growing in strength.

He took in a breath, leaning momentarily against the dais of dials and switches. Wreathed in the darkness of his sanctum, he turned a face hidden in shadow to where I stood.

'Do I disgust you, Stoker?'

Such direct questioning took me by surprise.

'Answer me, fool.'

I did as I was commanded. 'I know what it is to ail, Master.'

He laughed mirthlessly. 'You? What do you know of weakness?'

'I was not always as physically able as I am today,' I said. 'My childhood years were lost to illness. I was not expected to recover.'

My master pulled his cloak about him, shuffling around the dais, glaring in my direction. 'You believe me to ail like some consumptive child? You believe a human can comprehend the trauma I have endured?'

'I would not presume to know what suffering has brought you to this, Master. I understand that we all walk a narrow path between life and death. My own wife and son were almost taken from me in recent memory.'

'The philosophy of humanity is a blight on this universe,' said my master, before he was consumed by a fit of coughing. He looked into the darkness above us. 'Is this why you like them so much, Doctor?' The last word was spat with such vehemence. His coughing became bitter laughter as he swept away from the dais to step close to me.

'I burn to stay alive, Stoker. Can you comprehend that? Even as I die, as my body rots and decays, I cling to the edge of existence, desperate for revenge on the one who did this to me. Do you understand that?'

My master gazed at me, unblinking eyes blazing an energy and hatred I had not witnessed within him before. The stench of his fetid breath reached my nostrils, but I no longer flinched. His fingers reached up to me.

'Do you know what it is to stare death in the face? I have, so many times.' The mouth moved imperceptibly. Was he smiling? 'Here.' The burned fingers of both hands caressed my face. 'Let me share that gift with you.'

I cried out, but there was no pain. The sanctum receded into nothing. I stood in a room, bright sunlight falling in narrow beams through a shuttered window. There was a calm here, a calm I had never experienced. A bed was placed against the wall, a figure laying prone beneath white sheets. I took cautious steps across a wooden floor, approaching the bed. I looked down at the sleeping form. Eyes opened, looking up at me from a pale, thin face. The chest rose in shallow breath. The eyes closed. A final exhale.

I knew in that moment I was looking upon myself.

I gasped, sharply intaking breath. My master whirled away from me, stalking to the dais and the alcoves beyond. 'Enough of these tricks.' He ran withered fingers down the casing of an alcove. 'I am dying, Stoker. This technology is flawed. As quickly as we distil the life energies of the carrion you bring, the acceleration of Artron decay increases with each transfusion.'

'What can I do, my master?'

He paused, considering, then crept forward. 'It is time.' He fixed me with those eyes that could not blink. 'If I am to sustain this body, you must bring me human life.'

The words penetrated my reason like an arrow through the heart. Human life … I shook my head, as if awaking. 'Master. I cannot.'

The Master stalked toward me angrily, breath cracking in his lungs. 'You will do as I command!'

'I tell you, I cannot!'

'You must obey.'

The Master reached out a grasping hand and I recoiled, falling to the floor, scrabbling away across the cracked stone. 'I will not commit murder!'

The Master descended on me like an angel of death, tattered cloak billowing about him. I hauled myself to my feet, and he crashed to the floor where I had been. Another coughing fit took him, and I saw how weakened his body truly was. He hacked and wheezed, reaching out a beseeching hand. 'Stoker, please … !'

I turned and fled towards the wall of black marking the portal into the sanctum, plunging headlong into the darkness beyond.

'Stoker!'

I did not stop to look back.

5 August.

I slept a full twenty-four hours following my terrified flight from the churchyard. I didn't stop for breath until I reached the Royal Crescent and the safety of Mrs Veazey's boarding house. At every turn I had feared the talon grip of those withered fingers grasping from the shadows to bring me back under the Master's compulsion.

However, of pursuit there was none; I made it safely through the streets and was in my room as the sun came up.

I awoke and to my intense surprise felt as refreshed as I had in many a day. A clear gaze looked back at me from my mirror and a certain colour had returned to my face.

Was I truly free of my abhorrent servitude? Had it, in fact, been merely a nightmare, a figment of a restless imagination?

Washing and dressing, I cautiously came down to breakfast, fearing how I would be received by my fellow guests following the embarrassment of the dinner episode. I need not have worried. All three seemed cheered by my presence, saying how much fitter I seemed. Even Mrs Veazey appeared well-disposed to me, especially after I indicated I would be absent from my room if she wished to clean.

'Have you heard, Mr Stoker, of the talk down in the town?' enquired Miss Smith.

I admitted I had not due to my extended illness. In my mind, that's how I explained it to myself.

'A right to-do,' said Mrs Veazey, bringing in a fresh pot of tea. 'Poor Mr Swale.'

Fear gripped at my heart as the ladies proceeded to relate the news that a vagrant man, Mr Swale, had been found dead on a bench in the vicinity of the churchyard. Swale had been known about the town as harmless, and everyone agreed what a tragedy it was that he had lost his life in this way.

I sipped at my tea, as much to gather my tangled thoughts as it was to wash the sudden dryness from my throat. 'Do they say how he died?' I asked.

'Exposure to the elements on account of being abroad at night,' said Mrs Veazey with a matter of factness only one born of Yorkshire could express.

I breathed out in sudden relief. Had this been an act perpetrated by that fiend, the body would have crumbled to dust like the animals I had brought for him to feed on. Perhaps even now, the Master lay dying on the floor of his sanctum, starved of the very life force he needed to survive.

'How very sad,' I said, taking another drink of tea, feeling it warm through my body.

5 August. Later.

I spent the best part of that day down in the town. The sea air was sweeter than ever I thought it could be, and my spirits restored even further. I wandered along the harbour wall, relishing the sunshine that warmed the town, fully resolving to make full use of what time remained to me here. I had a few days before Florrie and Noel arrived and there was much to do. Over the next days, I intended to visit the public library at the Coffee House End of the quay, my thoughts clear enough to return to the work of fiction that had taken root in my mind.

I returned to number 6 Royal Crescent at the end of the day, a man at peace.

That peace was to be short-lived.

I chose to dine away from my lodgings on this evening and enjoyed a fine meal in one of the local hostelries. I found the company of the local fisherman restorative and enlightening, their hospitality to this incomer being without compare. I listened long to their tales, and it was dark when I left the confines of the inn.

On returning to Mrs Veazey's intending to retire, I found Mrs Smith and Miss Stokes anxiously awaiting my return in the dining room. I enquired as to what distressed them.

'Oh, Mr Stoker, it is my daughter,' said a visibly shaken Mrs Smith.

Miss Stokes attempted to calm the older woman, persuading her to sit. 'Marjorie did not return for her dinner,' said Miss Stokes, her face pale. 'She left around late-afternoon to take in some air.'

'I'm sure there is little cause for concern,' I said, putting as much conviction in my words as I could muster. 'Did she indicate where she intended to walk?'

'To the Abbey and churchyard,' said Mrs Smith.

The room span in that instant, dark dread dropping to the pit of my stomach. I steadied myself against the table.

'Mr Stoker?' said Miss Stokes, a hand touching my arm.

I opened my eyes and looked at her worried face.

I ran from the room, flinging open the front door and sprinting into the night.

5 August. 11 p.m.

I hoped against all hope that I would come across Miss Smith wandering the streets, having somehow become lost during her constitutional.

However, I knew I would not.

I came to the bottom of the Abbey steps. I stood for several moments, looking up as they curved away from me. I knew I must climb, as I had so many times in the last four days.

My thoughts of freedom had been short-lived. Angry determination took me; with a snarl of anger I placed my foot on that first step, bounding forward. With each step taken, my rage grew.

Breathing hard, I pounded through the churchyard. Clouds obscured the moon, but I knew the path I must take, weaving surefooted amongst the gravestones in the darkness. With grim dread I saw my destination, the pitted and pocked grave marker listing at that sickening angle. I grabbed the edge of the stone, as if to fortify myself with that strange fizzing power that seemed to emanate from its core. Pulling in a deep breath, I hauled myself forward, allowing the gravestone to consume me.

Shaking off the disorientation of passing through that dark portal, I stepped forward into the sanctum. It was as I had left it, as broken and rotted as the denizen that occupied its shadows.

I saw the master across the chamber, his back to me, cowled head lowered towards the left alcove. He settled an unconscious figure with something approaching reverence into the greasy yellow light. Miss Smith! I almost sobbed in horror.

My foot scraped across broken stone. The master whipped around to face me, eyes shining out of the darkness. 'Stoker,' he breathed. 'You should not have returned here!'

'Fiend!' I bellowed, diving headlong across the sanctum. He darted around the control dais with unexpected speed, face a gleeful mask as he reached towards the second alcove and the activation leaver. His hand gripped the wooden handle. Miss Smith moaned in her oblivious stupor.

Roaring, I fell upon him, wrenching him bodily away from the infernal apparatus, throwing him to the floor. Miss Smith groaned, her head lolling back. I ran to her, attempting to pull her from the alcove. But then claw-like hands closed around my face, pulling me backwards with a raw strength. I cried out, the Master hissing close in my ear, his talons probing towards my eyes. 'Witless human!' he rasped.

I bit down hard, finding bitter, rotted flesh. The master screamed out in agony, snatching his hand back, pulling away from me. I turned, aiming a blow at his exposed face. He dodged with the skill of a prize-fighter, coming back with a well-timed blow that caught me across the temple, sending me reeling. I grabbed at the edge of the control dais to steady myself, turning to face his next attack. He pulled back the hood to reveal the full extent of his horrific features, leaping towards me with vicious intent. Such was the ferocity of his attack I fell back against the dais. He was immediately upon me, fingers at my throat.

His eyes glinted and shone, boring into me with terrifying intensity. I had experienced that deathless gaze before, but now those eyes blotted out all reality, burrowing into my soul. I saw rage and depravity, a hunger for dominion over all life.

'What are you?!' I screamed.

'I am the Master!' he snarled, an animal growl drowning out all other sounds. 'And you will obey me!'

Sheer power flowed into me, consuming me. I was prepared to give myself to its seductive promise.

'You *will* obey me!' the Master rasped once more.

Images danced across my vision, a magic lantern of snatched moments from my life. The face of Florrie and Noel. So dear to me, and so nearly lost. I craned my head, seeing Miss Smith set within the alcove, so peaceful, an innocent in all this.

'I will *not* obey!' I shouted, bringing my hands up, placing them against the flayed flesh of his face, forcing him back. At once I felt his power wane, the body weak and thin beneath his cloak, as if energy were leeching from his soul. With a defiant bellow of rage, I heaved him backwards. The Master smashed against a pillar with a cry of pain, fragments of stone raining down on him.

Immediately he surged forward, cloak billowing, coming at me again.

I grappled with him, turning him bodily round, his strength gone. I flung him like a rag against the control dais. He screamed as sparks erupted from the dais, haloing around him in a glow of St Anthony's fire. The entire chamber shuddered, the floor shaking beneath my feet. A screeching banshee wail throbbed in the air.

'You poltroon!' hissed the Master, hands scrabbling at dials and switches. 'You've engaged the dematerialisation circuits!'

I knew not what these words meant. The Master's attention taken by the sparking and sputtering apparatus, I ran to Miss Smith. I caught her as she swooned forward from the alcove, the yellow light within fading to nothing. I lifted her slight form in both arms, the floor moving beneath my feet as I turned. The air was thick with sound and light, the wailing increasing in pitch like an anguished cry from the pits of hell.

The Master moved around the dais, stabbing at switches, that hideous visage a mask of desperation. 'It is not yet time! Stoker, help me!' he pleaded, but his dominion over my spirit was ended. I hefted Miss Smith and ran.

Dust rained down from above, chunks of stone crashing from the walls to smash on the pitted floor, which bucked beneath my feet, forcing me to keep balance. Turning, I looked back.

'No!' wailed the Master as bright light seeped through the dirty, burned surface of the glass valve at the dais' centre. It ground into motion, jerking upwards.

Across the dais, the Master's hooded features snapped up, eyes locking with mine.

It was the last time I would look upon that mask of terror.

I turned and strode forward into the rectangle of darkness.

Cold air rushed across my face, my feet touching on grass glistening in the dawn light. I laid Miss Smith gently on the ground. Suddenly heavy and tired, I sank to my knees next to her, pulling in a breath of sweet air.

Before me, the gravestone pulsed with light. I feared that at any second the denizen that lurked within would rise up from it to exact a sample of the revenge I knew to burn in his soul. But moments later, the stone began to fade, the air filled with the same wailing shriek. It may have been a trick of the dawn, but somewhere within that cacophony I swore I could discern a scream of savage anger. A second later, the gravestone vanished away to nothing.

A gentle moan pulled me back to the here and now. I bent to examine Miss Smith, who appeared to be sleeping peacefully. With luck, she would not remember her ordeal, or dismiss it as some fevered dream.

I, of course, was not so fortunate.

7 August.

My soul was restless.

The following day, I rose long before dawn, unable to find any sense of oblivion within sleep. I walked, events of the past week turning over in my mind.

I had returned to the boarding house with Miss Smith, who appeared none the worse for her ordeal, though with blessedly little memory of what had taken place. I concocted a story of how she became faint during her walk and had been given shelter by the landlord of a local hostelry while she recovered. This seemed to satisfy her concerned companions, and I felt no need to distress them further with any hint of the terrible truth.

In any event, who would ever have believed me? Stories such as this were destined for the fancies of fiction, passing entertainment for the masses.

As I walked, I pondered on what compulsion had taken me to carry out the bidding of that monster: simply a desire to aid a creature in dire need, or something more insidious?

I walked along the West Cliff. A gentle breeze flowed in from the sea, its chill touch refreshing me with each step. I was surprised to reach as far as Sandsend, where I turned and retraced my steps back towards Whitby. I felt light and free and could now look forward to the arrival of my dear Florrie and Noel later that day.

As I neared Whitby and the Royal Crescent, the sun was beginning to rise, the dawn light bringing warmth to the town below. I paused on the West Cliff, looking out to sea, which today glistened calm and still.

My eye was drawn to the East Cliff and the ruins of the Abbey, standing proud and tall. Below it, nestled St Mary's church and its graveyard, where the dead travel fast.

A shadow passed over me as I gazed across to this tableaux, where my ordeal had taken place just days ago. A face rose up before me, scarred and decayed, unblinking eyes locking me in their unflinching, mesmeric gaze.

I blinked, dispelling the vision.

I knew with all certainty that when I looked into the eyes of this creature called the Master – eyes full of such hatred and depravity – I had stared into the true heart of darkness; the quintessence of all that is evil. On dark nights still, I hear the death roar of his strange engine and glimpse the shadow of his cloak amid the clouds that brush the moon. And I wonder if he may return, and come to me again.

Missy's Magical Mystery Mission
JACQUELINE RAYNER

Daphne Nollis saw the good in everyone. She herself had frequently been told she had a heart of gold, and she fondly believed that everyone's heart was equally metallic, if sometimes in need of a bit of a polish. And polishing was her job, both literally and figuratively. She worked as a cleaner for Tivone of Enfis, whom most of the population thought didn't have a heart at all – but Daphne knew it was in there, even if currently almost totally tarnished. She didn't believe in abandoning people just because they did things she didn't approve of, like relentless judicial murder. Abandonment would just send them further into the dark, she thought, whereas a kind word and a Jaffa cake could potentially bring them back from the brink.

And so Daphne ('Mrs N' to her clients, although she wasn't married), scrubbed Tivone of Enfis's bathroom, steam-cleaned his oubliette and de-crumbed his toaster, hoping all the while her cheerful chat, homemade oat and raisin cookies and occasional casual mentions of how every person was worthy of rights and respect would make his heart shine, just a little bit. In return, Tivone of Enfis gave Mrs N a Festival of Snowtide bonus and a personalised holo-card, included her in Team Tivone awaydays, and had refrained from having any of her relatives killed (although admittedly she didn't have many relatives and if they'd shown any signs of seditious behaviour they'd have been for the chop, however well their sister / aunt / second-cousin-once-removed dusted his ornaments).

Which is why Daphne didn't think it at all peculiar when she walked into a cloud of sparkles hanging in the anteroom of Tivone of Enfis's office, just between the adjutant's Desk of Doom and the water dispenser, and found herself receiving a mind-message on behalf of someone called Iarbus, inviting her to a mysterious event on an unspecified planet.

Iarbus, Daphne thought, did sound slightly familiar. Her second-cousin-once-removed's husband, perhaps? Or was it that manager from the Marketing and Mayhem Dept, the one with the pointy beard? No, it was that little man from Enfisian Resources; she was almost certain. So, not a birthday party (shame) or a consultation.

It'd be one of those training days. But she wasn't going to complain, it was always nice meeting new folks and having a bit of a nose around a different planet.

The telepathic invitation came with automatic RSVP, so Daphne carefully transmitted her acceptance.

Five seconds later, she was a whirl of atoms.

Ten seconds after that, she was on top of a cliff.

Hundreds of metres below, purple waves crashed onto ebony-black rocks, each more pointed than the teeth of a needletoothed vipsnake. Still, it didn't do to criticise anything that came even vaguely under the purview of Tivone of Enfis, so she contented herself with a tiny mental shrug that it would have been nice if they'd let her get changed out of her pinny first, or maybe specified that outdoor gear would be desirable. Even the hologram standing there ready to greet arrivals had a holographic umbrella. Perhaps it was Daphne's lack of rainproof coat and wellies that was making the greeting hologram *stare* at her so wide-eyed; eyes which had far too much make-up on in Daphne's opinion. They weren't just smoky eyes, they were full-blown infernos.

Daphne and the hologram weren't alone on the cliff. Four men stood there too.

Daphne's first thought was that they, like her, hadn't been given adequate information on appropriate dress. Three of them were wearing cloaks (rather like Tivone of Enfis himself often did) and, while the material looked wonderfully dramatic blowing in the howling wind, they weren't practical – too busy billowing about to keep you warm. Worse, the fourth man was wearing (or trying to wear) a tall, spindly diadem; not only did it offer no protection against the elements, he'd had to replace it on his head three times already, just in the few moments since Daphne had materialised.

The female hologram with all the mascara (honestly – a bit of lippy was all you really needed unless you were going to a party or something) seemed reluctant to tear her eyes away from Daphne, but eventually she shook her head as if to clear it and included them all in a somewhat wolfish smile. 'Welcome to you all, honoured guests. Perhaps you would introduce yourselves?'

One of the cloaked men laughed. 'I hardly think I need any introduction.'

'Oh, honey,' said the hologram. 'You have to play along. Do what the nice lady says.' She leant forward and whispered confidentially. 'I mean me. I'm the nice lady. The nice lovely hologram lady who's just a hologram.'

'Yes.' Daphne nodded in agreement. 'Don't be nervous. Has anyone got a beanbag?'

The four slightly sinister men looked as though a tiny slug had decided to address them. Oh, they're *that* sort of people, thought Daphne. Probably why they'd been sent on the awayday, an attempt to get them to work better with others. Shame she hadn't had a chance to bring a box of flapjacks with her, that always broke the ice. Mind you, looking at this lot, she might have needed to bring out the big guns: chocolate brownies.

'Beanbag,' Daphne said again. 'Come on, you know the one. Getting to know you! You throw the beanbag and whoever catches it has to tell a fact about themselves.'

'Oh, I like that!' The hologram scrunched up her nose, and a small green beanbag appeared in mid air and fell at Daphne's feet.

Daphne picked it up. The four men were still staring at her. She sighed. Looked like she'd have to take the initiative herself, show them how it was done. 'My name is Daphne Nollis and I'm not married, although my gentlemen call me Mrs N as a courtesy. I have a pet turtpup and I make a mean oat and raisin cookie, if I do say so myself.' She threw it to the man who'd laughed.

He caught it, then seemed surprised at the reflex. He stared at the beanbag for a moment, then slightly uncertainly said, 'I, er, am the Embodyerment Rouge. I have destroyed empires. Grown men tremble at the sound of my name.' He hesitated, then tossed the beanbag to the next man, a squat being with pale blue skin and rather too many ears.

'I am Xnardo, son of Wnardo, son of Vnardo.' Xnardo's voice rose in volume. 'The blood of kings flows in my veins!'

The wind whipped the beanbag as it was thrown again and it caught on a jewelled point of the tall, spindly diadem worn by the fourth man (who was also tall and spindly). 'I am, of course, Dib the Magnificent. I need say no more,' he said as he unhooked the beanbag.

'Oh, go on, say a little bit more,' said the hologram. 'Pretty please?'

Dib the Magnificent shook his head regally.

'Pretty please with cherries on top? Lovely, lovely cherries?'

Dib suddenly looked worried. 'Is this part of the test?'

'Do *you* think it's part of the test?' said the hologram. 'Ooooh! Perhaps it's a test to see what you'll say. Perhaps it's a test to see if you'll stand your ground! Or …' She leaned forward and hissed, so Daphne could hardly hear her over the wind. 'Perhaps it isn't a test at all.'

Dib's face creased momentarily, then smoothed out. 'I choose to stand my ground. I will say no more.'

The hologram shook her head sadly. 'Well, if you've made up your mind, dear...'

'No!' yelled Dib suddenly. 'I'll say something else. Ah! I know.' He smiled. 'I have seventy-nine concubines.'

Daphne snorted in disapproval.

'Yes, disgraceful,' agreed the hologram. 'Why not round up to an even eighty?' She turned towards the last man, who had just caught the beanbag from Dib's disdainful toss. 'Come on, then. You're up, buttercup.'

This man was, in Daphne's eyes, 'normal', apart from a very long nose that resembled an eleraffe's trunk – and, as she discovered, a small round mouth that flared out like some sort of carnivorous plant or sea anemone when he spoke, spewing out tinny, staccato syllables. 'I. Am. ꓒ.'

The hologram nudged Daphne in the ribs (although obviously Daphne felt nothing). 'I was wondering how you pronounced that,' she said. ꓒ flung the beanbag away, his long nose wrinkling up as though it was something stinky, like Tivone of Enfis's vest after a heavy day's world-conquering. It passed through the hologram – who clutched her stomach and staggered around for a few seconds, before pretending to discover, in her astonishment, that there was no hole in her middle – and fell on the stony ground. Daphne, automatic tidier, picked the beanbag up and put it in her apron pocket.

'That's that, then,' said Daphne, seeing that none of the men were going to say anything more. 'I take it you're this Iarbus's assistant?' she added, turning to the hologram. 'You sent the invitations, didn't you?'

The hologram grinned and bobbed her head from side to side. 'I'm MISSY!'

'MISSY?'

'Mr Iarbus's Special Space Yummy.'

Daphne blinked.

'Are you saying I'm not yummy?' said the hologram, looking offended.

'I didn't say a word,' pointed out Daphne truthfully.

'Oh, all right then,' said the hologram. 'That didn't really work anyway. How about this. You're Mrs N – I'm Miss E!'

'What's the E stand for?' asked Daphne.

'Everything! Energetic, excellent, exciting – efficient, enjoyable, and extremely entertaining!'

While the others stood about looking baffled and unimpressed, Daphne gave a polite nod.

'Sounds like Iarbus is a lucky man to have you, then,' she said. She wasn't used to holograms having so much ... *personality*. Usually they merely fulfilled a function, a computer simulation with a face added to make it more relatable. And they were rarely programmed to wink at you like that, as though the two of you were sharing a thrilling secret. It was rather nice, actually. Daphne didn't have as many friends as she used to; they just didn't see why she stayed working for Tivone of Enfis. Why couldn't they understand? It wasn't as if she too didn't dream of a world full of peace and understanding, of smiles and joy, of sticky toffee pudding and birthday parties, a world where you were able to say 'That Tivone is a bit of a rotter' without yourself and your entire family being garrotted by the Enfisian Guard. Of course she did! She was just working to overthrow it from the inside. Well, overthrowish.

And doing well in this Tivone of Enfis-sponsored awayday would be another tiny step towards that goal. He'd be pleased with her, which would mean she might possibly dare to mention in passing something like 'Ooh, I've always thought the right to a fair trial is a really nice thing, don't you agree, Mr Tivone?' So she'd have to do her very best with whatever events had been planned.

Daphne smiled at the hologram. 'I bet you've got some good activities lined up for us, haven't you?'

'Oh, simply super,' said the hologram. 'One hundred per cent super dooper. Why don't you guess what we're going to do first?'

Daphne shrugged. 'Some sort of team-building thing, is it? Trust exercises? You know, where you have to fall backwards and trust someone to catch you. I've done that one before.' She eyed the four men with reservation. She'd probably squash the skinny Dib the Magnificent into a pancake if she fell on top of him. And while she'd always been proud of herself for not being prejudiced against anyone, whatever their colour, shape or size, she really didn't fancy landing on Ʒ's prehensile trunk; who could tell where it might end up? 'Or, maybe you were thinking of a scavenger hunt? Not that there's enough of us to divide into equal teams. And is there anything to collect here apart from rocks?'

Xnardo snarled. 'Stop this foolishness! I was summoned here by Iarbus himself! He considered me, and only me, to be worthy of inheriting his great power!'

'Ooh, now maybe you can help me,' said Daphne. 'This Iarbus – he's not my cousin Euphemia's husband, is he? Bald, dirty laugh, had a few too many cookies along the way, if you know what I mean ...'

Xnardo's eyes widened until there were huge circles of silver around the irises. 'Iarbus is the greatest sorcerer this universe has ever known! Holder of infinite power! Destroyer of the eighth galaxy! Mind-mage extraordinaire!'

'Oh, it's not Euphemia's husband, then,' said Daphne. 'He's a greengrocer. But that doesn't sound much like the man from Enfisian resources, either.'

The Embodyerment Rouge raised an eyebrow. 'Enfisian? Do you by any chance know Tivone of Enfis, you feeble female?'

Daphne folded her arms and counted to ten, so she wouldn't say anything rude. Out of the corner of her eye she saw that Miss E had also folded her arms and was staring hard at the Embodyerment Rouge. But Miss E didn't look annoyed about the sexist remark, she looked – what was it? *Triumphant*. That was it. How odd. Still, she was only a hologram. Maybe she didn't understand gender-based insults.

Having controlled her annoyance, Daphne said, 'Well, of course I know Tivone of Enfis. I assume everyone here does, it's him that's arranged this training day, isn't it? I mean, not him personally, he's too important, but it's because of him.'

'Enough of this!' That was Xnardo, sounding angry again. 'Commence with the tests! I hunger for the power I was promised!'

Miss E bobbed him a very deep curtsey. 'As you wish.' Then she straightened up and wagged a finger at all the men. 'Little reminder – there can be only one winner. But there will *be* a winner. One person *will* take the prize.'

Xnardo thumped his chest. 'And it shall be me!'

'If you say so, dearie,' said the hologram. 'Now, just very, very quickly, let's go through the terms and conditions.' She suddenly shouted out a string of sentences, too fast for Daphne to fully comprehend, but which sounded something like '*I referred to hereonin as the participant acknowledge that the participant enters the Trial of Iarbus hereonin referred to as the process through their own free will and once started on the process cannot exit the process and must continue to death or victory whichever comes first and the participant hereby agrees to accept all risks inherent in this process and acknowledges that Iarbus is not liable for the participant's almost certain death and the said participant grants the said Iarbus permission to use photovids and/or holorecordings of their inevitable corpse for promotional purposes voice sig-print here –'* Miss E waved a hand at the four men, who in quick succession announced their names, then at Daphne, who followed their example, being quite used to signing things she hadn't fully understood, because who had the time to take in all that stuff and you just had to trust that the people in charge had your best interests at heart, as she was quite sure Tivone of Enfis did, really, he just expressed it in slightly controversial ways.

'Attend!' cried the hologram. 'First, dear brave adventurers, you must cross to the field of combat, where you will face the first test!' She frowned. 'Shouldn't have used "first" twice. Initial test? Opening test? Test that comes before the second test?'

'Get on with it!' shouted Xnardo. 'Must we listen to the inane prattling of a woman?'

'Inane? Don't you mean, in-*sa-a-a-a-ane*?' Miss E rolled her eyes in what Daphne considered a rather offensive manner, but she was used to not calling out people on awkward behaviour (no one ever took it well and execution often followed) so just tutted inwardly instead. Anyway, while she didn't approve of Xnardo's insults, she actually rather agreed with him that things were taking far too long to get going. If they didn't start soon she couldn't see any way they'd be finished in time for her to get back and refill Tivone of Enfis's night-time slimepods.

The hologram had perhaps been programmed to pick up on social cues, because she stopped rolling her eyes and barked out, 'Oh, very well. Cross the bridge to the field of combat. Get on with it.'

And suddenly there was a bridge. No, there'd always been a bridge. Hadn't there? A solid, sturdy thing leading from the edge of the cliff into the swirling mists.

'You expect us to go on that?' said Xnardo.

'I do,' said Miss E. She growled, pointing a finger at him like a phaser, and adopted a funny accent. 'You godda problem with that, cowboy?'

'Of course not.' That wasn't Xnardo but Dib the Magnificent, who strode forwards on to the bridge and was soon lost to sight. The Embodyerment Rouge and Đ swiftly followed. Only Xnardo, Daphne and the hologram remained – and then the hologram flickered, giving a little wave as she vanished.

The wind was howling and they were very high up, but although Tivone of Enfis was a hard taskmaster he would hardly have arranged a training day somewhere unsafe. Daphne felt that it was up to her to reassure this man, even if he had been a bit rude.

'Is it the height?' she asked Xnardo. 'I had a friend once, oh, many years ago, who got all giddy if we went up in a balloonbus. But you don't need to worry. The bridge looks ever so strong, and if that skinny Dib fellow can get over without being blown away a more … *well-built* gentlemen like you will have no problems. Come on, you can hold my hand if you like.'

Xnardo recoiled from the proffered hand with a snarl. 'Xnardo, son of Wnardo, son of Vnardo is afraid of nothing!' He took a step – a ridiculously timid step, considering how stable the bridge looked – and then another. And – after a long pause – another. He was almost tiptoeing, swaying, foot in front of foot like he was on a tightrope rather than a wide, solid path. And then … Daphne thought her eyes were playing tricks, but no, it was really happening – he swayed again, and somehow fell *through* the bridge. She ran towards him, not really with any hope of getting there in time, and indeed she didn't. She tried to see where he'd gone, but there was nothing left of Xnardo except a faint trace of a scream in the air, and the bridge remained substantial beneath her feet. All she could do was hurry across to the other side, and hope one of the others would be able to help.

'It's Xnardo!' she cried, when she finally reached the end of the bridge. 'He fell! What's down there?'

Miss E popped back into existence and wrinkled her nose. 'Oh, just the never-ending darkness,' she said. 'Well, never mind.'

'But can't we do something?' asked Daphne. 'I mean, that's not really fair. We hadn't even got to the first test!'

'Ah,' said Miss E. 'Teensy little lie-ette there. That *was* the first test. The bridge manifested as a representation of your confidence. Anyone who actually doubted their ability to complete the tasks ahead would find it as flimsy as their faith. Whoops!' she added, looking as though she found the whole idea very funny.

Daphne privately thought that wasn't on at all. The hologram could at least have warned them. But she also slightly envied Xnardo. Presumably anyone who failed a test would be teleported straight back home, and it really was terribly chilly and she could definitely do with a cuppa. Lucky Xnardo might be having a hot bath and a bun before long. She was almost tempted to fail the next test deliberately, just so she could get out of here. But Tivone of Enfis would definitely not approve of that sort of behaviour, and she had the feeling he'd know, somehow. He always did. She'd just have to see this through.

Ⴣ, the Embodyerment Rouge and Dib the Magnificent were soon gathered on the field of combat. Miss E gestured to Daphne to join them. The name – field of *combat* – was worrying Daphne slightly. She could wield a feather duster with the best of them, but anything more weapon-y than that scared her a bit. Hardly a week went past in Tivone of Enfis's domain without someone accidentally phasering themselves or sharp-blading themselves through the heart, or even laser-axing their head right off. Weapons were *dangerous*.

Miss E did a little dance. 'Bye, bye, Xnardo!' she sang. 'That's one down and four to go!'

The Embodyerment Rouge snorted. 'I think you'll find there are only three serious contenders here,' he said.

He turned up his long nose. 'Three? Just. One. Me!'

'Now, now, children,' said Miss E. 'If you don't play nicely I'll just have to snip off all your heads and try again, and that would be so yawn-making. Do be good little boys and have a go at the next test, there's loves.'

Daphne hoped the next test would be a bit more interesting. The bridge thing might have been *clever*, but it wasn't what she'd call amusing. Maybe they could do the thing where you had a vulper, a chick-chick and a bag of grass pods and had to work out how to get them all safely across a river. Or where you put on a blindfold and felt something and someone else had to draw what you were describing, and the results were always *hilarious.* Of course, those sort of things tended to be indoor activities, and there was no sign of an indoors here – not even a tiny hut, let alone a conference centre. Which was particularly disappointing, as it was starting to rain.

Goodness, those men were making a fuss about a few tiny drops. Ꜣ was curled up on the ground, screaming, trying to pull his cloak over his head. Dib the Magnificent was running around in circles, waving his arms in the air. 'It burns! It burns!' – that was the Embodyerment Rouge.

'Oh yes. I should have mentioned,' said Miss E, popping open her parasol. 'It's raining the tears of your enemies.'

'Our what?' demanded Daphne. Enemies? Since when did she have enemies? Yes, OK, Mirabelle Quarant had been a bit miffed when Daphne hadn't wanted to share the recipe for her bipnut pie, but the secret had been passed down through generations of Nollises and she didn't feel it was hers to reveal. But *enemies*? People who hated her? People she'd hurt? People who blamed her for something unpleasant? Surely she didn't have any of those?

Suddenly the ground gave way beneath Daphne's feet – beneath all their feet. Four shrieks rang out as they tumbled into four separate holes. 'Oh dearie me,' said the hologram of Miss E, peering into each in turn. 'Looks like you're going to drown in your enemies' tears – if the acid in them doesn't eat you up first, yum yum. But don't worry, it's not *very* strong acid – don't want you dying straightaway, now, do we, where'd be the fun in that? It's just going to sting a teensy bit as you melt away verrrrry slooooooowly.'

A drop fell on Daphne's hand, but luckily she was still wearing her trusty rubber gloves. The rubber bubbled where the rain had fallen, though. That was annoying. She wondered if Tivone of Enfis would let her claim for a replacement pair.

A new face appeared above her. A very surprising face. 'Mirabelle!' Daphne cried. 'I was just thinking about you! What are you doing here?' But Mirabelle didn't answer. She stared down at Daphne with an expression of being just very slightly fed up on her face.

Then Miss E was there again. 'Little clue, because I'm the loveliest fluffiest helpfuliest kitty-cat in the whole of pussland,' she said, in a mock-cutesy little-girl voice. 'The only way to get out of the hole before you drown or dissolve in the nasty ol' acid is to persuade your deadliest enemy to pull you out, which is ridiculously embarrassing if they're, for example, some sort of pious prig with a shock of white hair and a young-old face – don't write in, it works for more than one of him – but you've gotta grit your teeth and do it.'

Well, that didn't seem too difficult, even if it was embarrassing – yes, the hologram was right, there! – to find out how much animosity that pie had caused. 'Would you mind giving me a hand up?' Daphne called to Mirabelle. The woman shrugged and reached down into the hole. Seconds later, Daphne was back on firm ground. 'Thanks,' she said. 'I am sorry about not sharing my mum's recipe. I guess I was being a bit selfish. After all, what's the problem with more people being able to make nice things? The more pie, the better. I'll let you have it as soon as I get back home.'

'She's not *real*,' said Miss E, rolling her eyes (she did that a *lot*).

'Doesn't matter,' said Daphne. 'The point stands. Sharing is good.' Just then a noise from Ⅎ's hole made her spin around, but out of the corner of her eye she thought she saw Miss E stick a finger down her throat and pretend to gag.

Ⅎ was struggling, and the being standing at the top of the pit where he was trapped – it looked rather like a Festival of Snowtime tree, but with glowing red eyes – wasn't doing a thing to help. Admittedly it didn't have any arms, but it surely could have done *something*. Daphne tried to cross to the hole so she could attempt to pull Ꮷ out, but there was an invisible barrier in the way – as there was between her and all the other holes too. There was nothing she could do but watch. Eventually, with most of their clothing burned away (Daphne tried not to look) and a fair few perforations in their skin too, the Embodyerment Rouge and Dib the Magnificent gained the safety of solid ground again, the rain above them stopped and their 'enemies' faded away. But not so Ꮷ.

'Don't want to miss the show, do we?' said Miss E, and Daphne found she could somehow see right into the hole, even though she didn't seem to be any closer. She wished she couldn't. The rain was streaming down onto the poor man. His anemone-mouth pulsed in and out, making tiny sounds of pain. 'A fiver says his nose falls off before his knees dissolve,' said Miss E, waving a small rectangle of bluey-green paper in Daphne's face.

Daphne didn't take the bet, but she would have lost.

The acid rain – a torrent above Ꮷ's prison – didn't let up for a moment, and the water level was rising. The worst thing was how slow everything was. Ꮷ's terror grew, with no hope of a quick release. Obviously he wouldn't *really* drown, and his skin, then flesh, then bones weren't *really* melting away, but was the pain real? It looked like it. Unfortunately she wouldn't put it past Tivone of Enfis to think a bit of pain built character. It was a relief when the last of Ð's bones liquefied, his tree-enemy faded away, and there were no more screams.

'Isn't it funny how people's insides are so much prettier than their outsides?' Once more Miss E had faded away for a couple of minutes, but now she was back. 'It would have been totes amazeballs to decorate that Christmas tree in strings of intestines and go rockin' around it. And eyeball baubles should totally be a thing. Shouldn't they?'

Daphne hastened to change the subject. 'At least there was no fighting,' she said. 'When you said this was called the field of combat …'

'Oh yes,' said Miss E. 'There is that. Ooh, look! Here are all your fallen predecessors come to attack you.'

And suddenly there were thousands of people all around them. People? Was that the right word? It was really going a bit far, in Daphne's opinion. Worse than the costumes the kiddies wore to go Jape-Joking on Witchborn Eve. Whoever had thought this up needed a good talking-to; she felt quite queasy looking at the decaying hordes. There was rotting flesh hanging from rotten bones. Some of the figures were bones only, ancient and bleached. A few whole, but with skin grey and eyes dull. Most of them wore cloaks. And the weapons! Miss E was swooping around, commenting happily – 'X-ray laser cannon, mmm! Oh em gee, don't tell me that's a plus-three broadsword? OK, so, tissue compression eliminator, that is, like, really cool, but you do know I'm going to sue, right?'

The Embodyerment Rouge and Dib the Magnificent both produced arms of their own. Daphne was a bit worried. The invitation hadn't said anything about bringing your own weapon – because while she hated weapons she hated being attacked by demonic dress-up mobs perhaps even more, and the only thing she had to defend herself was the beanbag that was still in her apron pocket. That wouldn't be much good against an X-ray laser cannon. She couldn't run away – there wasn't a gap anywhere in the ranks surrounding them. Goodness, Tivone of Enfis must have really pushed the boat out with this event – hiring that many undead would have cost an arm and a leg (no pun intended, she added internally). Right now, she wished he'd been slightly less of a perfectionist.

But strangely enough, although the army was attacking both the men, it was leaving Daphne alone. Once or twice a creature approached her when she waved a cleaning cloth in its direction, but actually attacking? No. 'Well done,' said Miss E, holding the back of her hand vertically by her mouth as though telling secrets. 'You've worked it out. The harder you fight, the harder they attack. The only way to win is to stop fighting.'

Dib the Magnificent, going hand to hand with a particularly large zombie, froze. 'Foolish female! I heard that!'

'Oh, shoot,' said Miss E, but she didn't look that unhappy about it.

In contrast, the Embodyerment Rouge *did* look unhappy. There was an arrow sticking out of his shoulder and a laser burn across his face that had taken out one eye. 'Stop fighting!' Daphne called to him. 'Then they'll stop!'

'Ridiculous!'

'No, it's true!' she cried.

'Only a weakling, a coward, would stop fighting!' shouted Dib the Magnificent.

'What are you doing?' said Daphne. 'That'll make him keep going!'

And it did. Faced with such an onslaught, the Embodyerment Rouge stood no chance. A final proton blast took him in the chest. The army of zombies vanished before his body had even hit the ground. Then his body vanished too.

For a moment, the survivors just stared. Then the one remaining man howled in triumph. 'Aha! Ahaha! Ahahaha! I am victorious! No longer will I be called Dib the Magnificent. Henceforth I will be known as Dib the Incredible!'

'Incredible,' Miss E muttered under her breath, just loud enough for Daphne to hear.

Daphne wasn't one who believed in putting herself forward – 'I'm not one for putting myself forward,' she'd said many, many times – but Dib's behaviour was, she thought, rather disrespectful, as well as inaccurate.

She gave a small cough. Dib ignored her. She coughed again. Dib just continued going 'Ahahahaha!'

'I'm not one for putting myself forward,' Daphne said, 'but I think you're missing something. I'm still here.'

Dib frowned, and finally stopped going 'Ahahaha!' 'As if you could possibly be a candidate for Iarbus's power! Your presence here is a mistake – a joke!'

'I received an invitation just like you did,' Daphne told him. 'Mr Tivone is very good at including me in things.'

'You ridiculous woman! Look around you! Xnardo. The Embodyerment Rouge. Even Ꮰ. None of them compare to me, Dib the Mag– the

Incredible – it is true. But you? You are so far below us! We held entire worlds in the palms of our hands! The power Iarbus controls – how could it be credible that he would consider you a worthy heir?'

Daphne was about to answer, about to tell Dib exactly what she thought of him and his rudeness, when she suddenly stopped, a thought drilling into her head. Was he … right? She replayed the scenario in her head. There she was, going about her business, having a bit of a dust, and then the invitation appeared in her mind … Tivone of Enfis had sent mind-messages to her before, she had no reason to doubt it was for her, but …

Could it have been? Could some silly sausage have sent an *unsecured* mind-message, a mind-message she had accidentally intercepted? Could it have been Tivone of Enfis himself who was supposed to be here? Could it be Tivone who was supposed to be competing for Iarbus's power? Could it be that this was all … *real*?

Daphne sat down heavily, not caring that the rocks were uncomfortable and cold, or that she was getting mud all over her skirt. 'Oh lordy,' she breathed. 'I shouldn't be here.'

Miss E rolled her eyes. 'Sorry, sister. You're quite right, of course. But hasn't it been *fun*.'

'And in truth, your presence is not unwelcome,' added Dib the Magnificent / Incredible. 'I shall enjoy having a witness to my ultimate triumph.' He took a mighty step forward and bellowed: 'I claim the power!'

The rocks trembled. Daphne hurriedly stood up, then fell over. The ground split. Rising out of the boiling earth came a man. In his hands was a shape – a sphere, a cube, an icosahedron? It was all and none of those, shining with darkness. Daphne stared. Was it her imagination or were there *eyes* staring out from the mad geometry of the shape? Thousands of eyes on thousands of faces...thousands of mouths screaming endlessly, silently, desperately...

'Welcome,' boomed the man in a voice like really horrible music. 'I ... am ... Iarbus!' There was such force in his words that Daphne started applauding, without really realising what she was doing.

Iarbus ignored her. 'Many years I have waited,' he said. 'I have been weary, bowing under the weight of the power I hold, power so great that a mere waft of it could compress an entire planet into a tiny diamond. But I could not let this power go. I had to pass it on to a man like myself, one capable, one worthy, one *ready* to wield such a force. So I designed tests, tests that only such a man could complete. I have waited years. Decades. Centuries! So many have tried. So many have failed. In failure they add their essence to the power, making it greater still, yet making it weigh even heavier on my shoulders. And finally – finally! – one has triumphed. The first! I have found my heir. I can pass on this power.'

Totally rapt, Dib the formerly Magnificent stepped forward, his twig-like fingers reaching for the shining shape. Forces swirled from it, engulfing him, he and Iarbus joined together within a galaxy of energies.

'Ahem,' said Miss E, with a little cough.

Both men turned towards her.

'Nice story,' said Miss E. 'But you missed out a little bit, didn't you. Just a tiny detail. The detail that Dib-Dab here *isn't* the first person to pass your little tests throughout the centuries, is he? The first person was actually little ol' me!'

'You!' gasped Iarbus.

'That's what I said. Me!'

'No, I mean – it's you!'

Miss E sighed. 'Yes, I mean – it's me! The bitch is back, bitches.'

'But you were ...'

'Destroyed? Yawn. You've no idea how many times I've been destroyed. In fact, I consider it a bit of a waste if I get to the end of an evil scheme *without* being destroyed. Being destroyed has never destroyed me! I always come back! Having my life essence drained into an ancient power source was a minor hiccup.' Miss E hiccupped as if to emphasise the point.

'Hang on,' said Daphne, 'I thought you were his assistant?'

'Nope,' said the hologram. 'I am the victim of a great injustice. I am no one's assistant. I am *Missy*!'

'Yes, you said earlier,' said Daphne.

'No, it's spelled differently,' said Missy. 'Will you just be quiet for a moment and let me tell you about the big injustice thing? I, Missy, was the first person ever to complete Iarbus's gruelling tests. I proved myself worthy of wielding the power! But he actually *rejected* me!'

'Well, you're just a woman,' put in Iarbus. 'You obviously only made it by some fluke.'

Dib nodded his agreement. 'No woman could make it through such trials. And even if she did – somehow – she would clearly not be worthy of such great power.'

Missy flung up her arms. 'Will you listen to yourselves? You're the fluke, Dib-Dab. *I* invited you here. Not Iarbus. *Me*. Yes, my life force got sucked into the power source when Iarbus spurned me, but I was stronger than anyone who'd come before – because I'd *won*. I was able to keep my identity. I found ways to manipulate the power from the inside. I picked five of the most gullible but nevertheless powerful and totally evil men in the galaxy, used the power I was trapped within to send them messages—'

'Which you didn't mind-secure,' put in Daphne.

Missy did actually look slightly uncomfortable. 'Well, I wasn't working in ideal circumstances, was I?' she said. 'But never mind that. Four of the men *did* come. I disabled as many tests as I could and guided them through the ones that were left – as if they could have made it on their own! Didn't it click how *easy* these ultimate games of certain death that no one has completed in centuries were? Of course, I only needed one to make it all the way. The life force of the others, as of so many failures before them, was drained into the power. Except … well, I am a clever cupcake and no mistake – I tweaked it oh-so-very slightly so that life force went straight into incorporeal me. So I could be me again. So I could *manifest*.'

Daphne stared, horrified. 'D'you mean to say that Ɉ, and Xnardo, and the Embodyerment Rouge – they *didn't* get teleported home?'

All three of the others turned to look at her, shaking their heads in disbelief.

'Of course not,' said Iarbus.

'It was a game of death!' said Dib.

'Oh honey,' said Missy.

Daphne felt embarrassed and insulted. It wasn't as though it had been an illogical conclusion. What would be the point of a training day that killed people? And it had seemed very like one of Tivone of Enfis's normal awaydays, they were never exactly fun. It would hardly be anyone's immediate deduction that a hologram woman was luring evil but credulous dictators to a deadly planet to get revenge on some misogynist bloke who hadn't let her have his big shape-thing of power.

'Anyway, back to me,' said Missy. 'As I was saying. So I could be me again, yadda yadda yadda. So I could … *manifest!*' Before their eyes, the hologram became solid. Well – more or less. There was still a little bit of flickering. Missy sniffed. 'Only three lots of life force. Another one would have been just peachy, but –' she looked at Daphne again, and blew her a kiss – 'you were so super-yummy I just couldn't bring myself to horribly slaughter you. Well, not right then. I probably will, in a minute or two. Tell a lie; I definitely will. But first –' And now she turned to Dib and Iarbus – 'I'm going to drain both of you nasty little boys, because that power belongs to me and it knows it. We've been quite intimate with each other for a while now, me and that sweet, heady power. *That'll* teach you to underestimate a woman!'

Missy gestured, and the shifting shape of power was no longer between the two men, it was floating just above her hands. It seemed to have three sides now, and through each one Daphne could see a different screaming face – one side showed Xnardo, another the Embodyerment Rouge, and the third ⅃. Then Missy gestured again – and Iarbus and Dib began to dissolve away.

'Nooooooo!' they both screamed.

'You could always try saying something nice,' said Missy. 'I am a lovely lady, after all. I might just change my mind if you do.'

'You – you are not an inferior just because you are a woman!' gasped Iarbus.

'I really like your hat!' choked the dribbling Dib.

'Aw, thanks hun!' said Missy. 'Tell you what, though. I'm still going to totally kill you, and then I'm going to use this big powery thing to squash your planets into two lovely diamond earrings, OK? Bye-bye, Iarbus the idiot! Bye-bye, Dib the Dead!'

As Daphne watched, the shape grew two more facets, and two more faces. Dib and Iarbus had been added to the eternal scream.

Missy pretended to tickle Iarbus's shrieking face under the chin. Then she began to laugh. She laughed and laughed and laughed. 'It's mine!' she cried. 'Mine, mine, mine!' She started to dance a jig around the power source, singing, 'I'm gonna smash your plan-et, gonna smash your plan-et … Total power is mi-ine, total power is mi-ine—'

And then a green beanbag flew through the air and knocked the – at that point spherical – power source out of her grip.

It actually took Missy a few moments to realise what had just happened – which was quite long enough for Daphne to run over and pick up the sphere.

Missy turned to Daphne. 'Naughty, naughty,' she said. 'That belongs to me, doesn't it?'

Daphne shook her head. 'You stole it. It's not yours. It shouldn't belong to anyone like you.'

'Of course it should!' said Missy. 'Come on, Daffers, me duck! Hand it over. Girl power! Up the women!'

Daphne was used to being told what to do. She'd never been the one in charge. Even before she'd worked for Tivone of Enfis, she'd always been at the beck and call of others. And now something was telling her that didn't have to happen ever again.

She was in charge now. Ribbons of power were swirling around her, like a magical maypole. 'Up the women!' she echoed. 'Except you did just what Iarbus did. Just what all the men did. You underestimated a woman.'

'No,' said Missy, like it was really obvious. 'I didn't. I mean, I couldn't! I am a woman! Look at me! I'm wearing a dress! I have a parasol! A lovely hat with actual cherries on top!'

'Women can underestimate other women,' said Daphne with certainty. 'It's nothing to do with hats.'

Missy sighed. 'Oh, whatever. Just hand over the power, hun, because you don't have a clue what you're doing.'

But Daphne did know. The power was telling her how to use it. She sent it a thought – and oat and raisin cookies began to rain from the stormy sky. Daphne laughed, a laugh of sheer delight. Because she suddenly realised that the sky didn't have to be stormy! A flick of her mind and it was sunny, blue, full of rainbows. The rocks below her melted away to be replaced by daffolips and tuladils.

Then she looked at Missy. And Missy held up a strange sort of device with glowing red circles on one side. A weapon. Daphne knew without any doubt that Missy was going to kill her.

Or she would have done, if the device hadn't turned into a bunny rabbit.

Missy growled and flung the rabbit away from her. 'Give – me – the – power – or – I – will – cuddle – you!' she snarled. And looked surprised. 'Or – I – will – *kiss* – you,' she tried again. 'I. Will. *Kitten!* You!' She was holding a kitten now. Lots of kittens. Missy was cuddling the kittens. She was cuddling the kittens and nibbling on an oat and raisin cookie and now she was *smiling*, she was humming a happy little tune and cuddling kittens and smiling and –

'Get away from me!' screamed Missy desperately. 'I'm turning nice!'

'All right,' said Daphne. 'I will. Because I think I'm going to go and stop Tivone of Enfis doing bad things now. After all, I've given him lots of chances to turn over a new leaf, and I'm actually beginning to wonder if he's ever going to. I'll probably pop in to the planets where those other men came from, too, and see if they need a helping hand. And then do you know what I'm going to do?'

Missy shook her head. 'You're going to turn this planet into a pendant?'

'I'm going to make everyone in the galaxy a nice cup of tea.'

Daphne smiled, thinking of all the good she could do. The rabbit hopped up to her foot, and she stooped to stroke it. When she looked up again, Missy had gone, and a nearby tree was fading in and out with a wheezing, groaning sound. Still, it didn't matter. Daphne was going to make sure no one ever underestimated a woman again. Because Daphne had the power now.

And munching on an oat and raisin cookie, Daphne headed off to change the universe.

A Master of Disguise
MIKE TUCKER

The storm on Djinn had been raging for centuries, and it would probably do so for centuries to come. It tore at the surface of the planet, the hurr-icane winds and driving rain scouring the bedrock and making it impossible for all but the most tenacious of lichens to grow. There were no trees, no birds, no animal life on any kind. The planet was deserted.

Almost.

Moses stared out at the storm through the window of the fortress that had been his home for over a decade. 'Well,' he murmured with a smile. 'Perhaps "home" is being a bit generous.'

The truth was this was his prison, and although there were no bars, no guards and no locked doors he was as trapped here as much as if he'd been thrown into the most secure Stormcage facility.

The fortress jutted from the side of one of the highest mountain peaks on Djinn, its thick walls carved from the very rock. Who had built it here and why was a mystery lost to time and the howling winds. Moses often imagined that, in its distant past, the planet had been beautiful and calm and green. Then the location of the castle made sense to him, with spectacular views across the majestic peaks and down into the river valley far below.

Or perhaps things were always this way, Moses mused, and the fortress had been constructed simply so that someone could be locked away in total isolation on a planet where leaving its shelter would result in a swift death from exposure.

It hadn't started out so solitary. During the first few weeks of his incarceration there had been dozens of other prisoners, working day and night to construct the power systems that provided him with heat and light. All of them had vanished within hours of the work being completed and, knowing the nature of the man who had brought them here, Moses couldn't imagine that their fate had been a kind one.

In the rare moments that the winds lessened, Moses always stopped to listen to the distant throb of the huge generator that must be buried somewhere deep in the bowels of the fortress, and to offer a small prayer to the memory of those who had constructed it.

Heat, light and power were the only concessions to comfort that Moses had been provided with. The furniture that he had been left with was crude and rudimentary, and the food and drink that he had access to was enough to sustain life, but there was little that could provide pleasure or variety.

And so he had contented himself with his craft – after all, it was his skill at that craft that had caused him to be brought here in the first place.

Moses was a sculptor; one of the finest sculptors that his race had ever produced. The fortress was littered with examples of his work. In every nook and alcove, on every sill or shelf sat exquisite sculptures of creatures of every description. Birds, animals, fish, insects; there seemed to be nothing that Moses couldn't turn his hands to, every scale and feather modelled in precise and exacting detail.

Impressive as the creatures were, they were not the reason that Moses had been brought here. They were personal projects, distractions to keep him amused on long evenings when the wind screamed outside the walls, tokens to remind him of his own world, a world bursting with life and colour and warmth.

No, the masks were the reason that he was kept here, and the talent that Moses showed in the animal sculptures that decorated the walls of his prison paled in comparison to the skill displayed in the clay heads that dominated his workshop.

Although every head was severed at the neck and placed on a simple stone plinth, it was easy to imagine they were alive. Moses often did. Every fold of skin, every pore, every nuance of the face was captured in the sculptures that he'd created.

He had always had this ability. Even as a young hatchling he had seemed to be able to coax his playroom clay into a menagerie of different creatures, to the astonishment of his elders and the jealousy of his classmates, but that talent had never been encouraged. He, like so many of his race, had gone to work in the Hives, making models only to pass lonely hours back in his brood nest.

But word of his lifelike works spread. Neighbours convinced him to exhibit. Moses smiled, remembering the day he first sold one of his pieces. That in turn had led to the sale of another, and another and another. Word travelled through the elitist, artistic community and sales increased to the point where he left the Hives to become a full-time artist in a studio in the northern forests. Late in life it seemed as though he had managed to find the perfect career, turning his childhood passion onto a way of making a living.

'Nothing lasts,' Moses reminded himself softly, staring out at the rain-swept desolation.

Times and tastes change, and over the years Moses found his work falling from favour. People stopped buying his art, exhibitors moved on to the next big thing. As the months went by, the future for Moses was starting to look bleak, but then salvation of a kind had presented itself from the most unexpected quarter.

He had emerged from his brood hive one day to find a humanoid waiting in the street outside his front door.

'Ah, Moses …' The man took a step forward. 'I have come a very long way to meet you.'

'To meet me?' Moses regarded him suspiciously. The man was slim, with a neat beard, wearing a simple black tunic with a high collar. As the man had begun to praise the quality of his workmanship, Moses could only imagine that someone was playing a cruel practical joke.

'That's very kind of you,' muttered Moses as he tried to push past him. 'But I'm not in that line of work any more.'

'Nonsense.' The man blocked his path. 'An artist such as yourself should not be left idle.' The man gave him a dazzling smile. 'I have a job offer for you that you simply cannot refuse.'

'Thank you, but I'm not interested.'

'Oh, but I insist.' It was only when the strange-looking gun had appeared in the man's hand that Moses had realised that the 'job he couldn't refuse' was exactly that.

Panicked, Moses had turned to run, but the man gripped him by the arm, fingers digging painfully into his flesh.

'I assure you that resistance is useless. You could shout for help, try and summon the authorities, but I assure you that is a decision you would regret.'

At that moment one of Moses's neighbours had emerged from her dwelling. As she turned and frowned, the man aimed the strange-looking gun at her. There had been a sharp, piercing whine and a flash of light. When the light faded, Moses stared in disbelief at the tiny, shrivelled figure lying on the ground.

The man had turned to him with a shrug. 'You see, Moses, I too am an artist in my own way. I can fashion the most beautiful creations in miniature.'

Moses had stared at him in horror. 'Who are you?'

'I am the Master ... and you will obey me!'

Initially, Moses had railed against his kidnap, refusing to cooperate with his captor, demanding to be taken back to his home world. He had swiftly realised how painful refusal could be, and how futile it was to believe that he could make any demands of the man who now owned him. Reluctantly he allowed his talent to be used, sculpting the faces that he was instructed to, turning them into masks, never knowing what final use they were being put to.

As the years went on, he honed his craft, the constant work making him a better sculptor than ever. Gradually the bitterness he had felt at his imprisonment had started to fade and he started thinking of the man who had put him here not as his captor, but as a kind of patron. Who cared what use the masks he made were being put to? At least his work was appreciated, and he didn't constantly have to haggle about cost or deadlines. His brief was to work to the highest quality possible, regardless of what the time or expense might be, and he had been provided with a vast reference library. What more could an artist wish for?

Except that in recent months he had started to slow down.

Moses turned and walked slowly along the long, grey corridor that formed the central spine of the building, back to his workshop. He hadn't seen any sign of his patron in what seemed like years and in the absence of specific instructions he had started to indulge himself, sculpting whatever face took his fancy: Hath, Jagaroth, Astingir ... But each sculpt was taking him longer and longer to complete, and his fingers began to stiffen after only a few hours' work. The bust he was currently working on, a fantasy sorcerer from the Eastern mythology of a planet called Earth, shouldn't have taken him more than a couple of days to block out, but he was still struggling to find the right character in the face.

He glanced up at the mirror that hung alongside his workbench, examining the sunken, lined visage that stared back at him. He brought up a hand, running his fingers over the contours of his face. It was nearly time ...

With a deep sigh, Moses was about to return to his work, when a new sound joined the constant howl of the wind, a grating rasp, rising and falling. It was a sound that he hadn't heard in years.

He looked up in surprise. 'Master?'

Moses brushed the dry clay from his hands, wrapped a damp cloth around the unfinished sculpture, and made his way towards the source of the noise, the laboratory at the far side of the fortress.

As he neared the laboratory door, a booming voice rang out, echoing off the cold stone: 'Moses? Where are you, you useless creature? Is this any way to greet your Master?'

Moses stopped, startled not by the tone of the voice, but by the voice itself. Moments later the doors to the laboratory were thrown open and a man stepped out into the corridor.

'Ah, there you are.'

Moses took an involuntary step backwards as blazing eyes regarded him with a mixture of amusement and contempt. Superficially this could have been the Master he remembered, the same jet-black hair swept back from the high forehead, the same neat beard and black suit, the same arrogant bearing, but the face … The face was altogether different, the nose broader, the brow wider, the mouth fuller. As Moses studied the face before him, that mouth curled into an unpleasant smile.

'Well? No comment on my new appearance?'

Moses felt a knot build in his gut. Had he been deemed redundant yet again? Had his patron too finally decided that he was 'out of fashion' – after all these years of holding him here? He struggled to find something complimentary to say. 'The features are truly lifelike. It is a fine piece of work, who did you employ … ?'

'This isn't a mask, you dolt! This is my new physiognomy. My true self!'

Emotions surged through Moses: confusion at what the Master was telling him, a strange elation that his talents were needed once more, and a weariness that his servitude was not yet over. 'So you have returned because you are in need of my masks again?'

'Yes.' The Master pushed past him, making his way back along the corridor to Moses's studio. 'I had hoped that block transfer computation might have been the way forward – digital disguises, created via pure mathematics – but recent experiences have convinced me otherwise. I wish to return to simpler solutions.'

Moses sighed. In the years that he had been alone he had forgotten the tone with which his patron addressed him. The absolute dismissal of him as anything other than a tool to be used. As Moses hobbled after him, memories of the mistreatments he had suffered over the years came flooding back.

The Master turned sharply. 'Why are you skulking back there? What's wrong?'

'Nothing, Master, nothing.' Moses did his best to move faster as his patron disappeared into the studio. 'I have been working constantly in the years that you have been away ...'

'So I see.'

To his dismay, Moses entered his studio to see that the Master had lifted the cloth from the unfinished sorcerer sculpture and was raising a quizzical eyebrow. 'A little more fanciful than your usual work?'

Embarrassed by the crude nature of the blocked-out head, Moses took the damp cloth from him and covered the head once more. 'An unfinished work in progress, nothing more. Here, these are the pieces I have been working on whilst you were away.'

He gestured towards the line of plinths, each supporting a different head. The Master walked down the line, nodding in satisfaction as he examined each bust in turn.

'Excellent, Moses, excellent. You truly are a craftsman.' He turned back to his prisoner, a frown crossing his saturnine features as he looked at him properly for the first time. 'There *is* something wrong, isn't there? What is it?'

Moses dithered.

'Tell me!'

With a weary sigh, looking down at the ground, Moses spoke: 'I fear ... I am dying, Master.'

'Dying?' A look of shock flickered briefly across the Master's features. 'No. I cannot allow that.'

'You have little choice in the matter.' Moses gave a wry smile. 'Dying is the one thing that I *can* do that you have no control over.'

'But why? Are you ill? If you can be treated ...?'

'My people have a ritual that must be performed when we reach a certain point in our life cycle, a liquid that must be consumed in order to prolong life.' Moses shook his head. 'When you took me from my home world, you deprived me of that liquid.'

'But you've said nothing before!'

Moses half-laughed. 'It has been many years since you first put me to work here, and many more since I last laid eyes on you. Much as I try to pretend otherwise, the solitude has taken its toll.'

Exhausted by the first conversation of any length he had had with anyone other than himself in an age, Moses lowered himself down onto one of the hard wooden chairs and gave another deep sigh. 'To die now will not be so bad. The truth is that no one wants these skills any more. You say yourself, even you sought an alternative ...'

'Be quiet,' snapped the Master, his features darkening angrily. 'I still have need of you, Moses. This liquid you require. What is it and how do I get hold of it?'

Moses looked up at him with quiet amusement. 'It is a revitalising fluid from the body of the Hive Mother herself, given in an ancient ritual that my people have practised for centuries. You cannot possibly think that you, one man, could successfully force the Hive Mother and all her attendant drones to agree to letting you have the secret? Besides, the point at which it must be taken is critical, and I passed beyond that point a long time ago.'

The Master gritted his teeth. 'Then there will be some way of synthesising the substance, of altering the timeframe.'

'Many have tried, none have managed it.' Moses paused, a distant look stealing into his eyes. 'Except …'

'Except?' The Master leaned close to him. 'Except what?'

'Before you kidnapped me, before you brought me here, I did hear rumours that a man, a scientist, was experimenting with a new artificially created compound. A compound called Carenophil.'

The Master stiffened.

'You have heard of it?'

'Yes.' The Master nodded slowly. 'Carenophil is a rare and dangerous ingredient indeed.'

For a time, the Master thought, and the only sound in the workshop was Moses's own laboured breathing. Finally the Master reached down, gripped Moses by the arm and heaved him bodily from the chair. 'Still,' he said, smiling. 'Where there's a will …'

Tovin, leader of the Planetary Council of Restovan, strode through the doors of the Senedd building and hurried to greet the man who was waiting for him.

The Doctor was just as he had remembered him, tall and gangly, with a shock of curly hair crammed beneath a broad-brimmed felt hat, clad in loose, bohemian clothes and enveloped in an extraordinary long scarf. He grinned broadly as Tovin approached, his teeth virtually gleaming in the gloom of the council chamber.

'Doctor.' Tovin shook him warmly by the hand. 'It is good to see you again. I came as soon as I got your message. Please, come to my office. We can talk privately there.'

The two men hurried across the polished marble floor and up a set of wide stairs, emerging onto a wide curving gallery overlooking the council chamber. Unlocking one of the ornate wooden doors that lined the gallery walls, Tovin ushered the Doctor inside.

'Now, Doctor,' said Tovin, seating himself at his desk. 'You say we are in danger?'

'You are indeed, Tovin, you are indeed.' The Doctor sprawled back into the chair opposite him, swinging his legs up over the arm. 'Have you heard of the Master?'

Tovin frowned. 'Yes … A criminal of some kind, I believe?'

'A criminal genius!' boomed the Doctor. 'A fellow Time Lord, utterly ruthless. A superb astrophysicist and chemist, a formidable hypnotist, highly advanced ESP abilities, expert marksman, probably a talented cook, and my oldest enemy.' He grinned. 'And I do believe he's after your Carenophil.'

'What?' Tovin stiffened in alarm.

'Yes. The Doctor swung his feet down from the arm of the chair and leaned across the desk conspiratorially. 'After the Master almost laid waste to Gallifrey, the Time Lords searched time and space for him. Their matrix projections suggest that he intends to steal a quantity of liquid Carenophil from your pharmaceutical vault. Now, correct me if I'm wrong, Tovin, but given the highly dangerous nature of Carenophil, we should be concerned as to what the Master might be up to with it, yes?'

'More than concerned, Doctor.' Tovin was grim. 'The thought of someone like the Master getting hold of it …'

'Well, then, let's make sure he doesn't,' cried the Doctor clapping Tovin on the arm. 'You can arrange its safe transport to another, more secure facility, hmm?'

'Our facility is secure, Doctor,' Tovin protested. 'The Master won't find the task easy.'

'I really wouldn't underestimate the Master.' The Doctor broke his solemnity with a sudden grin. 'What safeguards do you have in place?'

Tovin reached for a control on the side of the desk and the top lit up, becoming a holographic projector. 'Central Records, this is Councillor Tovin, identification 21281 / 61289. Request access to construction plans for pharmaceutical vault.'

Immediately a glowing network of lines flickered into life above the desk, resolving into a 3D schematic image of a large cuboid space station, its interior crisscrossed with corridors and layered with chambers.

'There you are, Doctor. Clinician Mills's original blueprints.'

'Of course. He always had a brilliant mind.' The Doctor leaned forward eagerly, eyes roving around the image. 'Yes. The security is quite … masterful.' He jumped up and jammed his hat on his unruly curls, turning to Tovin urgently. 'How quickly can you get me up there?'

'You want to go to the vault?' Tovin asked in surprise. 'Why?'

The Doctor turned from the hologram, his face stern. 'Because however good your security systems, we have to assume that the Master knows how to neutralise them.'

'But that's not possible—'

'I suggest that you let me rig up a couple of materialisation dampeners in the vault to stop him landing his TARDIS there. If he can't get himself in, he can't get the Carenophil out.'

Tovin considered the Doctor's plan for a moment, and then nodded. 'Very well, Doctor, I shall arrange an armed escort to the vault.'

'Your best people, Tovin,' said the Doctor solemnly. 'Make them your best.'

Medical Services Support Robot 2B watched as the three passengers mounted the ramp of the low orbital shuttle. Two of them it identified from their bio-chips as members of the Senedd security team, the third had been designated in its files as an off-world visitor called 'The Doctor'. Switching to a different scanning mode, 2B noted that the visitor had a dual circulatory system, and adjusted its calculations for acceleration into orbit accordingly

2B's orders were straightforward. Transport the three passengers to the pharmaceutical vault, transfer a series of security protocols to the service robots on board, and then wait.

The vault was currently unmanned: the navigation systems maintaining its geostationary orbit and the security systems that controlled the defence grid totally automated. That wasn't always the case; in any given month there were numerous research teams coming and going, conducting experiments on new drugs and materials, together with maintenance crews installing and enhancing equipment and correcting minor errors. 2B's job was simply to ferry those teams between Restovan and the vault.

Satisfied that its three passengers were safely strapped into their seats, 2B turned to the controls and began transmitting its flight clearance codes to Restovan space traffic control. Moments later, the shuttle was swooping in a shallow parabolic curve above the spires of the Senedd building and accelerating into orbit.

The journey to the vault took no more than fifteen minutes. During that time, 2B monitored the environment controls in the shuttle's passenger compartment, sent diagnostic telemetry back to traffic control on the planet below, and adjusted course to line up the shuttle with the vault. Satisfied that they were on the correct flight path, 2B transmitted security clearance to the vault's central computer.

The conversation between robot and computer took less than a nanosecond and, as the security grid closed down to allow access, 2B edged the shuttle forward into the docking bay.

No sooner had the shuttle's engines shut down than 2B became aware of a commotion in the passenger compartment behind its seat. It turned to see the Doctor grappling with one of the security team. Of the second guard there was no sign.

Confused by the apparent loss of one of its passengers, 2B scanned the compartment, immediately noting that the life signs of the second guard had flatlined, and that there was a mass discrepancy that made no sense. Before its processors could decide how to react, the Doctor gave an angry snarl, pushing the guard he was fighting off balance and sending him crashing to the floor. Staggering backwards, the Doctor reached down for a stubby tubular device that had apparently been dropped onto the deck in the struggle.

As 2B watched, the Doctor pointed the tube at the prone guard and there was a burst of energy that temporarily overloaded its visual circuits. When visual function was restored, the life signs from the guard's bio-chip were reading zero and the body was gone. No, not gone ... 2B could see a tiny, twisted shape lying on the deck plates.

The Doctor turned, sliding the tubular weapon into his coat pocket. 'Sadly, tissue compression is going to have no effect on you. I shall just have to resort to more traditional solutions.'

In a blur of motion, the Doctor pulled a second device from his other pocket. 2B had enough time to identify it as a compact laser pistol before there was a brilliant flare of light, and its systems shut down.

The Master regarded the smoking remains of the robot with satisfaction. Sometimes the old ways were the best. He slipped the laser back into his coat pocket and reached up to his chin, catching the edge of the mask and peeling it away from his face.

Moses had done an outstanding job; even hanging limply in his hands the mask had an uncanny resemblance to the Doctor. It had easily been enough to fool that idiot Tovin.

'Collapse,' he hissed, and the mask folded in on itself, becoming a tight roll of flesh and hair. It had been his idea to construct the final wearable item from Nestene plastic. The mask wasn't alive, as such, but it could respond to a strong enough mental instruction, and his mind was more than up to the task.

Slipping the mask into his pocket alongside the laser, the Master lowered the shuttle ramp and hurried across the landing bay to the entry hatch. With the security protocols deactivated, it was only the work of moments for him to access the locking code. With a whir of motors, the door slid open.

The Master slipped into the cold sterile atmosphere of the vault, mentally bringing up the layout of the interior that he had memorised from the hologram Tovin had shown him. It wouldn't take the authorities long to realise that there was something wrong and send a second shuttle. He had perhaps fifteen minutes in which to find the central computer bank. Once he had the ability to turn the defence screen on and off he would have the freedom to find and drain off the Carenophil he needed.

The Master hurried along the deserted corridors until he reached the main computer bank in a chamber at the very centre of the station. He didn't even bother trying to decipher the complex-looking lock. With the laser he cut a neat hole in the security door and slipped inside.

Despite himself he was impressed. The vault's automated systems were far more sophisticated than he had been expecting. He had underestimated Tovin and his people – except in as much as they would trust a crusading do-gooder like the Doctor.

The Master strode across to the main control console and punched in a series of complex commands that would prevent anyone on Restovan from re-establishing control. Satisfied, he made his way back out through the lasered hole and into the corridor, hurrying to the lift.

The Carenophil was stored at the very top of the station, in an isolated pod that could be jettisoned from the station in the case of emergency. As the lift sped towards the highest level, a flicker of doubt crossed the Master's mind. Carenophil was a volatile, unpredictable, highly *dangerous* substance and at present he could not see how it might aid Moses's condition. But ... Moses had insisted that someone had made progress in using it for just such a case, and if a lesser being was capable ...

The lift doors slid open, and the Master stepped out into the pharmaceutical strong room. The large metal chamber was bathed in a soft green glow, each wall lined with caskets with hermetically sealed doors. Service robots of various shapes and sizes trudged and glided around the floor, but none of them gave him any heed; his interference in the security protocols had made sure of that.

He made a quick circuit of the room, checking the readouts on each of the doors. Each casket held a different rare or dangerous chemical compound – Spectrox, Loyhargil, Chimeron jelly, XYP ... Finally he found the casket containing the Carenophil and activated the opening mechanism.

Immediately the lighting in the chamber changed from green to a deep, angry red and the lift doors slammed shut with what felt like a disturbing finality. 'Isolated,' the Master murmured as, with a hiss of hydraulics, the casket door swung open and a cloud of freezing gas billowed out into the room.

The Master peered into the interior of the casket. For such a dangerous substance, the Carenophil looked innocuous enough – an amber, slightly cloudy, viscous liquid half filling a large, transparent cylinder not much bigger than an oil drum. On one side of the drum was a control panel controlling temperature and pressure, and at its base was a system whereby small quantities of the liquid could be siphoned off into a series of slim flasks, each about the size of a cigar tube.

Quickly familiarising himself with the controls, the Master activated the siphon and watched in satisfaction as one of the flasks slowly filled with the Carenophil. The machinery gave a soft beep as the process finished, and a small warning light started to flash on the flasks top.

Gingerly, the Master reached into the casket and extracted the flask, peering at the pale, golden liquid inside. Carenophil was a substance that had been created just before his time of hibernation as a Melkur on Traken. Even then it had struck him that it could be an incredibly useful addition to his arsenal. Now he would have a chance to study it properly.

Placing the flask gently onto the floor, he reached for the control panel once more. The sample he had would be enough for Moses's needs. Now he needed some for his own experiments.

He keyed in the same sequence of commands as before, but this time, instead of a soft beep, the machinery gave a harsh disapproving buzz. Frowning, the Master tried the sequence again with the same results. He was about to make a third attempt when a harsh, electronic voice boomed around the vault.

'Warning, the substance you have selected is restricted. The quantity you have drawn from the reservoir is the maximum that can be dispensed in any given work period. Any further attempts to access this reservoir will result in security shutdown.'

The Master cursed under his breath. He should have anticipated that there might be a restriction on access to the Carenophil. If he attempted to override the automatic system then he risked being trapped in here, or worse, ejected out into space, and it was almost certainly too late for him to get back down to the computer room to try and override it from there ...

Accepting that he would just have to make do with the small quantity of Carenophil contained in the flask at his feet, the Master stepped back. He reactivated the lock, and watched as the heavy metal door swung back shut with a soft sigh. To his relief, the light in the chamber returned to its original green hue and, as the lift doors slid open once more, he scooped up the flask and hurried from the strong room.

The flask of Carenophil safely tucked into one of the pockets of his coat, the Master hurried through the cool metal corridors towards the landing bay. Everything had gone exactly to plan. All he needed to do now was pilot the shuttle back to where his TARDIS was hidden outside the city on Restovan and return to Djinn.

He had already decided that, once Moses was recovered, he would look into improving the standard of the fortress's living quarters. The old sculptor had proved himself to be a more loyal ally than the Master had ever anticipated and, with the right manipulation, could be encouraged to do still more. He had plans, and Moses was going to be a key part of those plans.

But as the Master reached the shuttle bay he found the steel doors were closed. He frowned, certain that he'd left them open in order to ensure a swift escape. He keyed the entry code into the pad and the doors slid open.

As they did so, the Master saw, lined across the steel deck of the landing bay, Councillor Tovin with a phalanx of guards.

'Ah, my dear Councillor Tovin.' The Master smiled, tilting his head in mock deference. 'What a delightful and, I might say, unexpected pleasure.'

'I wish I could say the same,' said Tovin. 'But the thought of a creature like you impersonating someone like the Doctor has left a sour taste in my mouth.'

The Master's smile faded. 'How did you know? My disguise was perfect.'

'Oh, the mask was good, yes, *very* good. But when you studied Clinician Mills's blueprints you said he'd always had a brilliant mind. Now, given that the Doctor and Clinician *Claire* Mills worked together for weeks on that vault ...'

'Ah ...' The Master gave a shrug of resignation. 'A simple mistake.'

'You might be *a* Time Lord, but you are nothing like *that* Time Lord ...'

'And you granted me access knowing that I was an imposter?'

'I needed time to prepare my guards. Sending you here, I hoped to avoid any needless deaths ...'

The Master's arrogant smile returned. 'You should tell that to the two guards that you sent up with me as sacrificial lambs.'

'You think I would be so callous as to send two men to their deaths? They were Slabs. Artificial constructs programmed to react as expected to either blaster fire or tissue compression.' He held out his hand. 'Give me your weapons.'

'Listen to me, Tovin. This is no simple robbery. I *need* the Carenophil. Not for me, but for a dying man.'

'Is that the best that you can do?' scoffed Tovin. 'To try and convince me that you are on a mission of mercy?' The Councillor gave a snort of contempt. 'The Carenophil will be returned to the vault and you will be placed on trial by the Restovan authorities. Now, the weapons!'

The Master gave a deep sigh and slowly reached into the pocket of his jacket. As he did so a dozen gun barrels swung up in his direction.

'I suppose that you'll want this as well.'

Slowly the Master removed the compressed bundle of skin and hair that had been his disguise. Tovin watched with a mixture of revulsion and fascination as it slowly unfolded in the Master's hand, until it once more resembled the face of the Doctor.

'A remarkable substance, Nestene plastic,' purred the Master. 'And one that I have used to great effect over the years. However, I must admit that I never expected to use it like this.'

With a flick of his wrist, he sent the mask flying towards Councillor Tovin. As it arced through the air, it seemed to swell and distort, the eye and mouth holes widening, distending, the flesh of the cheeks stretching. With a scream of terror, Tovin tried to duck out of the way, but the mask landed wetly on his face, engulfing his head.

His screams muffled by the writhing plastic, Tovin crashed down onto the deck plates, fingers tearing at the thing that was suffocating him. Taken by surprise, the guards closest to the Councillor rushed to help. In that moment of confusion the Master sprang into action.

He threw himself to one side, snatching the weapons from his pockets. With his tissue compression eliminator in one hand and his laser pistol in the other, the Master opened fire on the guards. Bodies – both full-sized and miniaturised – tumbled to the deck plates, and in a few, short, brutal seconds it was all over.

The Master made his way through the carnage towards the motionless body of Councillor Tovin. It wasn't Tovin's face staring up with lifeless eyes, but the Doctor's, grinning wildly. The Master held out a hand and the quivering mask flowed from the councillor's face into his palm.

'You were quite right, Tovin,' murmured the Master as the mask folded itself back into its neat bundle. 'I am nothing like the Doctor, and never will be.'

With that the Master turned and made his way towards the waiting shuttle.

As the last echoes of the TARDIS engines faded to nothing, the Master emerged into Moses's studio on Djinn. But the room was dark and deserted, the lifeless eyes of the dozens of disembodied head glaring at him as if in disapproval.

After all his efforts, had he arrived too late?

'Moses?' the Master barked. 'Have you died on me, you ungrateful cur, after all I've gone through for you?'

To his satisfaction, there was the sound of movement from the corridor, and a few moments later the old sculptor appeared in the doorway.

'My apologies, Master. I was sleeping and did not hear your arrival.' He looked at him hopefully. 'You were successful?'

'Did you really think I wouldn't be?' With a smug smile, the Master held up the metal flask.

Gingerly, Moses took it from him. 'No, Master. I never doubted you.' He gazed at the pale amber liquid swirling inside it.

'Now, you need to tell me everything you know about this person who you claim has been successful with Carenophil in his experiments. I was only able to acquire that one sample, and I have no desire to waste more than is absolutely necessary saving your miserable skin. I have plans for the rest.'

Moses nodded slowly. 'Of course you do …'

Before the Master could stop him Moses twisted off the lid of the vial and swallowed the Carenophil in a series of rapid gulps.

'What are you doing … ?'

The Master lunged forward as Moses collapsed to his knees, the vial dropping from his fingers and clattering onto the stone floor. Catching him by the shoulders, he stared in horror and disbelief as the old sculptor began to pale and shrivel in front of his eyes.

'I never really believed that you would be so easy to fool …' gasped Moses.

'You lied to me?'

Moses gave a weak nod. 'If we pass the point where we must take the nectar from the Queen without doing so, nothing remains except a long, painful and undignified death. The Carenophil will ensure a swifter end.'

'But why? Why something as rare and dangerous as Carenophil?'

'If I had told you that my condition could be cured with something that you *knew* was a poison, you would have been suspicious. Worse, you might have spent years trying to keep me alive with solutions of your own. I could not bear the thought of the pain that would cause.'

Coughs racked the old man's body. Beneath the Master's gloved hands he was becoming more insubstantial by the second. 'My story created enough doubt in your mind for you to believe it to be true. And by telling you that another man had succeeded in this endeavour, your own ego would not let you believe that you could not.' Moses strained to look up at him. 'You see, *this* is my means of escape. But my work will live on, in the masks, and in whatever use you put them to ...'

If Moses had anything more to say, it was too late. What was left of him slipped from the Master's fingers, consumed by the Carenophil.

The Master rose to his feet, staring down at what was left of his captive artist. The anger he felt was directed more at himself than at the old artisan. Perhaps he had underestimated the old man from the very beginning.

Slowly he stared around the room, at the dozens of heads staring blindly from their plinths. In the years that he had been away, the old man had created enough disguises to last him years. Moses was right, his work would live on. But his body....

Well, thought the Master. There was no need for him to spend any more time here on Djinn. Once the sculptures and mask-making equipment were safely stowed in his TARDIS, he would shut down the generators and let the elements do their work. The fortress had been Moses's prison; now it would serve as his tomb. The likenesses of these creatures from all corners of the universe adorning the walls would be his guardians as his soul entered whatever afterlife awaited him. And no one who might chance on this place would ever guess its history, or know the fate of its only occupant.

The Master chuckled softly. It would make a fitting monument to the Master of Disguise.

The Night Harvest

BEVERLY SANFORD

'By the gods, are you mad?' Tala whispered as she pelted down the row of plants. 'It's not safe!' She checked the tightly woven mask over her face, praying that it would be enough. Out here in the field, deep within the tall, thorny crops, there was nothing else to protect her.

Tala's pulse raced as she drew closer to her target. Sneaking out after curfew and watching the skies every night had finally been rewarded. She'd seen lights behind the fields before, but she'd never been able to catch them before they disappeared. She'd known there had to be other lands out there, other creatures, no matter what the Elders said. And now, for the first time in Tala's entire life, a stranger had come.

'I knew you would come,' she whispered. 'I don't know where you've come from, but at last, you're here!'

A stranger. Someone new. Someone who seemed to have no idea of the danger they were both in. Dressed in a dark hooded coat, the figure advanced towards a large plant, which glowered down, its soft purple flower-head dancing in the night wind.

The figure whipped out a gleaming knife and sliced the flower-head clean off.

'Oh no …' Tala halted. She put her hands to her mask. She knew what was coming next.

The decapitated plant thrashed wildly as all around the stranger the plants began to ripple as one. Rustling angrily, they released their silent weapon. The air glittered as the moonlight caught the tiny particles. The stranger laughed. A man's laugh.

Tala knew he would fall into a forever sleep if she didn't help him, but her conscience pricked furiously at her. He had harmed the plants – everyone knew they must only be cut during the Night Harvest. The stranger deserved to be punished!

But what if the stranger didn't know what he had done? What if he was an off-worlder? What if the gods had finally answered her prayers? Tala put her head down, conflicted.

A rustling sound made her look up. The stranger had gone. Peering into the shadows, Tala saw him striding away through the thrashing plants. 'Wait!' she called. She hurried after him. 'Please will you wait?' she called.

The plants reared over her and Tala prayed again that the fumes wouldn't get through her mask. The plants recognised her, she felt it. They rarely turned on their caregivers, the villagers had learned how to handle them over the years, but they were deadly for anyone who crossed them. She had seen it for herself. As small children, she and her cousins had sneaked into a field. Little Kalat was eager to prove himself and so, dared on by his brother, he climbed a thorny stem and picked a flower for Aunt Syla. As the plant thrashed, he slipped and hit the ground, knocking the mask from his face. The children watched, helpless, as the plants released their poison and Kalat fell into the forever sleep. He was still clutching the flower in his hand as the Elders took him away to the Shrine. Tala had never gone into the fields without her mask from that day on.

The stranger was approaching the clearing at the back of the field, where a tangled brown forest of bushes and thorns blocked his exit.

'Now you'll have to talk to me!' thought Tala.

She dashed up behind him but then, right before her eyes, he walked into a tree and vanished.

'That's impossible!' Tala gasped. She peered around the trunk, rapped on it and looked up into the withered branches but he was gone. 'A person can't just walk into a tree!' she said. Unless … he wasn't a person? He'd walked amongst the plants unharmed, hadn't he? What if he wasn't an off-worlder at all?

What if this was a visitation from the gods?

Tala dropped to her knees and began to sing a prayer song, her eyes closed.

'Hello? HELLO? Could you stop that? I've got a banging headache.'

Tala's eyes popped open and she saw a man's head poking out of the tree trunk. His short, blond rumpled hair was like moonlight and his round face was creased with irritation.

'Yes, you. No more of the singing. The stink from these plants is quite the migraine trigger as it is.'

Tala's mouth dropped open. 'I'm sorry,' she offered. 'Oh Bal'kalu, you are—'

'Bal'kalu? Who's he?' The man raised an eyebrow.

'Bal'kalu, God of the Fields, Bringer of the Harvest and Our Kind and Benevolent Master. I can't believe you've chosen to appear to me!'

'Kind and benevolent?' The man smirked. 'Missed by a mile. Bye-bye!' His head disappeared again.

Tala jumped up. 'Wait! You walked through the plants unharmed, I saw you! Only the gods can do that!'

The man's head reappeared, this time with what looked like a mask over it, but made from a strange, thick material. 'First thing you should know: I'm better than any god.' Then he vanished again.

'How are you inside the tree?' Tala picked up a large stone and rapped on the trunk. 'Is it magic? Are you a demon?'

Tala suddenly fell straight through the wood and into a brightly lit, spacious room. The man stood before her, glowering. 'Got it now? And before you start, don't,' he snapped. 'I mentioned the whole headache thing, didn't I?' He turned his attention back to a white table, where he was poking at the severed flower head with some kind of tool.

'By the gods ...' said Tala, her eyes roaming the strange sights around her. 'Are all trees like this on the inside?'

'Ha. Are all the people here as ignorant as you? Hope so.' The man sneezed then blew his nose on a cloth. 'These plants really are incredibly stinky. How do you stand it? Don't you hate stinking of stinky plants all day?'

'Is this tree your home? Did it fall from space?' Tala persisted.

'Listen, stinky ...'

'Tala.'

'… whatever your name is. Want to know a secret?'

'Yes.'

The man bent down close to her ear and whispered. 'It's not a tree.'

'I knew it!' Tala breathed. 'It's magic, isn't it? You really are better than the gods!'

'Way better. Way, way better. Want to know another secret?' He didn't wait for her answer. 'Any gods of yours should be very afraid of me!'

'But what's space actually like?' Tala asked for the third time.

The man straightened up from his strange tools and rubbed his eyes. 'Perhaps I'll let you see for yourself when we're done here. Without a spacesuit.'

Tala stared at the fascinating stranger. 'You really promise you'll take me with you?'

'If you do as you promised and help me. Now, without mentioning space for two minutes, tell me more about the plants. Where did they come from?' The man stood, arms folded and head cocked.

'I already told you – Bal'kalu planted them so that the first people wouldn't starve.'

'These first people,' the man pondered. 'Where did they spring from?'

'They came from space,' said Tala. 'They were the first people here.'

'They had the whole universe to choose from and they came here? If I was looking for a new place, I'd pick somewhere with a little more entertainment.'

'They were fleeing their burning home world. Their ship crashed and they got stuck here. Please will you tell me your name?'

'Why didn't anyone come and get them? Didn't they have any space mates? Spaceships have ways of talking to others in space, you know.'

'Can yours?' Tala went to the table with the buttons and levers on it. 'Can I talk to others in space with these?'

'No,' said the man. 'Now think. Are you sure you've never met anyone else from space? Someone other than me?'

'No one! Uncle says there's nobody out there. He says we're alone.'

The man held out his arms. 'And yet here I am.'

'But that's the thing!' said Tala. 'I've seen strange lights behind the field before. I knew I wasn't imagining it, and then you—'

'What lights?' the man interrupted.

'I don't know. They go before I can catch them.'

'So maybe your uncle's wrong.' The man cocked an eyebrow.

Tala chewed her lip. 'He's the High Elder. He's never wrong.'

'High Elder? That sounds very important,' the man said.

'It is. The gods chose him to lead us. He's very clever.'

The man beamed like the sun coming out from behind the clouds. 'I'm very important and clever too.'

'Are you a High Elder where you come from?' Tala asked, wide eyed.

'Better. Than. A. God,' the man reminded her. 'What did your uncle say about the lights?'

'I haven't told him! I'd be punished for being out after curfew. Are you ever going to tell me why you're here?'

The man sighed, then peered intently at here. 'I'm here on very important work, Tala. Can't have the rest of space finding out. What if you tell someone about me?'

'I won't, I promise!'

'One of my many considerable talents is science. I don't expect you know what that is. But I'm particularly interested in botany.' He paused. 'Plants.'

'Our plants?' Tala said, furrowing her brow. He confused her, like trying to feel the sun through a thunderstorm. His words poured down like rain, as if his mind put thoughts in his mouth before he even knew them, and all the while his face and hands danced about as if he didn't know how to keep still. But his eyes ... they weren't mean old eyes like Elder Yaba's or sweet, devout eyes like Asha's. They burned like fire.

'Gold star for Tala!' the man said. 'I'm trying to find out why your plants are so clever. It's very important work.'

'It's because the gods made them that way. Elder Zara says—'

The man sighed loudly. 'You still want to see space, don't you, Tala?'

'Yes ...'

'Then let's start again, from the beginning. Tell me all about the harvest and don't leave anything out.'

Tala hurried through the fields as the bell rang out. She didn't know how she was going to sit through prayers with all the excitement bubbling under her skin. She'd promised the man – or, as he'd told her to call him, Xanos – that she wouldn't tell anyone he was there, not that he'd needed to ask. If the Elders discovered he had harmed the plants, they would kill him, and she wasn't about to let her ticket to space vanish when she'd waited her entire life for it.

She touched the small device tucked inside her hood. What had he called it? A 'transmitter', that was it. He said that he could see through it, that the moving picture window in his ship would show him everything that she saw. So many new things to learn! Tala's heart pumped, the thrill of her encounter pulsing through her.

A teenage girl with hair the colour of sunset ran up to Tala. 'Look at you!' she grinned. 'Someone's happy this morning! Is it because of Cabu?'

'What?' Tala said, caught out. 'Oh! No. I haven't seen him.' Oh gods, Cabu! He'd fallen out of her mind the second she had met the stranger. 'I'm just in a good mood.'

'I bet Cabu volunteers when we do,' said Asha. 'We can all live at the new settlement together. Maybe that'll make him smile for once! I can't wait, can you?'

Tala forced a smile but her heart sank. She hated lying to her best friend about Xanos, but she knew Asha wouldn't understand. She'd be horrified that he had hurt the plants and she would go straight to the Elders. While Tala spent her nights stargazing, Asha pored over sacred texts, absorbing the knowledge that she hoped would make her an Elder one day. She could never understand why Tala would want more than this place, where every day was the same.

The pair made their way to the Shrine of the Elders, where the rest of the villagers were assembling outside in the prayer circle. Cabu stood at the edge, watching them approach. Asha elbowed Tala as the tall, serious-looking young man looked intently at her. Tala smiled politely in greeting and sat down in her usual place, trying to calm her beating heart. How she wished her aunt and uncle had not chosen him as her future companion! The idea of spending her evenings washing his tunics and listening to him talk about his dream of being an overseer – honestly, he was far better suited to Asha than her. Those two would be a perfect match. If they paired, they surely wouldn't even miss her if she escaped into space with Xanos …

'And where were you at breakfast?' a sharp voice admonished her as a woman sat down beside her, grunting with the effort. The dark circles under her eyes evidenced many years of hard physical labour.

'I woke up early, Aunt, and went to say a prayer by the field,' Tala lied. 'You know, as it's nearly time for the harvest.'

'Well,' said her aunt. 'And there I was thinking you had your head in the clouds again. Your uncle will be pleased with you.'

At that moment, Tala's uncle stepped out of the shrine. The purple leaf tattoos on his face marked him out as the High Elder, a holy man chosen by the gods. Behind him stood the other Elders, each wearing purple robes.

High Elder Masa didn't live with Tala and her family. The Elders lived in the Lodge, a sacred building behind the shrine where they contemplated and received instruction from the gods. As a little girl, Tala had tugged on her uncle's robes and begged him to let her peek inside the sacred buildings but Aunt Syla had slapped her hand away. 'Show some respect,' she had warned. 'The holy places are only for the chosen ones and the dead!'

The bell declared the start of prayers. Tala tried not to think about Xanos but her mind wandered. She smiled secretly, thinking of what he had called his 'TARDIS' – his spaceship that looked like a tree. He told her it could take any form. 'Even your house!' he had smiled. He had a big smile, Tala noticed, but lopsided, as though it was broken.

The High Elder thumped his carved wooden staff on the ground three times. 'Good morning, my devoted, dutiful people. Today, I bring news – good news! The gods have spoken. We have received a much awaited message about the settlement.'

Tala's ears pricked up. This was news everyone had been waiting for.

The High Elder smiled benevolently at his people. 'The gods are pleased with our progress. The plants in the new fields are healthy and strong. I know you miss your loved ones, but we must trust in the decisions of the gods. The new fields benefit us all.'

He was right, Tala knew. Each generation of villagers was bigger than the last and the fields were no longer enough. They relied on the plants, no part was ever wasted – they were food, clothing, everything. Sometimes the trees bore blue fruit and orange berries, but that didn't fill hungry bellies. However, the people feared leaving the village. It was said that some had once gone in search of what lay beyond it but had never returned.

But, some cycles ago, the gods had offered to help the people once again. In a shared vision, the Elders had seen a bountiful place with rich soil, where new crops could prosper. The gods promised to protect the unselfish volunteers who went north to do this important work, but word had not yet come from them until now.

'Elder Dasu has just returned and assures us that all is well there. Your loved ones are dedicated to the task; do not fear for them but be glad they prosper. Some perhaps will wish to join them, as to prosper requires hard work and we need more hands. Who amongst you will volunteer?' The High Elder looked up expectantly, surveying the crowd.

Tala felt Asha's finger prod her in the back but she ignored it. She couldn't go to the new fields, not now that she had met Xanos.

Tala turned her head and saw Asha standing proudly, along with others, including Cabu.

'Get up, Tala!' Asha mouthed.

High Elder Masa beckoned the volunteers forward. 'Now, if you'll come with me, we will begin the preparations,' he said. 'You are making a noble sacrifice today.'

'I thought we were volunteering together?' Asha said in Tala's ear.

Tala couldn't look her in the eye. 'I'll come with the next group,' she lied. 'Aunt Syla needs me right now, it's too much for her by herself.'

'We agreed,' Asha began, but then the High Elder's gaze fell on her. Her face loaded with disappointment, she muttered something under her breath and walked away without saying goodbye.

Tala struggled to concentrate all day. Her head was too full of new ideas and possibilities to think about dull things like raking soil or stirring soup. She'd been scolded by Overseer Jakul several times and Elder Yaba trained his beady eye on her during sunset prayers when she forgot the words.

The Elders' mood had turned sour that afternoon. They'd stalked up and down the fields over and over, checking that everyone was hard at work. Tala had tried to keep her head down.

'This is important work!' she'd whispered into the transmitter as she chopped at the brown vines growing around the plants' stems. 'We have to do it, Xanos, or they strangle the plants. The Elders say the vines are an immortal evil, we kill them but they always regrow.'

That night, Tala shovelled her supper down and hurried to her room, claiming tiredness. She said her prayers and, as always, asked the gods to bless the mother she had never met. 'She died giving you life,' Aunt Syla reminded Tala whenever she complained that her existence was boring. Tala wondered what her mother would think if she could see her now, preparing to visit the stars.

When she was sure the household was asleep, Tala slipped out into the darkness. As she sneaked past the prayer circle, her skin prickled. Pulling her mask tightly over her face and looking around, she saw nothing untoward, but the feeling persisted as she crossed into the field and made her way through the plants. Instinct told her that someone was following her but whenever she looked around, she saw nothing except the plants glowing softly.

She had almost reached Xanos's tree when a hand closed over her mouth and the point of a blade dug in her back. A low voice hissed, 'Don't move!'

Tala knew that voice. Overseer Jakul! She hated him; he worked everyone to exhaustion and took great pleasure in running to the Elders whenever anyone did something not to his liking.

'Why are you sneaking around here?' the Overseer demanded.

Tala struggled against him, then kicked him so hard in the leg that he yelled, throwing her to the floor. Enraged, he slapped her around the head. The transmitter fell out of her hood.

'What's that?' he barked, snatching it up. He examined the device in the moonlight and shook it, setting off a buzzing sound. 'Heretic!' he hissed, eyes wide with fear. 'Witch! Your uncle will learn of this!' He grabbed her wrist and started dragging her across the field.

'Get off me!' Tala yelped, trying to wriggle free. 'Xanos! Help me, Xanos!'

There was a flash of light, a strange sound and the Overseer fell to the ground. Xanos stood behind him, frowning through his mask. In one hand he held a strange tool that he pointed at Tala. 'I told you to be careful.'

'I didn't know he was following me!' Tala said. 'He just jumped out of the dark. Have you killed him?'

'Well, duh!' The man scowled. 'I'm disappointed in you, Tala. My work here is very important. I can't have anyone sabotaging it.' He kicked the Overseer's lifeless body. 'I shouldn't have trusted you. You're fired!'

'Please Xanos! I really am sorry. I'll do anything you want. Anything at all!' Tala begged. She couldn't bear to see her dream slipping out of her grasp. 'I'll get information, I'll find out whatever you want from my uncle. He's the High Elder, remember?'

Xanos pointed the device at Tala's head. 'Does he know you're here?'

'Of course not! I told you, if he finds out that you hurt the plants, he'll kill you. We never hurt the plants.'

'You don't mind hurting the vines, though, do you? Hacking up their poor little stems and burning them to death.'

Tala's shoulders slumped. 'They strangle the plants. The Elders say the gods allow the vines to be sacrificed to help the plants grow.'

'They talk a lot, your Elders. Do you believe everything they tell you?' Xanos pursed his lips.

'Of course!' said Tala.

The man tutted. 'Oh dear. And you were starting to grow on me.' He barked out a sudden laugh. 'Like a vine!'

'What?' said Tala, confused.

'Come on, then,' Xanos beckoned impatiently. 'I'll show you exactly what your precious Elders have been up to.' Dragging the dead Overseer with him, he stepped inside the tree.

Tala followed, and the lights of the stranger's home shone down on her once more. Xanos stood in front of her, blocking her view.

'Want to know what really happens to volunteers here?' he said softly. He stepped aside.

Tala screamed. Lying on a table, with silver vines and strange shapes poking in and out of her, was Asha.

Tala started forward but Xanos gripped her shoulders and held her still. 'What's wrong with her? Why can't she hear me?'

'Don't touch her,' he said. 'She's very sick. It's a good thing I found her or she'd be dead by now.'

'I don't understand. She was going to the settlement, how can she be here like this?' Tala wiped the tears from her cheeks. 'She was so upset with me. We were supposed to go together but I didn't want to any more.'

'Lucky you didn't or you might be the one lying on that table,' Xanos sniffed. He adjusted some of the hard shapes poking into Asha's skin.

'Are you healing her?' Tala asked.

The man stroked his silvery stubble. 'I'm trying to make things better.'

'But what's wrong with her?'

'Your uncle and his friends are liars. Big, fat liars. The faraway fields, the settlement to the north – it's rubbish. The volunteers never even left this village.'

'But there is a settlement, people are already there. Uncle said the plants are growing and—'

'Uncle said, Uncle said,' Xanos mocked. 'I told you I'm better than a god. Yet you still believe your uncle over me?' He skipped over to his screen and pressed a button, revealing an image of brown, empty land. 'I've scanned this nothing little planet over and over and there are no other fields, no other plants and no other people.'

'All right, all right! Just tell me what's happened to Asha!' pleaded Tala.

'The transmitter I gave you has an excellent range. Very useful when you want to eavesdrop. While you were watching your BFF and your boyfriend go off with your uncle, I was listening to the other Elders. Do you know what they were whispering?' He leaned forward and spoke in a loud whisper, a look of spite on his face. 'These ones are younger and stronger. The plants will thrive on their blood.'

Tala froze. 'What does that mean?'

'I saw Asha on my screen,' said Xanos. 'She was trying to crawl out of the shrine. The metabolic restructuring hadn't taken full hold, she could still function … sort of …' He grinned. 'So I came to her rescue.'

'How?' Tala said. 'You couldn't have got near there without being caught …'

The man's grin turned into a smirk. 'Unless I had a really clever tree.'

And then Tala realised. 'This ship doesn't just travel through space … you can take it anywhere?'

'Gold star for Tala!' Xanos beamed. 'Guess what else?' He tapped a few buttons, then the screen showed something that Tala recognised. 'The shrine isn't really a shrine.'

He walked past the sick girl. 'Oh one more thing. She brought a friend.' He dragged something bulky from the shadows beyond the table into the light. Tala moaned with fear. The silver vines led from her friend's body into one of the plants. It writhed gently, hypnotically, happily.

Tala grabbed her mask but Xanos shook his head. 'Protection field. Can't do any of that nasty stinky stuff now, can you, Planty McPlantface?' He wiggled his fingers at the flower, then continued. 'Thing is, when I tried to remove it she started dying horribly. Lots of thrashing about. Turns out she's feeding it, making it stronger, more potent. Primitive but very effective.'

Tala gripped the table until her knuckles paled. 'Did my uncle do this to her?'

Xanos clapped. 'Ooh, angry! Very good. Yes, it turns out that your uncle, the esteemed High Elder, is quite the plant lover.'

'Why?' Tala said. 'Why would he do this to her?'

'Not just her. I bet all your friends are plumping up the plants somewhere in that shrine.'

Tears sprang into Tala's eyes. 'I have to do something!'

She ran to the door but Xanos blocked her path. 'Like what?'

'I ... I'll tell my aunt.'

'Use your head. She's probably in on it.'

'You really think she knows ... ?' Tala touched the talisman around her neck, the symbol of the God of the Fields.

Xanos leaned against the door, his arms folded. 'This isn't the work of gods, Tala. This is the work of monsters. Let me help you put an end to them.'

Tala looked at Asha, her life force feeding into the plant, and swallowed hard. 'What do we do?'

Xanos smiled.

Tala crouched down behind the shrine, her body buzzing with adrenalin, her head swimming with rage. The terrible image of Asha lying on the table kept dancing in front of her eyes.

Xanos dashed around the side of the shrine and dropped down beside her. 'Only two guards inside the door. Not much of a fight, but still.'

'The shrine doesn't have guards,' Tala said.

'A missing prisoner will have rattled your Elders big-time. They're probably having an Elderly conflab right now about how to look for Asha without giving themselves away.'

Tala frowned. 'You still haven't told me the plan.'

'Relax. I've got it covered. You? You're going to distract those guards.'

'Why me? You're the one with the magic!'

'You distract them while I deal with them.' He held up a device. 'With the magic.'

Tala could see the shadows of the guards inside the doorway. Taking a deep breath, she crept forward but her elbow caught one of the hanging charms and it clanged against the wall. Instantly the men turned around, knives out. 'What are you doing here?' growled one of them. 'You're not allowed in here!'

'Cabu!' Tala exclaimed as the moonlight cast over his face. 'It's me, Tala.'

'The new penalty for being out past curfew is death,' Cabu said coldly. He grabbed her arm and she cried out.

'Silence!' The other guard lunged forward with his knife.

There was a high-pitched sound, and both guards shrank to the size of leaves before Tala's eyes. They dropped softly to the floor. Tala gasped.

Xanos snorted. 'Just look at them, the tiny little idiots.' He scooped up the men and put them in his pocket, as Tala watched open-mouthed. 'Oh, where are my manners?' he said. He pulled Cabu's tiny corpse back out and offered it to Tala. 'Something to remember him by.'

Tala recoiled with a shudder. 'Are they dead?'

'Well, the wedding's off!'

'How did you do that?' Tala stared at Xanos with new awe, new fear. 'You said you weren't a god!'

'I said I'm better than a god. Pay attention!'

Tala, still reeling, barely heard him. First Asha, then Uncle Masa, and now Cabu was gone forever. She felt numb, more alone than ever. Tears welled up again.

'Less of that.' Xanos tipped her chin up. 'You've got me now. No harm will come to you again, no matter whether it's your boyfriend, your uncle or your god.'

Tala gave a small nod.

'Now. While you were distracting the Pontipines—'

'The what?'

'They're friends of mine. Live in a house at the foot of a tree. They're very tiny. Anyway! While you were busy distracting them, I noticed something very interesting.' Xanos led her across the shrine and pointed at a discreet hatch in the floor. 'Let's see what the little guys were guarding, shall we?'

Using Xanos's light, they made their way down a steep, roughly hewn set of steps and arrived in a narrow tunnel. The air was thicker here. Tala paused to catch her breath as Xanos examined the walls. 'A-ha,' he said suddenly. He licked the wall, much to Tala's disgust, and then his face lit up. 'Fascinating!' he said. He waved his silver device in front of it, which made a whirring sound.

'I don't understand that tool,' Tala said. 'It does good, it gives light and makes sense of things, but it does bad things too. You killed Overseer Jakul with it.'

'Laser screwdriver!' Xanos said proudly. 'Don't get me wrong, I love me some old-school tissue compression. But with the functions on this – it's just too good to leave at home. And its readings tell me that what we want is close by ...' He dashed off and a few moments later his voice exclaimed from the dark: 'Bingo!'

'I can't believe all this stuff is down here. We could have been eating this!' Tala held up the shiny purple fruit, amazed. 'I wonder where it grows.'

'Nowhere on this planet.' Xanos ran his fingertip along the fruit's surface. 'It's a very rare delicacy from the Ardassian Sea. That's a very long way from here.'

The whole thing was like a dream to Tala. After going through the door, they had travelled down a white tunnel and entered a maze of rooms. Xanos kept pointing things out to her – food, drinks, picture parchments he called 'books', comfortable seats, soft purple drapes. Everything felt familiar yet unfamiliar, as if someone had sprinkled stardust on her house and filled it with rainbow colours.

'How did all this get below the shrine?' she wondered.

'Maybe it really is a gateway to your gods,' smirked Xanos.

Tala said nothing. She knew he was mocking her again. He did that a lot. She stroked one of the drapes and it slipped aside, revealing something on the wall. 'There's a painting!' she said.

Xanos stared at it and then suddenly laughed, making her jump. 'Of course there is,' he said. 'Of course there is.'

He scanned the walls and followed them along until he came to a heavy drape. He pulled it down, revealing a narrow silver door.

'There's a lot of doors in this house,' said Tala.

Xanos smirked. 'Guess what?' He zapped a panel on the door and it slid open. 'It's not a house.'

'So it's a spaceship but not like your spaceship?' Tala said, looking around the corridor that had been revealed.

'Nowhere near as cool as my spaceship,' said Xanos. 'Although I admit it has a certain retro charm.'

'It's the ship the first people came in, isn't it? They built the shrine over it!'

'Getting warmer, but no. I think the same something that pulled your people out of space pulled this ship out of space too. Might even be where your plant seeds came from. That painting? It's the emblem of the Gathari. This was once a cargo ship from Gathari Minor, and it would have had one person on board, the pilot – let's call him Captain Bones.'

'His poor family. They must have wondered what happened to him,' Tala said.

'Not for long. Gathari Minor was crushed to pieces when Gathari Major tested their new planet-eater on it for fun.'

'So that's what's out there? People who eat planets for fun?'

'Have you been to Gathari Minor? It's almost as dull as here,' Xanos said dismissively. He walked through another door, leaving Tala wondering if she wanted to go to space after all.

A triumphant yell came through the door. Tala followed the sound but then froze. The missing villagers were in a large, bright room, each secured to a bed while long tubes trailed out of them to the back of the room, feeding into …

'I love to say I told you,' called Xanos, who was already climbing to the top of a large tank containing a row of enormous quivering plants.

A moan came from the nearest bed, upon which lay Yamet, a boy who had worked in Tala's field. He had a sickly pallor and his eyes were tinged with purple. Tala sighed.

'You can't help him,' Xanos said, scanning the top of the tank.

'Can't you? You must be able to do something!'

'They're too far gone, they'll die if we unhook them. They're in perfect synergy with the plants.'

'But, why?'

'It's really quite beautiful …'

Tala shook her head. She couldn't quite take any of it in. She walked along the row of bodies and, as her eye wandered, she saw some bottles on a bench, each filled with a glowing purple liquid. She picked one up and twisted the lid.

'I wouldn't do that if I were you,' called Xanos. 'It'll send you into a forever sleep and I can't save you from that.'

A chill crept through Tala's bones. 'They're using the plants to make a weapon?'

Xanos dropped down with a thud. 'They're using them to make a drug. A very potent, very profitable drug. And your friends here are making that drug purer and more powerful. They nourish the plants with their bodies and it feeds back into their own neurotransmitters, receptors, transporters, metabolising the drug in their bloodstreams …' He tapped his head with his screwdriver. 'He's clever, your uncle. But not clever enough. The symbiosis isn't fully balanced. He'll be burning through the specimens here.'

'They're people, not specimens!' Tala said.

'Same difference.' Xanos smiled suddenly. 'I bet your uncle has been trying to boost the birth rate in your little community, hasn't he, replacements for this bunch when they're spent.'

Tala blushed uncomfortably. 'Everyone over 16 cycles must choose a "night companion" now. Elder Zara says that there have been more new babies because the God of Fertility has blessed us.'

Xanos grabbed Tala by the shoulders. 'Do you really still believe that gods have anything to do with this? Look at your people. Look at them!' He turned her to face the beds. 'I thought I had chosen well when I said I would take you with me, but—'

'And where, may I ask, are you planning on taking my niece?' the High Elder snarled from the doorway. Elder Yaba and Elder Zara flanked him. Tala could see the other two Elders behind them.

'What are those?' Tala gasped, wondering at the shining silver tools the Elders were pointing at them.

'Weapons,' said Xanos. 'Shiny ones. Now where did you lot get your hands on guns like those?'

'Identify yourself!' the High Elder barked, closing in with his gun aimed at Xanos.

'Oh, you first,' said Xanos with a smile.

'I am High Elder Masa. I am the Chosen One. Now identify yourself.'

'I've heard so much about you! Are those tattoos real?' asked Xanos. 'Mind if I..?' He reached out to touch the man's face, but the High Elder blocked the hand with his gun.

'This is a particle eliminator, stranger. I won't hesitate to use it.'

'Oh I know what it is. Wanna see mine?' Xanos smirked. He held up his other hand and zapped Elder Yaba. The man dropped to the floor as a tiny corpse. 'Tissue compression eliminator. Fun, isn't it?'

'You'll die next!' High Elder Masa hissed.

Xanos pouted. 'Oh, you big bully!' He pointed his screwdriver behind him and pressed it. 'Hello planties!' The plants thrashed suddenly, and the people on the beds moaned in pain.

'You'll kill the specimens!' shouted Elder Zara.

'Stop it, Xanos!' begged Tala. 'You're hurting them!'

'Guns on the table! Now!' bellowed Xanos. The Elders obeyed. Xanos gestured to an empty tank. 'Get in there!' The Elders filed in. Xanos locked it, pulled up a stool and sat down in front of the glass. 'Now, we talk.'

'The Elders have always protected the plants,' whined the High Elder. 'You must let us out to carry on our work. The first people knew they were a gift from the gods, the plants saved their lives – they still save our lives.'

'Not yours!' Tala spat at him. 'You've got all this luxury down here while we go hungry!'

'How did you go from having your people working the fields to having your people literally feeding the plants?' Xanos asked. 'You're not clever enough to have worked that out all by yourself.'

'The Breeder,' said the High Elder. 'She came from space. She showed us how to make the plants grow strong. We made a … deal.'

'The lights in the sky!' said Tala. 'I knew I saw them. That was the Breeder's ship?'

'It is forbidden to watch the skies,' the High Elder snapped, automatically

'A deal for a regular supply of the drug. Exactly who is this Breeder?' demanded Xanos. 'How did she know the plants were even here?'

'I don't know,' whined the man.

'But on the say-so of a stranger, you agreed to increase the drug yield by using your own people to metabolise the drug alongside the regular harvest? Just to get a bit more fruit?'

The Elder stared at him. 'Do you know what it's like to have nothing? To subsist on the same dull slop every day?'

'I think you've forgotten. Maybe you should ask your niece here.' Xanos leaned right in. 'You know, you should be careful of getting too loud. You never know if the universe is listening.'

Tala couldn't take it any more. She thumped the tank glass. 'So my whole life is a lie? We're all just slaves working ourselves to death so that you can feed on luxuries?'

'I think she's going to tell everyone about this, Elders. Hell hath no fury …' Xanos chuckled. 'So, last chance. Tell me the Breeder's real name.'

The sound of shattering glass ricocheted through the room. Tala stood in front of the tank, a gun in her hand. Elder Zara slumped against the glass, a smoking hole ripped right through her chest.

'She had a gun under her robe,' Tala said simply. 'She was going to kill you.'

'Always the women!' said Xanos to the remaining Elders. He reached out towards Tala. 'Give me the gun.'

She shook her head. 'No,' she tried to say, but the sound didn't come out.

'Give it to me,' Xanos said.

She dropped it with a clatter and fled, tearing through the ship like fire as she tried to outrun the creeping terror inside her.

'Sabat – I need to tell you the truth about the plants … It's Hana, she isn't at the settlement,

she's dying! There is no settlement … Listen to me
– the Elders have been selling our harvest to a
visitor from the stars and keeping the profit while
we go hungry!'

Uneasily, the villagers backed away as Tala
went from person to person. She begged them to
listen, but they snubbed her, ridiculed her. 'She's
sick,' they muttered. 'She's always been strange.
She hasn't got a mother, you know.'

'Why won't anyone listen to me?' Tala pleaded.
'I'm trying to save you!'

A hand gripped her wrist. 'Tala!' hissed her
aunt. 'What are you doing? Are you ill?'

Tala nearly cried with relief. 'Aunt Syla, please,
you need to listen to me. Uncle is a liar. He's a
murderer!'

Aunt Syla slapped Tala around the face. 'How
dare you speak that way! He is the High Elder! Say
your prayers at once before the gods strike you
down.' She gestured apologetically to the people
around them.

Tala crumbled to the floor as the prayer bell
rang out. The buzz of chatter faded away but then
a chorus of whispers arose. Tala was too broken
to look up.

Beside her, Aunt Syla wailed loudly and a
familiar voice boomed out. 'My loyal followers.
My devoted people. I am finally come. I am

Bal'kalu, the God of the Fields, and I ask for your forgiveness.'

Tala looked up. Xanos stood outside the shrine, smiling benevolently at the villagers. He wore a simple black tunic with long, wide sleeves. A deep purple leaf tattoo trailed from his cheek down to his neck. Beside him, flanked by two other Elders, stood High Elder Masa, his hands tied and nose bleeding, his scowl a jagged rip across his face.

Xanos spoke again. 'You must hear the truth: I have failed you. This man is no chosen one, he is a charlatan who has deceived us all. In my name, he has been creating an unholy cordial from the sacred plants. An unholy cordial which he sells for profit so that he may live in luxury while you work your fingers to the bone. My devoted people, I chose this man badly and so I walk among you in my simplest form to show you that I am sorry.'

Tala looked around. The villagers stood, open mouthed, none brave enough to speak. Her aunt broke the silence. 'He's my companion!' she bleated.

Xanos smiled kindly and pulled out his black, stubby weapon. 'And now you will see what happens to those who abuse the sacred privilege that I have given them.'

He pointed at High Elder Masa, who seemed to disappear. The villagers fell to their knees in awe in front of his tiny corpse. Aunt Syla clutched the woman next to her, weeping.

'Let this moment herald a new way. An honest way. I will begin by identifying the new High Elder. Someone who has shown themselves worthy this day. Without knowing my true identity, she came to my aid when the charlatan tried to kill me.' He threw his head back and laughed. 'Do not fear, my devoted ones. I can never be killed.' He held out his hand to Tala. 'Come my child. I have chosen you for my new High Elder. Step inside the shrine and receive your blessing.'

Hypnotised, Tala took his hand and followed him inside.

'Woohoo! That was fun!' exclaimed Xanos, dancing about on the spot. He winked. 'Do you like my tattoos? Fruit juice!'

The fog was clearing from Tala's mind. One minute she'd been outside, watching Xanos deliver his speech, and the next minute she was inside the lab in the shrine. She wasn't sure how she'd got there.

'Your uncle was so busy filling his belly that he didn't think about the limitations of this operation,' said Xanos. 'But I'm in charge now. Time to increase turnover.' He made a change to a setting on one of the tanks and the enormous plant inside thrashed violently.

Tala watched as the surviving Elders moved around the beds, adjusting tubes and checking hosts. She crossed her arms. 'So you're still not going to help these people?'

'I'm helping them to be more efficient,' Xanos said. 'They're fulfilling a much better purpose now. And so will the rest of the village.'

'They have lives, families … !'

Xanos laughed. 'But no futures! You couldn't wait to get away from here when I met you. Don't pretend you've changed your mind. I know you Tala, you're like me. You want more.'

Tala stared at him. 'What's in it for you?'

'The. Drug.' He spoke slowly, as if she were a small child. 'I'll do a new deal with this Breeder, or maybe open up the market a little to the highest bidder. But before that, a little bit of trouble-shooting.' He grinned. 'There's a really annoying bunch of Malviids on Kereval-5 and I need a big batch of purple juice to put them into that forever sleep.'

'Why would you even do that?' said Tala.

'Well because they didn't reply nicely to my letter about letting me have some very shiny and very deadly weapons that they've been guarding.' said Xanos. He held his forefinger up and grinned,

'Oh – and because I can!' Whistling, he began to stack the bottles into a crate. 'You've been loyal to me, Tala,' he said. 'So I'll give you a choice. Be grateful for it, it's more than I've offered to most.'

She waited.

'I promised I'd take you with me, didn't I? The thing is, I need someone I can trust. So, you can work as my envoy and run this operation, or you can be dinner for Planty McPlantface and his pals.' He sealed the crate and turned around. 'Just one more thing. Whichever one you choose, it's time you used my proper name. I am your Master.'

Tala sat down in the booth and drank a bitter ale while she waited for the contact to show up. A green-skinned brute at the bar gave her an approving look until she slipped open her jacket, smiling sweetly, to reveal her gun. 'Bite me,' she mouthed. Relaxing into her seat, she grabbed a handful of nuts from a bowl and munched them as she reflected. If only her aunt could see her now! She wouldn't approve, of course. The look on the woman's face when Tala told her she was leaving was magnificent. Of course, Aunt Syla had already begun to metabolise the drug by then, so her scowl soon slid down her face. 'At least you'll finally get some rest now, dear aunt,' Tala had smirked before leaving the plant lab.

Yes, if only they could all see her now. Who knew that real work could be so much fun? She and the Master were a good team. She'd already persuaded him not to wipe out those Malviids in favour of expanding his base of operations. In fact he'd hinted that if she pulled this meeting off, she'd be in line for a promotion. After all, he needed someone to run the place. She liked the sound of that.

An imperious-looking brunette sat down opposite Tala and slammed a wallet on the table. It could only be the Breeder. 'I was expecting someone else,' she said.

'Yeah.' Tala leaned back and smiled. 'He said you'd say that.'

The Master and Margarita
MATTHEW SWEET

We know you'll have questions, because we know everything. And we know everything because we've always been here.

We were here before you. We were here before the trees and flowers, before the air. We toiled among the rocks for millennia. Biting at this planet. Burrowing into it. Creating the possibility of your existence. Giving you somewhere to put down roots.

So much depends on us. When you gaze upon verdure, you gaze upon us. When, at the end, they put you into the earth, you enter our embrace. We're in the space between your children and your lovers. We dream with you: we are the stuff of your dreams. We eat with you: we taste everything you taste. You breathe us in. You move through our atmosphere. You could see us tumbling in a ray of daylight, if you ever looked. If you ever stopped thinking of yourselves.

We are less self-involved. We think of you. And we see everything. We see you now. We can feel your inhalations and exhalations. We can sense the heat of your breath. The beat of your pulse. Your eyes moving over these words. We are scattered over this page. You just touched us. Somewhere within you, inside the space of your flesh, is the knowledge that you live in the net that we have woven. That your lives are gathered up in it. That if it was broken, you would fall.

We're so close to you. Close as the last person you kissed.

Remember that, when we reach the end of this story.

We creep through every word of it.

They looked like body bags. It was everyone's first thought, on entering the Garden. Therefore it had been the first thought of Ekaterina Yegorov, who, in her Stalingrad childhood, had seen more than her fair share of corpses. Back then, she'd helped her mother peel the wallpaper and boil it up for soup. She'd scrabbled for green herbs on the bombsites. She'd listened to the jokes about the butcher, who, unwilling to eat his own dwindling stock, was said to have murdered his mother and disarticulated her corpse with tender professionalism.

The Garden was warmer than Stalingrad. Oil generators, not nature, could take the credit for that. It had been cultivated thirty feet below the earth of Sakhalin Island, where, in the winter, the air was so cold and the ground so hard that it was difficult to remember the existence of summer. A natural cave system provided its home; winding prehistoric lanes and thoroughfares repurposed for the business of human agriculture. But there was something about the Garden that put Ekaterina in mind of her childhood of siege and famine. The gloom. The earthy smells. That sense of being part of a group of people waiting for good news. She did not mention this to her colleagues. Siege and famine were the plagues that the Garden had been founded to banish. They were dreaming a dream, down in the darkness. The abolition of queues, empty shelves, expensive foreign imports. The Soviet people, liberated from hunger by resources cultivated beneath the earth of the Motherland.

All this was the Director's favourite speech. He'd make it daily, amplifying his words with slightly extravagant hand gestures and a glint in his eye that was alarming if there was nobody else in the room. He'd patrol the endless rows of polythene sacks, suspended in the darkness on bright steel hooks, each one hefty with soft black matter. He'd press his hand upon one, as if it were the belly of an expectant mother. And he'd say: 'Listen! Can you hear it? You know what's growing in here? You know what's fruiting? *Saliota venetatum!* The hero of the next revolution.'

Ekaterina, with her clipboard and head-torch, picking her way over the plank-walk between the rows of bags, could hear nothing but the faint hum of the generators and the shifting of the boards beneath her feet.

If she had been listening a little harder, she might have survived the night. She might have registered the second set of footfalls up ahead, so that when she turned the corner, she would have been better prepared for coming face to face with a monster.

But she didn't. And then there it was, caught in the beam of her torch.

Reddish-green skin, scaled and muscular like a well-fed snake. A full and strangely sensual mouth. Languid, heavy-lidded eyes, set in a skull of elaborate crests and ridges.

Ekaterina gaped in horror. A scream refused to emerge from the dry depths of her throat. The monster began moving its head. Ekaterina had the impression it was nodding its encouragement; urging her to cry out. Then she noticed the light.

A blood-red brightness that burst from its waxy forehead like the flare of a phosphorous match. Somehow, heat was surging towards her through the air. It lit the damp walls of the cave. It entered her bones and her open silent mouth.

Ekaterina tumbled backwards. Her body fell against the fat form of one of the suspended polythene bags. The plastic blistered in the heat, spilling the contents. Coffee grounds, leaf mulch, pig's blood, wood chips from the sawmill. The perfect medium for fruiting fungi. She felt herself crashing onto the plank-walk. Her attacker, still lit by the beam of the torch, loomed above her, like a warplane caught in a searchlight. Its reptile head juddered in mad violent exertion. Ekaterina remembered her mother, trying to keep up her spirits by making the boiling of the wallpaper into a game. Then the light went out.

Major Lev Surikov was from a long line of military men, longer than he cared to admit. His great uncle, Alexei, had fought on the wrong side in the mutiny of 1921, and been shot as an agent of the Entente. Major Surikov didn't advertise that, not least because he didn't want to be drawn into uttering some dreary catechism of denunciation against Uncle Alexei. He had loved him. One of his earliest memories was sitting on Uncle Alexei's knee at the dacha, in the last summer before the revolution, the old soldier singing out some toned-down version of a barrack-room ballad. Had the weather been better under the Tsars? No. It was simply that Major Surikov's career in the Soviet Army had taken him to some of the coldest places in Russia, and the coldest missions of the Cold War.

He was cold now. Sitting in the back seat of an ice-adapted jeep, swaddled in a greatcoat, leafing through his briefing notes and wondering whether a subterranean facility on Sakhalin Island would have a decent canteen. Behind him, a military convoy rolled through the snow. A truck stacked with crates of gas grenades. Two gleaming polar-white BMD-1 amphibious fighting vehicles, fresh from the factory at Volgograd. The mobile HQ, a large clumsy van adorned with communications aerials and green paintwork quite out of season. The half-impressive sight of that top-secret government outfit Yedinitza on another assignment to protect the Soviet Union from the consequences of the odd, the unexplained; anything on Earth, or even beyond.

Major Surikov squinted at a document marked with a forbidding red stamp. It was difficult to read. The light was fading, and the jeep was making increasingly violent progress over a road that barely seemed to exist.

One word leapt out at him from the page.

'Mushrooms, is it?' he said.

'Apparently so, sir,' replied Captain Tsybukin, craning his neck from the passenger seat beside the driver. 'The place is stuffed with them.'

'Like a dumpling?' asked Surikov.

'Like an underground farm,' replied Tsybukin.

'I love a nice mushroom,' said Major Surikov. 'Was it a mushroom that killed her?'

Tsybukin didn't register the joke. 'She burned to death, sir. The pathologist wondered if a welding gun might have been the murder weapon. But that wouldn't account for the scratches. They occurred after death. Like she'd been mauled by a tiger.'

'A tiger? With a blowtorch? In a mushroom farm?' Major Surikov chuckled indulgently. 'Got Yedinitza written all over it. No wonder they called us in.' His thoughts returned to his stomach. 'Any chance the mobile HQ could radio ahead?' asked Surikov. 'I want to know the soup of the day.'

'No need, sir,' said Tsybukin.

'I suppose not. It'll be mushroom, won't it?'

'It's not that, sir. It's just that we're already here.'

Surikov squinted through the window. The sight was not encouraging. A concrete blockhouse sunk with a heavy steel door. Stacks of empty pallets, banked with snow. The vehicles in the convoy rumbled to a halt. Major Surikov clambered from the jeep and exchanged a glassy look with Captain Tsybukin. Then the door of the blockhouse opened inwards, spilling yellow electric light over the snow. A man in a white lab coat and a bearskin hat was waving at them with unselfconscious enthusiasm.

'We're so glad you're here,' said Mikhail Afanasyevich Gospodinov, grasping Major Surikov by the shoulders and kissing him on both cheeks. 'Welcome to the Garden!'

'You're the Director, I take it?' asked Tsybukin.

'Oh yes,' he breezed. 'And we've a very interesting problem for you here, Major. And when I say interesting, I mean deadly.' Gospodinov was a restless, skittish figure with glittering dark eyes and a dagger-like beard. Was he Armenian? Turkmen, perhaps? Surikov did not usually appreciate kisses from a civilian. This man's informality, however, stirred no objection in him.

'We've made a discovery,' said Director Gospodinov, ushering Surikov and Tsybukin through the door to the blockhouse. 'The Garden was built inside a pre-existing cave system. We just put in some heating and plumbing and added a few extra rooms to make life bearable if you weren't actually a mushroom. But the day after Ekaterina was killed, we were examining the tunnel where we found the body. And we came across something rather intriguing.'

'Oh yes?' said Major Surikov.

Gospodinov blinked, as if suddenly remembering the correct protocol for the situation. 'You must be hungry,' he said. 'Come and have some soup. It's not bad. It's tomato. Well, it's red anyway.'

He led them past the front desk, through a pair of double doors, to a room that contained a circular hole in the ground about ten feet in diameter. Two metal runners protruded from its depths.

The Director grinned at Surikov and Tsybukin. 'How are you with ladders?' asked the Director.

They began to climb.

At first, Major Surikov couldn't understand the point that the Director was trying to make. Gospodinov was sitting on the cave floor beneath one of the farm's uncountable rows of pendulous polythene sacks. The Major did not much care for the strange fruit of the Garden. Black mulch bagged like the contents of an enormous blood pudding; naked white mushrooms of the genus *Saliota venetatum* sprouting from the plastic skin. But the Director, grinning and semi-recumbent, was asking him to look at geology, not agriculture. He was indicating a sulphurous yellow patch in the rock, about the size of a rouble.

'Impact mark?' suggested Surikov. 'Shots were fired here, I understand.'

A Yedinitza soldier was setting up a row of powerful magnesium lamps along the length of the tunnel. Captain Tsybukin swung the nearest one in the direction of the Director's discovery. Its cold glare illuminated nothing. The yellow mark was a yellow mark. The Director pulled a metal tape measure from his pocket and asked Tsybukin to hold it against his discovery. He paid out two metres until he had found something else of interest. An identical area of discolouration at the same distance from the ground. Tsybukin let go of the tape and let it stream back into its housing. The Director repeated the process three more times. At each two-metre measurement, another yellow mark became visible in the beams of their torches.

'So what is this?' asked Surikov. 'Some sort of signposting? This way to the woolly mammoth?'

'No,' said the Director, his eyes alive with excitement. 'Much more interesting than that.

These marks weren't made on the rock. These marks are *part* of the rock.'

Major Surikov looked blank.

The Director scrambled to his feet. His sudden movement made the polythene sacks swing like carcasses in an abattoir.

'Have you ever seen them putting up a new housing development in the suburbs, Major? They go up almost overnight. That's because they're made of prefabricated panels. The builders slot them together like a cardboard toy.'

'My sister in Tomsk has newlyweds next door,' said Tsybukin, sonorously.

The Director ignored the remark. 'This tunnel, this whole cave system, was built in sections in a factory,' he declared. 'It's millions of years old – and completely artificial.'

'What?' Surikov stared. 'Then who built it?'

Gospodinov rapped a knuckle against the rock and his face lit up with surprise. He rapped again. He turned slowly to Surikov and Tsybukin, his eyes as full of wonder as a monk who has just met God in the forest.

'Gentlemen,' he breathed. 'I think this section of the wall is hollow. There's something behind it.'

Breaking through was easy. It reminded Surikov of the time that his mother had locked herself out of her apartment in Leningrad. He had found her sitting on the stairs, sullenly and indecorously, chewing the heel from the loaf of black bread in her shopping bag, flirting with the locksmith who had arrived to extract her broken key. Surikov blushed to recall it.

The door had been discovered by Captain Tsybukin. He'd been examining the rock face and, quite by accident, had activated a concealed mechanism that caused a section of the wall to rise before him like a theatre safety curtain. Behind it was a granite slab of door, into which was sunk a metal grille that looked like part of an antiquated communications system. The door proved no obstacle. A Yedinitza engineer, unlit pipe clamped between his teeth, examined the door and announced that it operated on a pulley system, like a portcullis. The process was embarrassingly simple. He drove a wooden wedge beneath it, then added more blocks until he'd created sufficient space through which a man could crawl.

And Tsybukin, Surikov and Director Gospodinov crawled through.

Beyond the door, the air was cool, ancient, motionless. Surikov and his companions strained their eyes to understand the space before them. They were standing on the mezzanine floor of an excavated chamber that stretched several storeys below them into darkness. They shone their torches into the abyss. Since it was an abyss, the light was easily swallowed in its immensity.

'Mikhail Afanasyevich,' asked Surikov, 'this isn't one of ours, is it?'

'No,' said the Director.

'Or something the Japs left behind?'

'No,' said the Director.

'How old is it, do you think?'

'Eocene?' said the Director, a little catch of pleasure in his voice. Major Surikov watched three torch beams skitter across the walls of the chamber. Its surfaces were colourful. A faintly iridescent green and amber. They seemed to welcome the illumination and amplify it; an impression that increased as a squad of Yedinitza troops pushed through the doorway and began raking their own lights across the shadows.

As the gloom lifted, Surikov could see that the walls of the chamber were lined with box-like structures, glass-fronted like the vitrines in a museum. Their bases were twined with creepers and vines, some of which bore large, seductive, lotus-like flowers. Surikov examined the nearest plant.

'How do these things flower in the dark?' he asked.

'I've no idea,' whispered Director Gospodinov.

'I thought you were a botanist?'

'I'm a mycologist, Major Surikov,' said Gospodinov. 'Fungi aren't plants. In some ways they're more like animals.'

The Director was standing right beside Surikov. So close that the Major could feel hot breath on his skin. Ordinarily, he would have shirked such close contact, but he chose to stay exactly where he was. Had he fallen a little in love with this man? Perhaps something in the scent of the flowers had affected his judgement. The Major moved the torch closer to the nearest plant, inspecting its languorous purplish petals. The light spilled through the glass of the vitrine, revealing what was housed inside.

Major Surikov gave a sharp exhalation.

Inside the cabinet was a skeleton. Upright. Articulated. Clothed, partially, in body armour that glinted like mother-of-pearl. It was not a human skeleton. Its jaw was trumpet-shaped, like the mandibles of a bottom-feeding fish. The orbits of its eyes were hugely exaggerated – the greatest exaggeration being that it possessed three of them. Around the third eye, spurs and spikes of bone rose like the points of a medieval crown. It was something that Hieronymus Bosch might have dreamed after eating a bad pork chop.

'Astonishing,' whispered the Director. He glazed unblinkingly. 'Bipedal. Trinocular. Is that armour for combat, I wonder? Or ritual?' He was dragging the creepers away from the glass to get a better look. 'Or perhaps it has some funerary significance?'

Surikov shook his head silently. He shone his torch into the next cabinet. This too contained a monstrous skeleton in elaborate armour. The party moved along the walkway, passing from compartment to coffin-like compartment.

'It's wonderful!' whooped Gospodinov.

'It's the Valley of the Kings,' said Tsybukin.

'Kings of what, though?' muttered Surikov.

Then he came to a halt. The next cabinet in the row did not contain a skeleton. Its occupant was clad like the others. It had two arms, two legs and three eyes, like the others. But its body was fleshy, corporeal. Its hands were like human hands, but the skin was a mass of dry scutes and each finger terminated in a knife-like talon. It had tight strong musculature and scales the colour of a ripe plum. Above the drooping flesh of its eyelids, a third eye gleamed like a blood-red glass bead. It was a reptile. It was a man. It was impossible.

The Director moved in for a closer look, his breathing quick and urgent. He whipped a magnifying glass from his pocket and began drinking in the details. He was halfway through a speech about the preservative properties of the subterranean air when Surikov noticed another difference between this cabinet and the others they had so far inspected. It contained no glass. There was nothing between them and the monster inside.

And it was at this moment that Surikov registered that the eyes of the creature were open. That they were wide and glassy and alarmingly cognisant. That a clawed hand was planted firmly around the throat of the Director.

Surikov pulled his revolver from its holster. Six Yedinitza soldiers raised their weapons. The lizard sprang from its cabinet, spun the Director round and subdued him by placing one hand around his wrists and the other over his face. It was a curiously intimate gesture. The monster's thin green tongue tasted the air. For a moment Surikov though that it was going to kiss its captive. Instead, it dragged him sharply backwards. The Director's heels dragged helplessly over the stone floor and into the darkness.

Surikov had barely put a foot forward when a huge dull thud shook the air of the cavern. The beams of standard-issue Yedinitza torches revealed the source of the sound: the grave-like bulkhead of an anteroom. The lizard had pulled the Director into its lair and slammed a great stone door behind it.

Surikov stared at the impassive block of limestone. He imagined what was happening behind it. The lizard was probably picking the meat from its victim's bones.

The Major yelled for the engineer, who came stumbling into the chamber, dropping his pipe in the process. Tsybukin watched the object clatter to the floor, and, in an act of disciplinary malice, kicked it over the edge of the mezzanine. He did not hear it land.

The engineer examined the barrier, tapped at it with a small hammer, attempted to drive a wedge beneath it. The wood splintered against it. He tried this, over and over again, for twenty minutes, then shrugged in an infuriatingly casual manner. Tsybukin briefly pictured him blindfolded before a firing squad.

'What about this thing?' snapped Surikov. The Major was indicating a metal grille embedded in the door. 'Could you remove it? Then at least we could look through and see what was happening.'

The engineer nodded and plucked a chisel from his apron but, before he could begin work, the grille crackled into life like a radio receiver. It was relaying a conversation between two voices. One was a deep guttural bellow, the other smooth, reassuring and persuasive. It sounded like a conversation between analyst and client. It sounded like therapy.

'My father was a farmer,' said the harsher of the two voices. 'I remember him standing in the field, picking off those filthy little beasts as they ate his crops. Ape vermin. He could throw heat at them from thirty paces and kill them stone dead without burning the corn.'

'They're in charge now,' said the second voice. 'They read, they write. They have governmental systems.'

'But how could they have survived? The little planet removed the atmosphere. They should all have suffocated.'

'They clung on to the rocks. They hid, like you hid.'

A snort of disgust. 'I can smell them now. Revolting creatures. You have something of that stink.'

'If you weren't feeling angry,' asked the second voice, 'what would you be feeling now?'

Surikov recognised its tone. This conversation was happening on the other side of the door. It was Mikhail Afanasyevich Gospodinov, talking to the lizard as if they were in a book-lined study in Vienna.

'I'd be feeling homesick,' said the lizard.

'You say you remember your father's farm,' said the Director. 'What else do you remember?'

'Everything.'

'Really?'

'Everything. It is a habit of the reptile brain.'

'Do you remember being born?'

'I remember before that. I remember the egg. The pale red light of the nursery glowing through the shell. And the sensation of breaking through. The fluid spilling. The first sweet gulp of air.'

'Do you often think of that moment? Without being asked, I mean?'

'I do.'

'It's natural. You've been in total sleep for millions of years. You are the only one of your community to survive. I can only surmise that the mechanism to wake you up was never triggered because the disaster your scientists predicted never quite happened. The air never left this planet. Not completely. Your machines must still be working on the assumption that the little planet has yet to arrive. So keep thinking of the egg.'

There was a low, sputtering sound. Surikov realised that the monster was weeping.

'I know it's a lot to take in,' said the Director, a new, cold note in his voice. 'But you can't hide from it. You may be the very last of your kind.'

The creature hissed gently to itself.

'You should consider my offer,' continued Gospodinov. 'On the other side of the door are Major Surikov and his men. They are well-meaning, but they are also armed and nervous. They are the representatives of the authorities here. Benign authorities. We've created a kind of paradise here in the Soviet Union. Or we're on our way there, at least. So it strikes me that you have a choice of two futures. You could keep me prisoner in the dark, and we could both rot in here. Or—'

'I could eat you,' spat the lizard.

'Eat me?' replied the Director. 'An ape? No, we're unclean. We're untouchable. You wouldn't eat me. That would be beneath you.'

Surikov thought he heard the lizard give a rueful laugh. 'You're right,' it said. 'I wouldn't feed you to my turtle.'

Gospodinov was laughing too. 'The other way is a happier one,' he said, softly. 'Walk from here. Embrace Major Surikov as a comrade, as I have done. Learn about Marxist-Leninism. Study the world in which you've woken. The old world is gone. Become a citizen of the new one.'

Words tumbled from the metal grille. The reptile voice was losing its edge of rage. The Director's poured like honey. The conversation went on for half an hour. The men from Yedinitza hunkered down outside the door, as if listening to a play on the radio.

'It's insane,' muttered Captain Tsybukin.

'It's beautiful,' said Major Surikov. His eyes were full of tears.

The stone door rumbled open. The men leapt back, half shocked, half sheepish. Standing before them was the Director, his glossy black hair disarranged and a jagged rip disfiguring his well-cut jacket. Beside him was the lizard. Six feet tall, armoured, its scales bright and clear, its third eye glowing like the star on the Spasskaya Tower. They were arm in arm, and walked through the doorway like two married film stars arriving at a movie premiere.

The Director cleared his throat. 'I'd like to introduce you to K'vo,' he said. 'She hatched 40 million years ago. She rode a Diplodocus across the plains of Pangea and swam in the prehistoric superocean of Panthalassa. Then she was put into suspended animation. Now she's awake. And she's ready to become a citizen of the Union of Soviet Socialist Republics.'

K'vo had never seen the frozen ocean. The sight shocked her; the steel prow of the trawler splitting the grey crust of the water. The cold also shocked her. In her wildest nightmares she had never conceived of a world so starved of heat. The journey from the Garden to the port had chilled her blood. As the jeep rattled over the ice-scarred ground of Sakhalin Island, she had tried to gather warm prehistoric thoughts. She pictured the deserts; the egg-eating lizards whipping over the dunes in tight little packs. She recalled the hot, wet air of the cycad forests. And still she shivered.

When they arrived at the quayside, the Director stretched out his hand as if inviting her to join in a nuptial ritual. He led her aboard the trawler and into the captain's cabin, where she settled gratefully in a chair by the oil heater. A soldier brought in two army blankets. The Director wrapped them carefully around her. The crew peered through the door, fascinated by their green-gilled passenger. The Captain gave her hot vodka and sugar cubes. One of the fishermen, under the impression that she was some variety of mermaid, presented her with a box of chocolate-covered prunes that his sister had sent for his birthday. K'vo accepted the gifts, more for the opportunity of observing the physical variety of their donors. She had assumed that all apes looked the same, but the more she encountered, the more their differences became apparent. Some were smooth-skinned. Some had greasy pendulous hair drooping from their faces. Some had bulbous noses red with broken veins. All of them, however, possessed a common stink. She tasted the air around them. Gross mammal smells. Alcohol. Fish guts. She sipped the vodka, and enjoyed its fiery sweetness.

The Director ushered the fishermen from the cabin. Only he and Surikov remained. Gospodinov crouched by the reptile's side. He held her hand and spoke soothingly. 'That drink will do you good,' he said. 'It'll warm you. Keep listening to my voice. You can trust me. You can trust Major Surikov too. He's got a very kind face.'

K'vo looked slowly into the Major's eyes, and concurred.

'She's so much calmer,' observed Surikov. 'How are you doing it, Mikhail Afanasyevich?'

The Director put a finger to his lips. K'vo's eyes were closing. The Director gently removed the vodka glass from her hand and downed the rest himself. The reptile slumped slowly sideways.

'Is she asleep?' whispered Surikov. Gospodinov nodded. Surikov pressed further. 'Hypnosis, is it?'

The Director said nothing.

Surikov sighed indulgently. 'Don't worry,' he said. 'I know Comrade Stalin banned such things, but only on the stage as entertainment. He didn't say anything about more serious work. There was some experimental research done a few years back, you know. A bunch of dervishes, lamas, whatever they're called. They came to HQ for weeks. Stared at my men. Tried to put things into their minds. I had high hopes, but the results weren't up to much. And it certainly wouldn't have worked on a lizard.'

K'vo was snoring quietly. The Director turned around. 'She is astonishing,' he breathed. 'Forty million years old. To hold her hand, to look into her eyes. It's like travelling through time.'

Surikov sat down and removed his cap. He found a glass and poured himself some vodka. 'I've been thinking,' he said. 'About her usefulness. She survived in that cave for millions of years. And now, here she is, fighting us, talking to us, drinking with us. Her powers of endurance are extraordinary.' His eyes drifted over K'vo's scaly, sleeping form. 'She's travelled in time to meet us. But perhaps she can also travel in space.'

Gospodinov looked blank.

'Imagine, Director,' said Surikov. 'A Soviet spacecraft making landfall on Mars. The ladder rolling from the module. And down comes K'vo. Or her daughter. Doesn't matter which. Placing a foot on the rocks. Making a speech. Taking socialism to the red planet.'

The Director stifled an immoderate surge of laughter.

'What's funny?' asked Surikov, deflated.

'Sorry,' said the Director breathlessly. 'I was just imagining Nixon watching it on television.'

The Major peered into his glass of vodka. 'Your staff at the Garden,' he murmured. 'They're pretty competent, aren't they?'

'They're exemplary workers,' conceded the Director. 'Highly skilled. Toiling tirelessly to ensure that the Soviet Union never again suffers from shortage or famine.'

'Good,' said Surikov. 'That's settled, then.'

Gospodinov frowned.

'The Ministry of Agriculture can appoint another head. You're coming to work for me at Yedinitza,' stated Surikov. 'You're going to be my new scientific adviser. And your lady friend is coming too. She can be your guinea pig.'

'What?'

'Your assistant, then. Whatever you want.'

Gospodinov appeared stunned.

'All right,' he said at length, distantly. 'I was bored of mushrooms anyway.'

Surikov drained the glass of vodka and nodded. 'See you in the morning,' he said, briskly and cheerfully, and left the cabin.

The Director enjoyed the silence. Then he began to laugh.

K'vo was also laughing. She had not awoken. She had never been asleep in the first place. She stretched out in the captain's chair like a long green cat.

'Scientific adviser, eh?' she teased, reaching for the vodka bottle and pouring out two glasses. 'Don't let it go to your head, Mischa.'

'I think it's a pretty impressive title.'

'Not as impressive as your real one, though, is it?'

'Go on,' he urged. 'Say it. Nobody's said it for years.'

K'vo sank the last of her drink.

'*Master*,' she hissed.

The ship ploughed on through the sea of ice.

Before the Revolution, Yedinitza HQ had been a palace of Catherine the Great. A minor palace. So minor that no record existed of her ever having visited. The Empress had once intended it to become a way station on journeys between Moscow and one of her country retreats, but the destination fell from favour, and the building failed to become anything more than a storage space for dust-sheets, a small retinue of complacent servants, and a thousand pieces of

Wedgwood creamware, each emblazoned with a jumping green frog.

Since 1917, the palace had been put to several uses. A hospital during the Civil War. In the Comintern days, when global revolution was a key enthusiasm of the Party, it had become a training centre for the International Lenin School. Teenage radicals from all over the world had arrived to study how to handle bayonets, explosive devices, and that tricky third volume of *Das Kapital*. Yedinitza had been the official occupants for a decade. Almost immediately, Major Lev Surikov, its founding senior officer, had moved into a cottage in the grounds. This was partly for security reasons, partly to ease the pains of his divorce. The apartment in the Tverskoy District he relinquished to his wife. It was not a great wrench. He had barely visited the place, and hardly knew its occupant. Surikov preferred the routines of the mess hall and the gymnasium: the diversions of military life. And in the last six months, that life had undergone a transformation, thanks to the activities of Yedinitza's most unusual new recruits.

Everyone gossiped about them. Mikhail Afanasyevich Gospodinov and K'vo. The dark-skinned Ukrainian with the neat little beard and his elegant green girlfriend. They did not share quarters.

Gospodinov kept a small flat on the Cheryomushki estate, a new concrete housing development half an hour from HQ. K'vo was accommodated in a modest suite of rooms in the basement of the main building.

Her status was uncertain. There were bars on her bedroom window and she had yet to acquire citizenship of the USSR. But she lived in relative luxury, with a heat lamp and mirror surrounded by light bulbs, like something from the dressing rooms of the Malinsky Theatre.

The basement was the location for the scientific work carried out by K'vo and Gospodinov. Few were privy to the details, but their demands for equipment tested the abilities and the patience of the Yedinitza clerical staff. For weeks, porters arrived in pantechnicons loaded with wooden crates and hauled their contents down the stairs. Microscopes. The pale blue cabinets of an Elbrus computer. A theremin. A prodigious cheese plant. A chaise longue covered in green velvet. An ormolu clock.

Opinion on the base was unanimous: the scientist and his protégé were doing more than research down there.

Sometimes, there were music nights for the staff. K'vo would play hostess, darting around the room with a plate of blinis, shaking cocktails in an

Erlenmeyer flask. (Green ones, naturally.) Mikhail Afanasyevich, dark and handsome in his black roll neck sweater, would loll on the chaise with his guitar and sing 'Sympathy for the Devil'. People danced. Mikhail Afanasyevich asked daring personal and philosophical questions and appeared to be making note of the answers. Visitors who made a good impression at one of these soirees received a message in their pigeonhole inviting them to return for further discussions.

On the base, invitations to these sessions were both coveted and feared. It was faintly astonishing that anything so unorthodox was permitted, but Yedinitza had always enjoyed a reputation for existing slightly outside the normal mechanics of the state. Pletrov, for instance, the newly appointed KGB liaison officer, had rarely visited. When he did, his main interest was in sharing war stories with Major Surikov.

Had old Pletrov ventured down to the basement, risking his knees on the stairs, he would have detected enough ideological deviation for a whole season of show trials. He would have seen Surikov's pet scientist encouraging those assembled – soldiers, scientists, even some of the maintenance staff – to shut their eyes, empty their minds, sit cross-legged on the floor and call him Master. He would have seen the reptile woman from Sakhalin Island, dressed in a flowing white djellaba, putting Beethoven's Ninth Symphony on the record player, and Mikhail Afanasyevich Gospodinov, arms aloft, moving between the meditators and making one of his silky, irresistible speeches:

'We have gathered here to go on a journey. A journey beyond psychology. Over the period since last September, we here at Yedinitza have been given preliminary exposure to techniques that will offer a means of directly overcoming the fatal internal flaw of all socialist organisations up to this time, Lenin's included. We have been compelled, like Marx before us, to discover within ourselves qualities of mind which extant psychology does not imagine to exist. Those of us gathered here, this little cadre of seekers, will make that discovery. We need not be held back by fear of intellectual error. We need not be afraid of anything ...'

And if old Pletrov had lingered, he would have seen the quiet smiles of the men and women sitting on the floor. Such smiles were rarely spotted in real life, but beyond it they were ubiquitous. In murals, at bus stops, at the entrances to the metro, hung in banners on the street. Workers who knew that the Soviet Union was a form of paradise. Young revolutionaries gazing optimistically into a headwind. The citizens of tomorrow.

Major Surikov was always pleased to receive a memo from Mikhail Afanasyevich Gospodinov. This one, though typewritten on the thinnest paper, was like a valentine. An invitation to see the latest results of the research project in the basement.

Surikov had attended many of these sessions. Watching Gospodinov put K'vo's capabilities and limits to the test had begun to seem a form of entertainment, like a night out at the circus. The Major had seen her sit calmly for an hour in a tank of water, her great speckled eyes gazing out through the glass. (When she emerged, he felt like applauding.) He observed her use her red third eye to burn her way through a variety of materials. (Copper, for some reason, defeated her.) He had also witnessed evidence of her telepathic competence: Gospodinov had asked Surikov to draw the first thing that came into his head; seconds later, a blindfolded K'vo had also produced a pencil sketch of the Pushkin Monument on Tverskaya Street. It convinced Surikov instantly. He had rendered the statue simply, as a child would. K'vo's version was the view from the bedroom window of his wife's apartment.

When Gospodinov asked the Major for permission to take his experiments in a more psychological direction, Surikov signed the paperwork without a second thought.

The result of that largesse was now displayed before him. His scientific adviser had cleared a large room in the basement as if for physical exercise or theatrical performance. He had used chalk to mark out a grid on the floor. In each chalk square he had placed a metal-framed chair. In each chair sat a volunteer. Surikov recognised some of them. Captain Tsybukin. Magda, the divorcee from the canteen who always flirted with him at the tea urn. Boleslaw Bobkov, the quartermaster with the lazy eye. Eleonora Kalashnik, who cleaned Huts 1–17 and whistled like a blackbird while she mopped. They looked as if they were in a doctor's waiting room. Or, thought Surikov, lined up like those awful reptile skeletons they'd discovered in the cave on Sakhalin Island.

K'vo and Gospodinov were dressed in white lab coats. Each had a clipboard bearing a sheaf of typewritten papers. They nodded to each other like two actors about to begin a performance.

'Come left four degrees, Comrade Navigator,' said Gospodinov, reading from his notes.

Tsybukin looked ahead. 'Sir,' he said.

'Make your course three-four-zero,' ordered Gospodinov.

Tsybukin nodded. His hands moved in the empty air.

K'vo joined in. 'Sonar?'

'Yes sir?' replied Magda from the canteen.

'Let me know when we pass fifty fathoms.'

'Hitting it already, sir,' said Magda.

Surikov gazed in puzzlement. Had they learned this dialogue? Or had Gospodinov and K'vo led these people into a kind of dream, in which they were the crew of a submarine?

'Comrade helmsman?' said Gospodinov.

'Commander?' returned Eleonora Kalashnik.

'Rig for silent running.'

'Sir,' she snapped. 'Reducing engines to quarter speed and opening outer doors.'

'Left full rudder,' said K'vo.

'Rudder is left full,' reported Eleonora Kalashnik, making a motion not entirely unlike mopping the floor of an army hut.

'Course two-five-zero,' said Gospodinov.

'Affirmative,' said Captain Tsybukin. It was a word that Surikov had never heard him use. He wondered whether he knew what it meant.

'Engine room?' barked Gospodinov.

'Yes sir?' Quartermaster Bobkov jumped with surprise, as though he had expected his role to be a silent one.

'How is she running?'

'Running well, sir.'

'Pressure normal?'

'Yes, sir.'

'Are you sure about that?'

'Sir?' Surikov could hear the panic in his voice.

'Look again, Comrade Bobkov. At the dial.' Gospodinov was no longer looking at his clip-board. He seemed to be enjoying himself.

Bobkov was beginning to sweat. His eyes were darting around the room. Then he was looking at his hands, as if they contained needles whose movements might bear interpretation.

'It's in the red zone, sir.'

'Might there be a fire in the engine room, Comrade Bobkov?' said Gospodinov, with flat, heavy emphasis.

'There's a fire in the engine room, sir!' wailed Bobkov. He was gripping the sides of his chair and staring straight ahead.

'Comrade Navigator? Comrade Helmsman?' said K'vo. 'Leave your posts and seal the engine compartment. We must contain the fire.'

Something horrible was happening. Suddenly Surikov felt that he was attending an atrocity.

Bobkov started screaming. Tsybukin and Eleanora Kalashnik leapt to their feet. Their hands gripped an invisible locking wheel. Together, they turned it. Bobkov, howling and hyperventilating, fell from his chair. He banged his fists on the cement floor, loosing great guttural sobs that filled the air of the basement. And then he stopped, because the dead do not sob.

'What did you do?' gasped Surikov.

'We have abolished reality,' said K'vo. 'These people are in a submarine in the Baltic Sea. Because we told them they were.' She hardened her voice and turned to her experimental subjects. 'Return to your posts, Comrade Navigator, Comrade Helmsman. You have both acted with courage and propriety.'

Captain Tsybukin and Magda from the canteen sat down in their chairs. Tsybukin looked content and weepy, like a grateful lover.

Bobkov's body lay lifeless on the floor. Surikov knew he ought to protest about the murder of one of his staff, but when his scientific advisers came to sit beside him, he could summon nothing but admiration for their work. He felt that it would be a moral and social error to object to their killing of Quartermaster Bobkov. Surikov noticed that the scales around K'vo's mouth were flushed crimson. He could see little waves of colour moving over her body. And Gospodinov's voice was like cold sweet champagne on a hot afternoon.

'Imagine the possibilities, Major Surikov,' he said. 'We wouldn't have to send a spaceship to Mars. We could simply persuade the Americans that we had done it. We could make them live in a world built by us. Built inside their heads.'

'And you can't escape your own head,' said K'vo. 'All we have is our own subjectivities.'

Mrs Pelageya Vlasova had once been a plump little girl, the sort who is always indulged with sweets and biscuits. There had been famine in the twenties, but nobody had told her, and the cannibalism in the Ukraine was impossible to deduce from the evidence of a box of sugar mice, wrapped in tissue paper on the counter of a Moscow confectioner. The war burst such little bubbles of ignorance. Now, when Mrs Pelageya Vlasova looked in the mirror, she could see the deprivations of '42. So she concealed them with rouge, less subtly than she would have liked.

'Don't look at me,' she said.

'Don't look,' replied Margarita.

Margarita had heard the phrase before. A human companion might not have been compelled to repeat it, but the compulsion to echo was deep in Margarita's nature. As deep as the carmine hues of her feathers. She shuffled along the edge of the dressing table, and stuck her beak into Mrs Pelageya Vlasova's little box of costume jewellery.

Outside the window, the snow lay thickly on the avenues and greens of the Cheryomushki estate. It had turned them whiter than the concrete from which they were formed. It made them silent.

Margarita bobbed her head. She liked to sit on the shoulder of Mrs Pelageya Vlasova. Breathe in her perfume. Inhale the odour of the fixative that clung to her shock of grey hair. But not when she was in front of her mirror. Margarita knew when she was welcome, and when to fly.

'I saw him at breakfast this morning,' said Pelageya. 'I was looking through the spyhole, but he wasn't to know that. So I went out onto the landing. Such a good-looking man. I don't like them too pale, you see. My husband was pale, wasn't he, Margarita? Particularly towards the end.'

Margarita stuck out her little black tongue.

'He was on his way to work, our neighbour. And I said to him: *You're always up so bright and early. So dedicated. Your students at the university must love you. I would love to see you in front of that lectern. Showing your erudition. Lecturing on those beautiful wretched Tsars and Tsarinas, may they remain forever in infamy.* And do you know what he said, Margarita?'

'Don't look at me,' said Margarita.

'He said – *Mrs Pelageya Vlasova, history is not my subject. I'm interested in the future.* And I knew that, of course. That he doesn't teach history. It was just my little test. And it was a moment between us.'

She dabbed some Troynoy cologne behind her ears. The bottle was almost empty.

'I think he knows I know that he isn't quite what he seems to be. But I find that a very attractive quality in a man, don't you?'

Margarita offered no opinion.

'And once he'd gone, do you know what I found?' She pulled something bright and shiny from the pocket of her housecoat. A house key on a small brass ring. 'Dropped it on the doormat, didn't he?' she explained.

The parrot followed the bright metal object with a beady yellow eye.

'I'm just popping out,' said Mrs Pelageya Vlasova. 'To the heel bar.'

She was gone for an hour, after which she went to the window to wait for her neighbour to return. She did not switch on the television; it spoiled her concentration. She perched on the edge of her armchair and gazed through the net curtains. She watched the shadows lengthen on the snow, noted the clockwork streetlamps click into life.

Margarita waited with her. Pelageya Vlasova did not turn on the light.

At ten o'clock, the sitting room in darkness, she decided to warm up a slice of kulebyaka from the day before yesterday. But just as she was striking the match to light the oven, Margarita gave an agitated squawk. Pelageya Vlasova shook the match to death and leapt back to the window.

There he was. Crunching across the snow from the metro station, and unmistakably handsome, even as a dark shape moving down the boulevard. Soon he would be entering the lobby of Tower Number Eight, getting into the lift, pressing the electric button, making his way to the shared landing.

She had no excuse to intercept him, so she decided not to concoct one. She simply opened the door of her flat and waited to hear the lift doors judder open. A little bell chimed, and then he was moving towards his own front door, fumbling for his keys.

'Good evening Mikhail Afanasyevich,' said Mrs Pelageya Vlasova. 'It's such a cold night. I was just about to put on a bit of dinner for myself, but it will easily stretch to two.'

He smiled. 'It's very kind of you, Mrs Pelageya Vlasova. But I still have work to do. No rest for the wicked.' He rummaged in his pockets. 'Isn't that parrot of yours hungry?' he asked.

'All the time. But she only likes sunflower seeds. That'd bore me to death.'

The keys refused to be found. Mrs Pelageya Vlasova wondered if he'd taken a drink before he left the lecture theatre.

'I've got a little bottle of strawberry liqueur, too,' she said.

Gospodinov stopped looking for his keys. 'I think I must have left them at college,' he said.

'You can stop on my sofa,' she said.

'You're a very good neighbour, Mrs Pelageya Vlasova,' he said, stiffly. 'I'd very much like to join you. And Margarita, of course.'

Margarita fluttered coquettishly around the sitting room. When Gospodinov entered, she came to perch on his shoulder.

The cushions on Mrs Pelageya Vlasova's sofa were too thin for a good night's sleep. Knowing this, she brought her guest two boiled eggs for breakfast. He ate them quickly, expressing his gratitude for her hospitality. She thought him insincere. Much of Gospodinov's conduct, she suspected, was about appearing as normal and as ordinary as possible.

Once he had finished, he bowed low in a way that struck Pelageya Vlasova as disturbingly bourgeois, and left for the Cheryomushki metro station. She watched him from the window, as she often did. When he had disappeared from view, she turned to Margarita.

'Is it safe now, do you think?'

Margarita appeared not to understand the question. But she gave what might have been an approving squawk when her mistress produced their neighbour's key. 'You stay here,' said Pelageya Vlasova. 'Have some seeds.'

Pelageya Vlasova opened the door of her flat. The fat ginger tomcat from the floor below was sitting in the stairwell, cleaning his paws. She slipped across the landing and tried her neighbour's key in the lock. It opened easily. She crossed the threshold.

The apartment was laid out exactly like her own. A sitting room with a small dining table next to the kitchenette; a bedroom and bathroom off to right. There was no television. The only picture on the wall was an inoffensive photographic print of a forest scene. The bookshelf drew her interest. A biography of Yuri

Gagarin. The inevitable cheap edition of Lenin. A row of scrapbooks, clearly collated over a number of years. She pulled down one of these and opened it up. Newspaper cuttings had been pasted on the sugar-paper pages. Most of them were in English. 'Killer Mist Panic – Londoners Flee!' An interview with the diplomat Sir Reginald Styles. Something about a computer in the Post Office Tower in London. A report from *Pravda* on the World Peace Conference in London, with a photograph of the American delegate, Senator Alcott. As she turned the page, a loose clipping drifted to the floor. It was an advertisement for soap powder, illustrated with a bunch of plastic daffodils. She bent down to pick it up from the carpet – which was when she noticed the object taped to the underside of the dining table. A hand-sized metal device with a stubby neck and a brass ring through which a finger might be inserted. At first she thought it was a hip flask. Then she wondered whether it was a grenade. Then she noticed its tiny buttons and dials and a small patch of mesh. This was a radio. Was it a bug? Or a device that her neighbour used for contacting his handlers in the West?

Reflecting on her actions later that day, Pelageya Vlasova reproached herself for her recklessness. But in the heat of the moment, emboldened by the excitement of forbidden territory, she forgot caution, slid herself under the table and unpeeled the device from its hiding place. It was a surprisingly beautiful thing, like a gold cigarette case of the kind you saw on stage in Chekhov plays. She handled it delicately – until she glimpsed a dark shape from the corner of her eye, and found that her sudden movement had caused the device to emit a sudden shrill sound and burst of light like a magnesium camera flash.

For a moment, she could not compute what had happened. Then she saw what she took to be a toy dropped on the carpet. A model of a cat. But when she examined the object, she realised that the little feline shape in the palm of her hand was not a manufactured object, but the miniaturised corpse of the ginger tom from the flat downstairs. She had left the door ajar and the animal had wandered into the flat. Somehow, the little machine from under her neighbour's dining table had discharged and reduced the animal to doll's house dimensions.

Wide-eyed, Pelageya Vlasova gathered up the scrapbook and replaced it on the shelf, returned the device to its hiding place under the dining table, scooped up the tiny dead creature, and ran back to her flat and pressed her back against the door, breathing loudly.

Margarita flapped around the room. She perched on the sofa, nosing over the cushions, as if trying to detect some trace of the visitor from the night before.

Pelageya Vlasova walked to the window, released the catch, and tossed the shrunken animal out into the air.

'Don't look at me,' said Margarita.

The Master strummed idly at his guitar, lazing his way through the chords of 'Brown Sugar'. He watched K'vo at the laboratory bench, doing what he took to be a small chemical experiment, until he realised that she was painting red nail varnish onto her claws. 'Magda from the canteen gave it to me,' she said. 'Nice lady. Good comrade.'

'What do you think of this world, K'vo?'

'It's cold,' she said. 'And it smells.'

'True,' said the Master. 'But it's yours.'

'What year did you arrive here?' asked K'vo. The Master did the calculations. K'vo gave a snort. 'I was twenty-three summers out of the egg when the Little Planet came and we were sent down to the shelters. You have spent more time in this world than I have.'

The Master conceded the point.

'I'm trying to think of these as my gap years,' said the Master. 'Exile is too pretentious a word for it. Half a century more and I'll be back in business. Then I've got a plane to catch.' His fingers slid up the neck of the guitar. 'Plenty of time to learn the whole of this album.'

K'vo said nothing. The Master felt criticised.

'It's time I told you how I ended up here,' he said. 'Mix me a vodka martini.'

K'vo shook her head. 'It's breakfast time.'

'Not on Gallifrey it isn't,' said the Master.

K'vo opened the drinks cupboard.

'I'm here because of a woman,' said the Master. He did not put down the guitar, but continued to noodle through the chords of the song. 'She's not around at the moment. I'm going to see her again one day – but only to humiliate her. I know all her secrets. You have power over people when you know their secrets.'

K'vo stirred the drinks with a glass rod, and passed one to the Master.

'What are yours?' she asked, as the cocktail moved from her hand to his. 'Are they about … mushrooms?'

The Master laughed. 'Mushrooms, yes!' he boomed. 'Oh you're good, you're very good. You've seen right into me. You should do this professionally.' He took a sip of his drink and sank back on the chaise longue. 'Take notes if you like.'

K'vo fetched a pencil and a spiral-bound pad, then sat on the floor with her back resting against the wooden frame of the chaise.

'There's this man, you see,' said the Master. 'Old school friend of mine. He's on the other side of Europe. The Doctor. He has a laboratory and an assistant and a position in a top-secret United Nations military taskforce. He likes velvet cloaks and fast cars and gorgonzola cheese.'

'And you admire this doctor,' said K'vo, matter-of-factly. 'You want to be like him. So you made a copy of his life.'

'Admire him?' scoffed the Master. 'He lives in a police box!'

'With his assistant?'

'No. Not as far as I know, anyway.'

K'vo paused. 'What is she like, this assistant?'

'Loyal. Brave. So brave. I've seen her courage overturn the world. Banish demons.'

'You sound envious,' reflected K'vo.

'Perhaps I am.'

'Have you ever inspired such loyalty?'

It was a blunt question. The Master stayed silent.

'What's her name?' asked K'vo.

'Miss Josephine Grant. Well, she was back then. She's married now. To a professor. They left England and went up the Amazon together.

Exploring in the jungle. Hacked their way upriver in Brazil, I understand. They're still there.'

'What are they looking for?' she asked.

'Mushrooms,' said the Master.

K'vo scribbled busily in her notepad.

'And your interest in fungi? When did that start?'

'About eight months ago. I'd never heard of them before then.'

K'vo's pencil stopped on the page.

'I'm a fast learner,' protested the Master. 'I knew there was a reptile base under Sakhalin Island. So I persuaded the authorities to let me build a garden under the snow. I made them a promise. Mushroom steaks for everyone. It'll be a key policy of the next Five Year Plan. Russia is going to win the mycoprotein war. It's only a little revision to history. Enough to spoil an expedition. Wreck a marriage.'

He lifted his head to drain his glass, then bit the olive from the cocktail stick.

'What's your diagnosis, doctor?' he asked.

'I think you need to live your own life,' said K'vo. 'I think you need to be the master of your own destiny.'

The Master smiled. 'That's a daring conclusion,' he observed, 'for someone who has spent the last few months under hypnosis.'

'I'm not under hypnosis now,' she said, turning round and fixing the Master with her variegated eyes.

'No,' said the Master. 'You're not. It's no longer necessary. Unless, of course, you want me to put you back under.'

The Master thought he detected a gentle glow in K'vo's third eye. Was she going to burn him a little?

She turned away, embarrassed, picked up a copy of *Pravda* from the lab bench and threw it at the Master. 'I want to go out to the city tonight,' she said. 'We can borrow Major Surikov's staff car. Find us something to do.'

The Master obeyed. *The Blue Angel*, he noted, was showing at the Orion.

'I think you'll like it,' he said.

Major Surikov loaned them his driver as well as his car. The Master and K'vo took the scenic route. They drove round and round the Gagarin monument, watching it shine under the electric light. They watched the stars turning on the spires of the Kremlin. They stole into the cinema just as the lights were going down, and sat on the sparse back row, where a six-foot lizard would attract less attention. The Master hypnotised the usherette into bringing a box of chocolates to their seats.

K'vo was mesmerised by the picture. She watched Marlene Dietrich parade over the little stage of a cabaret club in Weimar Germany; delighted in the star's posture and the sheen of her silver top hat; chuckled to see Marlene's lover, the old bearded professor, beaming down from the box, surprised at his own capacity for romance.

They left as soon as the credits rolled and ran down the concrete stairs of the cinema into the waiting car.

'I would very much like some Cuban cigars,' said K'vo.

'I'll see what I can do,' said the Master.

The driver turned the ignition and they sped back to Yedinitza HQ. The Master walked K'vo back to the door of the basement, then turned and made his way to the metro station, and caught the train back to Cheryomushki.

The metro carriage bowled through the tunnel. The Master followed his progress on the map, counting the stations home. It was a curious sensation. Of all the lives he had enjoyed and endured – the professorships, the prison sentences, the diocesan duties, those uneasy working relationships with various wet and tentacled co-conspirators – he had never anticipated becoming *suburban*.

A fellow commuter had abandoned a tattered copy of *Krokodil* on the seat beside him. The Master leafed through it, looking at the cartoons. They were mainly incomprehensible. The KGB sometimes used the magazine to relay messages to agents out in the field; he stared at the image of a dog eating a cuckoo clock and surmised that they were having a busy week.

The train stopped. The carriage emptied out. One new passenger came aboard. A hunched old man in a dusty grey raincoat with the collar turned up. He sat directly opposite the Master. He was also reading a copy of *Krokodil*. The train gathered its skirts and moved off.

'It's on trains like this,' said the man, from behind the magazine, 'that you begin to wonder where you're really going in life's great journey.'

The Master did not look up. He did not enjoy this kind of conversation. The metaphysical speculations of humans were, in his experience, invariably trite. But the man persisted.

'Like you, for instance, Mikhail Afanasyevich.'

The Master was surprised by this, but still did not look up. 'Do you know me?'

'Well enough to know that you're not really called Mikhail Afanasyevich,' returned the man.

'You KGB people are preposterous,' said the Master, casting his eyes over a cartoon that showed two men marooned on a desert island, pulling the wishbone on a chicken. 'That raincoat. Hiding your face behind that magazine. You need some new clichés.'

'I'm not KGB,' said the man. His voice was dry and discomfiting. 'I'm not from any three-letter agency. I represent a different kind of authority.' He lowered the copy of *Krokodil*. 'Allow me to introduce myself,' he said. 'My name is Cap. Comrade Cap, if you prefer.'

The Master looked up. The sight did not please him. Comrade Cap was an appallingly ugly man. His skin was mottled and desiccated like a baked potato left overnight in the oven. His eyes were two little black raisins. His sandy yellow hair was an obvious toupee, kept in place by a Cossack hat. The Master could not quite disguise his disgust. Until it struck him that this man was not a member of the human species.

An alien was importuning him on the Moscow subway.

'Pardon me for asking,' said the Master, 'but are you by any chance—'

'Extraterrestrial?' replied Comrade Cap. 'Sure. I'm like you. Just passing through. Making investments here and there. Chasing that elusive big deal. Earth is one of the most interesting developing markets in this sector. It has incredible potential.' He put the copy of *Krokodil* back into his briefcase and snapped it shut.

'You don't mind a cold call, do you?' he asked. 'Only I think that right now we have a very strong offer to make to an operator of your experience. I've been taking a look at your business model. And I have to say that it all looks a bit scattergun. You've been on this planet since the 1940s. And what have you got to show for it? An experimental facility in Siberia, dedicated to the mass production of mushroom stroganoff.'

For the first time in several decades, the Master was genuinely surprised.

'Not exactly holding the universe to ransom, is it?' said Mr Cap, laughing a little arid laugh. 'Not exactly Peoples-of-the-Universe-Please-Attend-Carefully, is it?' He chuckled wheezily. 'We all thought that was your best one in the office. And don't look so offended. You've got that shifty look of a man who's doubled back on his own timeline. You might think you're passing as a dead-straight linear kind of guy, but you don't fool me, honey.'

'It was Sakhalin,' said the Master.

'Eh?'

'Sakhalin Island. Not Siberia. The fungi place.'

Comrade Cap looked disappointed. He snapped open his briefcase, pulled a little notebook from the pocket in the lid, and jotted down the correction. As he wrote, he made his sales pitch.

'Have you ever thought of expanding?' he asked. 'The people I represent are keen to give their backing to business people opening up the new Earth markets. You're a pioneer and we salute you. But to secure our finance we'd need assurances that your work was going to go to the next level. Have you ever thought about seizing control of the Kremlin?'

'It's big and it's draughty,' said the Master.

'Or,' wheedled Comrade Cap, 'perhaps establishing a sister operation on one of the other planets of this system? The economies of scale would kick in sooner than you might imagine.' He stopped writing in the notebook. His mouth became a thin and serious wrinkle. 'Thing is, you see, this economic system isn't going to last forever. I know it's impossible to imagine that right now, when you see all those men standing on the platform and waving those nuclear missiles over Red Square, but it's in a terrible state of decay. Something new is beginning to grow. Some of my contacts are fifth-dimensional and give very good tips. But you don't need the time advantage to work that one out. You can just see it in the faces of those guys. They're all so *old*!'

The train stopped at another underground station. Nobody got on or off. The doors clattered shut and the carriage moved off down the tracks.

'Comrade Cap,' began the Master. 'Over the years many people have speculated about my motives. They have suggested I am vengeful. I am sometimes. Well, often. They have suggested I am power-mad. Well, I know my faults, and I know that madness is next to genius. And you'll think it terribly snobbish of me, but in all this time – and there has been much of it – nobody has ever accused me of being an *entrepreneur*.'

'You've lived in the Soviet Union too long, my friend,' said Comrade Cap, with an expression that did not plausibly convey friendliness. 'You've gone native.' The strange old man got to his feet, crossed the carriage, and sat directly next to the Master. Proximity did not improve his sales pitch. The Master was forced to examine the thick parched flesh of Comrade Cap's face; its fissures and patches. A strong smell, he noticed, rose from Cap's skin. Something rotten and powdery.

The train rattled from a tunnel and out into an overground section of track. The evening light burst through the windows and bathed Comrade Cap's grey features in the fire of a winter sunset. His little black eyes shone.

'Think of what you could do, though, in this mean little culture, with all its pettiness and moral mediocrity and stifled desires. It's so hard to live here and remain a virtuous citizen. But imagine if someone brought them the message that they were free to grab what they wanted. Imagine the money you could make. You could be their guru.'

Comrade Cap's words filled the Master with anger and contempt. Who was this man to speak to him in this way? His smell also had an irritant effect. The Master felt a prickling sensation in his nostrils. He sneezed.

'*Bud zdorov*,' said Comrade Cap. 'Bless you!'

This, for the Master, was the last straw. He considered himself capable of great self-control. Only the prospect of victory or defeat inclined him to emotion. But Comrade Cap's insinuations, his vulgarity, stirred a murderous rage in his hearts. He leapt to his feet and grabbed the wizened old man by the lapels. He was as light as an old stick. The Master hurled him against the doors of the train carriage. The pneumatics were elderly and poorly maintained. It occurred to the Master that it would be perfectly possible to pull the doors apart and push Comrade Cap through the gap.

He did so.

Comrade Cap made a rasping, bleating sound as he tumbled backwards into the air. The night was gloomy, but the Master thought that he saw the old man's body snap in two before it hit the ground.

When the Master got back to Cheryomushki, Mrs Pelageya Vlasova was waiting for him on the landing.

'Mischa,' she cooed. 'I've made *pelmeni* with sour cream.'

'Thank you,' he said. 'I am very hungry.'

'And I found your front door key. It was just lying on the stairs.'

The Master sank into the armchair while his neighbour lifted the dumplings from a pan of boiling water. He thought he detected something odd in her manner – as though she knew something about him that she hadn't known when he left in the morning. But he was too tired to speculate. They watched television together. Programme Two was showing a costume drama about Ivan the Terrible.

'You would have made a good Tsar, said Mrs Pelageya Vlasova. 'You've got the beard for it.'

Margarita was perched on top of the television. She squawked immoderately.

'Get off there, Margarita,' chided Pelageya Vlasova.

The bird did nothing.

'Come on, Margarita,' said Pelageya Vlasova's guest. 'Back to your perch. I am the Master and you will obey me.'

Margarita obeyed.

The killing of Comrade Cap was not reported in the papers. The Master anticipated that. But he had expected Yedinitza to be brought news of a mysterious non-human corpse discovered by a railway track ten minutes from its own base. Four morning briefings came and went, at which the conversation concerned an unsubstantiated UFO sighting near the Paldiski submarine base in Estonia and some satellite photographs revealing that the RAF had bombed a manor house in Surrey. And yet, every time the Master took the train to or from work, he could see the evidence with his own eyes. Comrade Cap's butter-coloured hairpiece, hanging from a buddleia bush on the embankment.

Comrade Cap's words also persisted. Not his business proposition. That held no attraction for the Master. He had no desire for four-poster beds or beach-houses or using mink coats to secure the affections of others. But the old man with the briefcase had suggested that the Master was underachieving, and this was uncomfortably close to some of the observations made by K'vo.

These thoughts were still gnawing away at him a few days later, as he stood in the basement laboratory with his prehistoric assistant, toying with the mind of an army volunteer. The experiment was going smoothly. They had successfully convinced him that Shirley Temple had been elected to the White House on a platform of unilateral disarmament and was flying into Moscow to give a special concert in Red Square. The volunteer believed he was in the crowd, singing along to 'On the Good Ship Lollipop'.

'The joke is,' the Master explained, over the noise, 'that Shirley is more hawkish than Nixon. During the Vietnam War she told him to mine the approaches to Haiphong in order to cut off the supply lines from Russia and China. Five years later he did it.'

K'vo absorbed the information mirthlessly.

'It's all right, this work, isn't it?' asked the Master.

'It's fine,' replied K'vo. It was not the response he would have liked.

'What's wrong?' he asked.

'It works on small groups of individuals,' she said. 'But I've yet to see how it could be used on a whole population. We have to be present in the room, sweet-talking them. It's not much use as a weapon of the state if we can't broadcast the effect.'

The Master nodded grimly. Their experiments in this area had been failures – though setting up a radio station at Yedinitza HQ had sharpened his ability to talk between records in a relaxed manner.

'You're right,' he said. 'It's just a parlour trick.'

The army recruit was singing blithely. His cheeks were hot and pink.

The Master decided to silence him with a shout. 'Oh no!' he yelled. 'Shirley's been assassinated!'

Colour drained from the volunteer's face. He stopped like a clock. The Master was relieved.

'Should I be thinking bigger, K'vo?' he asked.

'Like your rival in London?' asked K'vo. 'The one who likes cheese?'

The Master felt suddenly defensive. 'Is it my fault that the alien invasions are all happening on his turf?'

K'vo cocked her head to one side. 'Since you claim to have started most of them, yes.'

'I suppose so. But I wish just one alien race would launch a full-scale invasion of the Soviet Union. Or threaten to start the apocalypse from here. I could save the Earth. And eventually the Doctor would get to know about it, and that would be delicious. Wouldn't it be bliss if the

Daleks landed a saucer in front of the Lenin Library and went out to patrol the banks of the Neva? Then in I come, improvising something immensely clever and repelling them all back into space. For once I could be the foiler, and not the foiled.' He loosed a deep sigh. 'But no. When Daleks come, they come to Bedfordshire.'

K'vo reached into the top pocket of her lab coat and pulled out a cigar. She lit it on a Bunsen burner and then threw herself down on the chaise longue.

'You can save the Earth,' she said. 'What sort of threat does this Doctor usually tackle?'

'Well,' said the Master, 'I suppose the textbook situation would be a base of some kind. Military or scientific. And there'd be aliens doing something quite subtle, at first. Crawling around the pipes, for instance, or hiding in the basement, or poisoning people, and then waiting for the moment to emerge from the shadows and announce their intention. To colonise the world, or blow it up, or eat it, or some such.'

'Doesn't sound too difficult,' said K'vo.

She blew a smoke ring into the air.

Major Surikov was not good at writing letters of condolence. That is not to say he was inexperienced in the craft; simply that he found each new one as difficult to construct as the last. He tried to think kind thoughts about Quartermaster Bobkov, but could not recall any particularly pleasant interaction with him, nor summon any memory of having met his family. Surikov tore his first draft from the machine and found that, rather than expressing his regret, he had somehow managed to compose a graphic account of Bobkov's last moments on the basement floor. The man's family would gain no comfort from that; Surikov threw it into the wastepaper basket. He stared out of the window, and wondered whether he ought to make an appointment with the medical officer. Something was not quite right.

The phone on his desk screamed for attention. Surikov answered. The line was bad, but the voice on the line spoke clearly and urgently. It belonged to the commanding officer at the Paldiski nuclear submarine base on the Estonian Baltic coast. He was ringing in confidence. He didn't want his men to think he was losing his mind. He spilled his story. Surikov heard an account of strange lights out at sea. Shining figures that swam up to shipping and peered through the portholes. A break-in at the submarine base. Items of equipment going missing. And the Commander's best explanation for these mysterious events, which involved an alien spacecraft on the seabed, damaged and in need of repairs – and its crew looking to the submarine base as an obvious source of electronic components.

'I sound crazy, don't I?' said the voice of Commander Yuri Gerasimov. 'It's just a hypothesis.'

'Don't concern yourself, Commander,' said Surikov. 'This is core Yedinitza stuff. Our bread and butter. Now get a good night's sleep and I'll see you in the morning.' He put down the phone and dialled the basement laboratory.

'Mikhail Afanasyevich!' he exclaimed. 'Christmas is here. We're going to fight monsters on the Baltic coast. Pack your suitcase and tell that big scaly lady to do the same.'

'K'vo isn't very well, I'm afraid, Major. I've put her into isolation in her quarters.'

'Nothing serious, I hope?'

'Her immune system remains positively Palaeolithic. We just need springtime to come.'

'Ah well,' said Surikov. 'It might have been difficult to take her to a naval base. You know what sailors are.'

The following morning, a Yedinitza jeep stopped at the checkpoint at the entrance to the Paldiski base, a thickly forested high-security zone that no Estonian citizen was permitted to enter. The guard on the gate confirmed news that

Tsybukin had received by radio an hour before. The situation had escalated. Poison gas had been released on the site, and all non-essential personnel had been evacuated. Commander Gerasimov was still trying to establish the origin of the attack.

Major Surikov checked his respirator, but was unfazed. 'Much warmer here, isn't it?' he beamed, as their jeep cruised through the wooded avenue that led to the main street of the little town. 'I'm going to enjoy this, Gospodinov. Did you bring your costume? I love sea bathing.'

Yedinitza's scientific adviser shook his head.

'I brought mine, sir,' said Tsybukin, cheerfully.

The concrete mass of the submarine dock jutted out into the waves. Beside it soared the administration and strategy building, a brutalist slab thrown up without art or compromise. Neat barrack-like houses made up the rest of the town. On an ordinary day, the street would have been bustling with activity: the wives and children of the submariners going about their business. Now everything was silent. The little supermarket was shuttered, the school unoccupied, the swings in the playground motionless.

Commander Gerasimov, a weary Cold Warrior with sad patrician eyes, met the Yedinitza party at the door of the administrative block. A gas mask hung around his neck. The cares of the world seemed to do the same.

He apologised for the ghostly quality of the town. 'We removed all the families and civilian staff,' he explained. 'They piled out first thing this morning. It was the gas attack, you see. We had one fatality. We didn't want to take any chances.'

'What kind of gas attack was it?' asked the Master. 'Shells fired from the sea, perhaps?'

'Shells fired from the sea,' repeated Gerasimov. 'I saw one fall as I stood on the bridge.'

'Did you get a sample, Commander?' asked the Master. 'If so I'd be most grateful if you'd let me analyse it.'

Gerasimov led the Yedinitza group upstairs to the bridge. It occupied the entire top floor of the building, but with only a skeleton staff on duty, it looked bereft, like the bar of an unpopular seaside hotel. The long slate line of the Baltic bisected the view from the observation window. Major Surikov gazed out at the rolling grey waves, and thought of childhood holidays with his mother.

Gerasimov began to describe the events leading up to the gas attack. About a month ago, he said, he had witnessed something extraordinary. He'd been walking his dog on one of the coastal paths, and seen a light out at sea. A large, luminescent structure just below the surface of the water.

'I hadn't been sleeping well,' he confessed. 'I thought it might be all in my mind. But I wrote up a report all the same. I thought it was my duty.'

'We received that report,' confirmed Surikov. 'You did the right thing.'

'I regretted it straight away,' said Gerasimov. 'Naturally they wanted to give me a psychological evaluation. I was due to have it today. I'm spared that at least. Because two days ago, I saw it again. Pulsing in the water. Gathering its power. And there was a witness this time. Captain Glaskov, God rest his soul.'

'He's dead?' asked Surikov.

'Killed this morning in the gas attack,' said Gerasimov. He looked as forlorn as a figure in an old painting, kneeling at the foot of the cross. 'But we have had no time to mourn him, as you will appreciate. The last forty-eight hours have been … unusual.'

He handed his visitors a sheaf of reports. Tsybukin read through them. Telexes from the coastguard relaying eyewitness reports of fast-moving silvery beings glimpsed in the water. Sonar data describing the presence of a large object a mile from the Paldiski shoreline. Inventories showing items missing from the stockroom.

The Master cast his eyes over these. 'Interesting,' he mused. 'Somebody seems to be building an electromagnet.'

'Sir!' called out one of Gerasimov's lieutenants. He was hunkered over the teleprinter. 'I think you might want to see this.' The machine was chuntering madly, the cradle moving backwards and forwards with diabolic speed, paying out a photographic image, line by line. It was like watching something materialise at a séance. Something demonic. Two hollow demented eyes. The thin slit of a mouth. Skin that reflected the light back into the camera, burning out the image.

'Who is transmitting this picture?' barked Gerasimov.

The lieutenant did not reply. He was staring, slack-jawed through the observation window. The others turned to follow his gaze.

There, hovering thirty feet above the choppy water, was an alien spacecraft. A silver disc as large as the dome of St Basil's. It was marked with bright orange signs and symbols that Major Surikov surmised were a propaganda message directed, uselessly, at the occupants of the bridge. Gun turrets twitched and twisted on its under-carriage. Some were already crackling with pale blue light, as if preparing to discharge a rain of thunderbolts towards the coast. As they watched, the disc shifted position in the sky. And then it charged. The scream of its engines tore the air. Warning signals flashed on control panels all over the bridge. Klaxons shouted for attention. The small band of men looking through the window darted under desks and behind radar units, bracing themselves for the inevitable impact.

Which proved miraculously evitable.

Captain Tsybukin was the first to raise his head.

The saucer had cleared the top of the bridge. The screeching engines were silent. So were the alarms and klaxons, cut dead by some mysterious force. Tsybukin could hear the gulls crying down on the shore. But then came a second barrage of sound. Something slower and more measured that caused a mild vibration in the steel skeleton of the building.

The Master announced what everyone else was thinking.

'Gentlemen,' he said. 'That flying saucer has landed on the roof.'

The following day, when the debriefings occurred and the reports began to be drafted, the small band of people in that room on the Paldiski base found it hard to recollect the precise order of events. Tsybukin was sure that the silver figure had materialised on the bridge like a genie in a fairy tale. Surikov spoke of seeing the emergency exit flung open, and the enemy standing there, as provocative and defiant as a gunslinger entering a Wild West saloon. But they all agreed on the qualities of its voice – its pitch, its notes of violence, its fathomless contempt. They remembered the surface of its skin, which was like scrubbed aluminium. They also remembered that during the incident, Mikhail Afanasyevich Gospodinov was nowhere to be seen.

'Humans,' began the silver being, flaunting its hostility towards them like an expensive organza evening dress. 'We did not intend to visit your world. That was our punishment for a fault in our starship. We have now completed our repairs. But in our brief sojourn here on Earth we have made an unwilling study of your species. And we have come to this conclusion. I regret to say it will not please you. You are wretched stinking vermin. You do not deserve this planet. You have stolen it from others.'

Surikov recovered his voice. 'What others?' he asked.

'Your interjections are not required,' boomed the silver being. 'We are communicating this message because you have been selected as the designated survivors. In a few moments all simian life on this world will be extinguished. As you are a group of males, there is no possibility of you repopulating the planet. But we thought it appropriate to spare the lives of a small group in order to produce a record of this moment, so that it may be read by the species that evolves to take your place. We will provide you with the writing materials to do this.'

'Very generous,' said Surikov drily.

'And we will also tell you what to write.'

A second silver being entered the room. It was carrying a box like a picnic hamper, or a carrier you might use to take a small dog to the vet. It placed the box on the floor, lifted the lid, and produced a stack of silvery notebooks and a handful of metallic styli. It distributed these to the men present in order of rank – first Gerasimov and Surikov, then Tsybukin and the six naval staff officers who had stayed on the bridge. The second silver being then left the room, like a discreet maître d' who has just delivered the first course.

'Open your books,' said the alien. 'You will take dictation.'

The men fumbled with paper and pencils.

'We, the human race, have been polluting this beautiful world for millennia,' the being declared. 'On reflection, we have decided that it would be better for the planet, and for this region of space, if we were simply to take a bow and leave the stage.'

In the debriefing, nobody admitted to having obeyed these instructions. As the notebooks did not survive the incident, the denial was plausible. From this point, though, all their accounts agreed. The silver being had lorded it over them, listing the sins of humanity. Special mention was made of the hideous nature of viviparous reproduction, of the damage to nature caused by the factories and furnaces of Magnitogorsk, and the dismal crime of snakeskin shoes and belts. And while the silver being was dictating its suicide note for the human species, its reluctant secretaries noticed a presence behind its back. A figure was crouching in the emergency exit. He had two bulky objects in his arms: a large coil of copper wire, about the size of a wastepaper basket and a cardboard drum looped with insulated cable. Between his teeth, making a T-shape with the dagger-like line of his beard, was a screwdriver.

Surikov watched his scientific adviser moving around the room, paying out the cable. Gospodinov concealed himself behind desks and computer banks, lithe and quiet as a cat. At one point he stood up and peered over the top of a filing cabinet, and the Major was sure that the silver being had spotted him. But it seemed too engaged with the task of adding new crimes to the charge sheet.

'... we atone for the inadequacy of critical writings on the life and career of Miss Marlene Dietrich – for the unsatisfactory nature of nail varnish under Communism ...'

And then the cable went live. Electricity sizzled around the room, so much that Surikov, Gerasimov and their men could actually smell it. The effect on the silver being was instantaneous. Its mean loud mouth fell silent. Sparks coursed over its metallic frame. A white vapour poured from its joints. Like a doll held together by an elastic band that has finally rotted away, the creature disarticulated before their eyes, its constituent parts tumbling to the carpet tiles. After a couple of seconds, these fragments began to crackle and fizz with the fierce vigour of soluble aspirin. Moments later, nothing was left. Not even a stain on the floor.

Surikov and his comrades reeled in amazement. Then a great roaring sound rushed at them from above their heads. The saucer was taking off. Its engines shook the building, hurling everyone to the floor. Gerasimov was sure that his workplace was going to collapse. He thought he could hear the concrete cracking; imagined himself falling through the empty air. But the block remained upright. And as the men looked skywards, they saw the shape of the saucer recede to a tiny white speck on the horizon, and then disappear.

The Master enjoyed the scene. Not the sudden disappearance of the alien aggressor, but the sight of nine uniformed Russians crouched on the bridge floor, bidding good riddance to a hostile spaceship that had never arrived, getting up to brush invisible dust from their clean uniforms, and running, joyously, to congratulate him for having saved them from a peril that never existed.

The Master did not look at them. He was gazing at the figure of K'vo, loitering in the doorway of the emergency exit, clipboard in hand, smiling a thin smile of triumph. It was only when she had slipped from view that he acknowledged the handshaking and the backslapping.

'A simple solenoid,' he said, with the airiness that he knew the Doctor favoured in such circumstances. 'I had an inkling that these metal creatures were held together by electromagnetic force. So I interrupted it.'

Nine men with very little understanding of physics gave a loud cheer, raised the Master to their shoulders, and began a loud chorus of 'Kalinka'. They carried him in a circle around the bridge, until someone looked in a cupboard and discovered an unopened bottle of Polish bison grass vodka.

The celebrations went on for two days – first at Paldiski, then in the train compartment on the way back to Moscow, then at Yedinitza HQ – interrupted only by the Master's interview with the head of the investigation, who had very little idea of how to assess an event of such a nature, and was reduced to asking questions about the colour of the flying saucer.

At the end of the second night, a great honour was conferred. The Master and Surikov were invited to a drinks reception at the Kremlin. A sleek black car delivered them to Red Square, from which they were ushered into a thickly carpeted drawing room dominated by the most immense chandelier that either of them had ever seen. The Deputy Chairman of the Council of Ministers was there to greet them, fill their glasses, and introduce them to the august company assembled. Ancient military veterans, some almost invisible behind barricades of medals, offered their respects and told long stories about tank and aerial warfare against the Germans, which mostly dwindled into detailed accounts of their recent health, or – in one case – the memory of a girl last seen near a Georgian haystack in the summer of 1912. Old Pletrov of the KGB was there, too, though he did not seem sociable. He stood to one side of the room, apparently content to listen to the rambling anecdotes of others.

At precisely ten o'clock, the General Secretary of the Party entered the room. Hush descended. Leonid Illyich Brezhnev moved across the carpet like a sclerotic mole certain of the proximity of a juicy worm, but unsure of its precise location. Eventually he found it. He shook the Master's hand, his bright little eyes suddenly visible beneath the thick grey hedgerow of his eyebrows.

'Mikhail Afanasyevich,' he rasped. He smelt of soap and cigarettes, and would not release the Master's hand. 'At the battle of Malaya Zemlya, I got into a bit of a scrape. Germans. Hordes of them. Coming right at me. I wasn't a combatant in the Great Patriotic War. I did political work. But I ran to one of the machine gun posts and let rip. *Blam-blam-blam!* They're very loud things, machine guns.'

A cohort of generals had gathered around their leader, forming the kind of adoring audience familiar from a thousand socialist realist paintings.

'So the rest of the boys came running,' said Brezhnev. 'The trained men. And one of them touched me by the arm and said, *Let the machine-gunner take over now, Comrade Colonel.* And a few minutes later, all those Fascists were dead in the mud.'

The generals laughed immodestly.

The General Secretary relinquished the Master's hand and nodded to a nearby official, who produced a silk-lined box. It contained a shining medal suspended on a crimson ribbon.

'The Order of Lenin,' wheezed Brezhnev. 'The highest honour the Soviet state can bestow upon a civilian.'

He placed it around the Master's neck. Surikov and the generals applauded with the same manic vigour they displayed during speeches at the Party Congress.

That night, the Master slept a sound heroic sleep. Was this, he wondered, how it felt to be the Doctor? He awoke at six and went to the bakery at the end of the boulevard. He bought custard tarts and a bag of sunflower seeds, and rushed back with them to the apartment of Mrs Pelageya Vlasova. It took him a moment to locate her doorbell. He realised that he'd never had cause to press it.

Mrs Pelageya Vlasova opened the door in a state of discombobulation. She did not like to be seen without her make-up.

'Sorry to be so exuberant at such an early hour,' said the Master. 'But I had a very successful day at work yesterday. So here's something for you and something for Margarita.'

Mrs Pelageya Vlasova accepted the gifts with pleasure. Then her neighbour clicked his heels and went on his way to the Cheryomushki metro.

The same atmosphere of jollity prevailed at Yedinitza HQ. A knot of secretaries waved cheerily at the Master. A maintenance man painting marks on the road stood to attention. Even K'vo was in the mood to celebrate. When the tea break came, they shared her first cigar of the day. The Master felt like he was in the opening number of one of those Soviet musicals about a boy, a girl and a tractor.

Then a memo stopped the fun.

'It is most grave,' muttered Major Surikov. 'Most grave.'

A limousine was waiting to take them back to the Kremlin. Surikov, Tsybukin, the Master and K'vo climbed inside. K'vo brought a small forensics kit, with surgical knives and sterile plastic bags. They rode into the city in silence. The Master realised that it was the same car that had brought them to the party the night before.

When they arrived, a retinue of unsmiling, untalkative men ushered them through vaulted halls with polished floors and into the private quarters of the Deputy Chair of the Council of Ministers.

The room was richly furnished. On the wall there hung an enormous canvas of Prince Alexander Nevsky leading his forces across the frozen surface of Lake Peipus to put the Livonian Order to the sword. A bust of Lenin was facing the painting, as if absorbing points on strategy. In the bed, under a thick burgundy-coloured eiderdown, was the Deputy Chair. He was clearly very dead – but in a deeply unusual fashion.

The Deputy Chair was lying on his back with his eyes staring madly at the ceiling and his mouth wide open. It was if he had died in the act of swallowing something. But the traffic, as it were, was moving in the other direction. The pink space of his mouth was occluded by the thick fingers of a fruiting fungal body. It had pushed its way up from the depths of his throat, like a fist groping towards the light. A pale mass of flesh shaded his neck from view.

The Master moved closer to inspect the body. There was something odd about the dead man's eyes. It took a moment for him to register that they had disappeared, their places taken by two wet grey mushroom caps.

Another thought struck him. These fungi looked very much like the same species that he had cultivated under the ground of Sakhalin Island. *Saliota venetatum*. They were sprouting from the Deputy Chair just as they had sprouted from the polythene bags of wood chippings and coffee grounds and abattoir waste that hung in the avenues of the Garden. The man's skin, he noticed, was covered in little bumps and hives. Would more fruit soon be pushing its way through his flesh?

'We'll need to take some samples,' said K'vo. She used a scalpel to slice away a section of fungus, then placed it in a sterile bag.

Surikov was deep in conversation with one of the taciturn men. He was not smiling. They were both looking at something on the floor. The Master followed their gaze. In the corner of the room, next to the bust of Lenin, was an indentation on the carpet. A mark of the kind that might have been made by a heavy piece of furniture.

K'vo produced a tape measure from her kit bag and sank down on her hands and knees. The indentation, she announced, was exactly four and a half feet square. She measured the frame of the bedroom door. It was four feet across.

The Deputy Chair's personal assistant was summoned. 'Did anybody remove a wardrobe from this room in the last few hours?' asked Surikov.

'Or a statue, perhaps?' added K'vo.

The assistant shook her head and burst into tears, her eyes darting from the fruiting corpse of her boss to the six-foot lab-coated lizard who was asking the question.

A cold wind blew the following day. It whipped around the walls of old palace where Yedinitza made its home, raising little spirals of dust and grit. It also brought more bad news. When the Master arrived in the laboratory, old Pletrov of the KGB was already there to deliver it. He was sitting on the chaise longue, drinking a cup of black tea that had been made for him by K'vo. As if the laboratory belonged to him.

'Gospodinov, my dear fellow,' he said. 'I have a question for you. What's your favourite mushroom?'

The Master floundered. 'Well, there are so many.'

Old Pletrov did not wait for an answer.

'What was Comrade Lenin's favourite mushroom, then?' he demanded.

'I've really no idea,' said the Master.

'I do,' said Pletrov, inordinately pleased with himself. 'Ask me how I know.'

'How do you know?' said the Master, dutifully.

'Because I used to go mushrooming with him, Mikhail Afanasyevich. In those final months, back in '24, when the old Vladimir Illyich was all but gone, and he lived on the farm at Gorki. Are you going to ask me about the experience?'

'I am,' confirmed the Master.

'Splendid,' said Pletrov. 'At the end, you know, he moved closer to the mushrooms. They were a substitute for politics. Mushrooms exerted no pressure on his brain after politics caused his stroke. Ah, how that stroke brought him down. It robbed him of his words. It left him to struggle with a children's ABC, relearning the world through dogs and cats and tables and chairs. Futile, really. It just made him angry. I told him not to bother. *Vladimir Illyich*, I said: *Why die at school if you can die at home?*'

He took a sip of tea, complimented K'vo on its quality, and barrelled on with his anecdote. 'We'd go out together, he and I, and that little dog Aida. And the old man would hunt for mushrooms in the birchwoods on the estate, peering at wet rotten stumps, listening to the birds, observing the spores drift on the wind. And when he chanced upon some good fungi – a little outburst of them, in the grass – he would reach down and cut each one from the ground with a little penknife he carried in his pocket. Each nut-brown fleshy fruit.'

Pletrov peered coldly at the Master. 'And I'm leading up to my question again, Gospodinov, old chap. Which variety did it most delight Comrade Lenin to harvest?'

'I still don't know,' said the Master.

'*Boletus edulis!*' he crowed. 'The aristocrat of fungi. So you see, even in those last years, with that little penknife, Lenin was engaged in important revolutionary activity.'

The Master managed a polite laugh. Old Pletrov drank the last of his tea.

'And if you've forgotten your favourite mushroom,' he said, 'let me remind you. It's *Saliota venetatum*. That's what your friends on Sakhalin Island have led me to believe. Such decent people. The Garden is growing without you, it seems. But here's the difficult bit, Mikhail Afanasyevich. We've been talking to General Gerasimov, the commanding officer at the Paldiski base.'

'Oh?' said the Master. 'How is he?'

'Not very well, I'm afraid. The psychology report wasn't exactly glowing. He's been under a lot of stress. For some months, too. Poor man. That first report of UFOs he filed. Did you ever read it?'

'No,' said the Master.

'Quite cracked. Some of it was rendered as equations.'

'Oh dear,' said the Master.

'Odd thing is, when our doctors examined him, they noticed something else was wrong. Something peculiar in his mouth. A kind of infection. Fungal, it turns out. And the species? This is the interesting bit. *Saliota venetatum.* Extraordinary coincidence, don't you think?'

The Master nodded silently.

Pletrov turned to K'vo. 'I don't suppose you've identified the species found growing in the oesophagus of our dear late Deputy Chairman?'

'Not yet,' said K'vo.

'Well,' said Pletrov. 'Do let me know the results, once you get them.'

With a little difficulty, he raised himself from the chaise longue, placed his empty tea glass on the bench, and ascended the stairs.

As he opened the front door a gust of wind disturbed the building. A wheezing, groaning sound echoed in the stairwell. It seemed far too loud to be caused only by the wind.

The Master listened. And remembered the square indentation on the bedroom carpet of the Deputy Chair of Ministers. And understood.

'You cunning old goat,' he breathed. 'You devious, scheming weasel.'

'What is this mammal talk?' sighed K'vo, dismissively, relighting the butt of last night's cigar.

'That was him!'

'Who?'

'The Doctor.'

'That old boy with the knees?' laughed K'vo, inhaling. 'Fast cars and velvet? Impossible, darling.'

'It's a disguise. That's one of his things. Actually, it's one of mine. He's what I'd call a gifted amateur.' The Master looked imperiously in the direction of the staircase. 'But he can't do the close work. Now I think of it, the hands weren't quite right. Too young for the face.'

K'vo sucked the last bit of smoke from her cigar and stubbed it out in a petri dish. 'I suppose I'd better do what Colonel Pletrov says,' she said, opening up the specimen cupboard.

As she did so, she noticed a faint orange-green glow. It was coming from the bagged sample taken from the mouth of the Deputy Director.

'Master,' she said. 'Look.'

The Master looked. The flesh of the mushroom had acquired a network of tiny veins. They pulsed with a gentle but distinct luminosity.

'This isn't *Saliota venetatum*,' he frowned. 'What is it?'

K'vo issued a tiny sob of emotion.

'I'm sorry,' she said. 'I've not seen anything like this for, well, for forty million years. They used to give us them as hatchlings. Baked, like little cakes. A treat for if we'd been good. We'd eat them with lime-blossom tea. I remember how the warm liquid mixed with the fungus in your mouth. If you ate them in the dark, you could see a little light coming from behind your teeth.'

'You're sure it's the same species?' asked the Master.

K'vo dipped a talon into the plastic bag, and gave it a cautious lick.

'Unmistakable. As I taste this, I'm back there. In my world.'

The Master thought she might be going to weep.

'Did your people cultivate mushrooms?' he asked.

'Of course,' said K'vo. 'For food and medicine. For pest control. And for war, too. We hollowed out a mountain and grew them there. I went there once. It was like a great cathedral. You went up to the summit on a cable car, and then descended a spiral staircase into its heart. There were clouds of spores flying through the air. Great fluorescent clusters of fruit. It was like going to the bottom of the sea. And they grew so quickly that you could actually hear them – grinding and twisting and expanding. They wouldn't let you stay in there for too long.'

'Because of the toxins?'

'Because it was so beautiful. They thought people wouldn't come out.'

'What about the farmers? The maintenance workers?'

'It was a self-sustaining system. Like our shelters. We built technology to last. And the labour came from young people who'd go and pick the fruit before they went to university. It was a rite of passage. Like national service.'

'Are you telling me,' said the Master, 'that this farm might still be viable?'

K'vo watched the fungus filaments change colour. Red, green, orange. 'Perhaps,' she conceded. 'But how did the spores get from the mountain to Moscow? Into the Kremlin?'

The Master's mind was racing. K'vo had described a great wonder of the reptilian world. And unlike the others she had mentioned from time to time, this one seemed to have persisted into the modern period. He imagined himself scaling the rocks, searching out the entrance, descending into the interior of the mountain, his skin bathed in the phosphorescence of ancient life.

'Where was this mountain, K'vo?'

She took out her notebook, sketched a map of the great supercontinent of Pangea, and added its location with a cross. The Master tore it from her hand and pulled an atlas from the shelf. He spent the morning making furious paper calculations. He spent the afternoon punching sequences of numbers into the Elbrus computer. At seven in the evening he used a Bunsen burner to make a very nice omelette. He had his plain. K'vo augmented hers by lashing out her tongue and catching a fat bluebottle trapped by the window. At nine, the computer concluded its calculations, and produced a long roll of printout.

The Master read it quickly and laughed. 'I know where it is,' he said. 'I know where it is.'

K'vo's third eye pulsed in excitement. 'We should go there,' she said.

'The cold would kill you,' said the Master.

'I could wrap up,' said K'vo.

The Master considered the practicalities. 'We'll tell Major Surikov,' he said. 'We'll need transport. A military helicopter. A small plane, possibly. And climbing equipment, of course.'

'In the morning,' said K'vo.

She got to her feet and moved towards her bedroom door.

'Don't forget to turn out the light when you leave,' she said.

The Master rose, wondering whether he'd missed the last metro to Cheryomushki. As he reached the stairs he flicked the light switch, plunging the laboratory into darkness, except for the line of light under the door to K'vo's quarters. And something else. A gentle orange glow from the cover of the chaise longue.

The Master fell to his hands and knees. The green velvet was flecked with tiny spores. They had been invisible in the daylight, but were now clear and lucent in the gloom. The spores were not spread evenly over the fabric. They were concentrated where their guest from the KGB had spent an hour, drinking tea and making insinuations about his complicity in a murder.

'Oh, my dear Doctor,' he whispered. 'You have been naive.'

The map was so enormous that it draped over the sides of Major Surikov's desk. Much of it was obscured by the body of the Master, whose arm was soaring over the Transhimalaya, marking out a route that skirted Lake Manasarovar, Lake Rakshastal and the great peak of Mount Kailash.

'Tibet!' exclaimed Major Surikov. 'This takes me back.'

'You've been there, Major?' asked K'vo.

'No, not quite. Nearly, though. It's one of the reasons why I'm doing this job. Before the war I was assigned to the Cheka.'

'Never had you down as a secret policeman, Major,' said the Master. 'You're much too nice a fellow.'

'I wasn't one of the thumbscrew brigade, if that's what you mean,' replied Surikov. 'I was in the Special Department. Run by a queer old bird named Gleb Bokii. Gleb had a passion for anything outré. He thought that we could bring down bourgeois capitalism with telepathy.'

'Don't recall that bit of *Das Kapital*,' said the Master.

'Did you read to the end, Mikhail Afanasyevich?' The Master admitted he had not.

'Well don't bother,' he said. 'Marx never mentions telepathy once. Nor does he mention Shambhala.'

The Major left a dramatic pause, as if he hoped someone would ask him what this was. Nobody did. He went on anyway.

'Gleb wanted to find Shambhala,' he explained. 'Shangri-La. The lost utopia on top of a mountain in the Himalayas. He was convinced that it was the first communist civilisation, and that they were still up there, controlling the means of production, living on milk and lotus flowers and surplus value, and singing about it all day long, I shouldn't wonder.'

'Is this correct?' asked K'vo.

'Who knows?' said Surikov, a note of melancholy in his voice. 'We never went. I was an enthusiast at that time. My head was a little turned. And it was different in the twenties. There was no Chairman Mao running around and imposing himself on the lamas. Comrade Stalin had yet to declare war on metaphysics. We were encouraged to be original. Not like now. Everyone's a bootlicker these days.'

The Master moved back as Magda from the canteen bustled in with the tea tray and, to his faint annoyance, laid it down upon the Qing-Zang Plateau.

'So,' said Major Surikov, decisively, 'we know why I want to go on this expedition. But why do you want to go?'

The Master poured the tea from the metal pot.

'Because we need to take the fight to the enemy,' he said. 'He's there. On that mountain. I'm convinced that it's his base of operations. He's using what's inside it against us. Against me.'

Surikov's eyes narrowed. 'And what is inside it?'

'The treasures of the reptile people,' replied the Master. 'And the means to feed our motherland, win the Cold War and bring late-stage capitalism to its final end. Tell him, K'vo.'

'I believe Mikhail Afanasyevich is right,' said K'vo. 'This is the mountain of plenty. The Holy Mountain. Forty million years ago, when reptiles ruled the world and apes knew their place, its fruits fed us throughout the year. But other crops grew there too. Seeds and flesh and juices that were useful in the art of war. They could poison the air or the land. They could poison the mind, too. I recall a violent dispute between my clan and that of the next province. A water war. Each laid claim to the resources of the River Ahn. Our clan won that war without a single burning. We offered them food for the winter, but we spiced it with seeds from inside the mountain. They ate them and forgot the river. Literally forgot it. I remember swimming in the Ahn as a child and calling out to people on the other side. None of them could see I was there.'

The Master was delighted by K'vo's speech. It filled him with a monstrous enthusiasm. It made him feel ambitious and powerful; the way he'd felt when he'd watched that pompous Mr McDermott drown in a plastic armchair, or when he'd stuffed that dull little astrophysicist into his own lunchbox.

He could see that it had wrought a similar effect on the Major.

'Why is it,' said Surikov, as he signed the stack of authorisations brought to him by Captain

Tsybukin, 'that I can never quite say no to you, Comrade Gospodinov?'

'Isn't it obvious?' replied the Master. 'It's because you always make the right decisions.'

The night before the expedition left for Tibet, the Master stood in the kitchen of his flat in Cheryomushki Tower Number Eight, knife in hand. Bone-white forest mushrooms were piled on the Formica worktop. He sliced them speedily, laid them out in a neat blue oven dish, and poured over a sauce made with sweet transparent onions, thick sour cream and a Georgian white wine that was not quite as crisp as he would have liked. As he was putting it in the oven, the doorbell rang.

K'vo was wearing a man's dinner suit, white tie and a cummerbund. She produced Sovnarkhoz champagne from her forensics kit, told the Master to put the bottle in the refrigerator, and settled on the chair nearest to the radiator.

'But why can't I come with you?' she asked.

'Because you're cold-blooded,' he replied, emerging from the kitchen with bowls of olives and unshelled peanuts.

'Oh yeah?' said K'vo, a varnished talon plucking a pimento from the bowl.

'I need you here,' said the Master. 'With the Doctor in Moscow, trying to frame me for murder …'

'He might be on the mountain. In that horse box.'

'Police box.'

'Of course,' said K'vo. 'A horse box! That would be absurd.'

The doorbell rang again.

'Here she is,' said the Master. 'Be nice.'

The Master was concerned that Mrs Pelageya Vlasova would have an adverse reaction to finding a prehistoric lizard woman in his apartment. He need not have worried. She was delighted to make her acquaintance.

'Live and let live, I say,' declared Mrs Pelageya Vlasova. 'I'm a woman of the world. And Margarita is a parrot of the world. Aren't you, Margarita?'

Margarita, perched on the shoulder of her owner, did indeed look entirely untroubled.

'Mrs Pelageya Vlasova,' said the Master. 'It's time for me to be honest with you. You have been a very good neighbour to me, and I think you deserve to be told the truth. I am not a university lecturer. I am engaged in work for the Motherland about which I am not free to speak. But I can reveal my area of expertise. Mushrooms. That's my subject. Well, fungi generally. Lichens. Bloom and blight and rust. Mycelia, to give them their proper name.'

'I like a nice mushroom,' said Pelageya Vlasova. 'Going down to the woods with a basket. Taking them back to dry on the windowsill. Do you know, Mikhail Afanasyevich, this is such a relief to me. I thought you were a counter-revolutionary. A bourgeois objectivist!' She took a gulp of champagne and fanned herself with her hand. 'Are those olives?'

K'vo offered her the bowl.

For the Master, the evening was much more pleasurable than his drinks reception at the Kremlin. K'vo told stories of the prehistoric world. Of the sky chariots and the dinosaur rides and the day she saw a beast called the Myrka – a supposedly monstrous beast bred for war, which the children found cute and wanted to pet. Mrs Pelageya Vlasova spoke of her late husband. Mainly of his faults and infelicities, but she did concede that he had excellent teeth and a beautiful singing voice. The Master got out his guitar, and let his neighbour choose the repertoire. She sang 'The Blue Kerchief', a song from the war about a woman who gives a scarf to her lover who is leaving to fight at the front.

> And even though you're not
> with me today, my dear, my love,
> I know that you still wrap lovingly
> this blue scarf
> around the bedhead . . .

When she got to the end, the Master nodded gently to himself.

'While I'm away in Tibet,' he murmured, 'you two must look after each other.'

The Master's first thought, on being woken up in Tibetan airspace, was how much the topography of the country resembled the map laid out on Major Surikov's desk. Blue-green salt lakes, thick bodies of granite and basalt, wide fields of elevated ice and snow. The pilot of the military cargo helicopter moved skilfully over its peaks and valleys. He was a diplomat as well as an aviation expert: if detected by Peking, their journey would be considered an act of war.

When the helicopter landed, the men from Yedinitza jumped from its open belly and slammed their boots into the ice-bitten tundra. Surikov went first, Captain Tsybukin next. Four troopers followed confidently after. One, Kosygin, carried the extra burden of the radio pack. The Master smarted at his lack of military physicality. Tsybukin helped him from the helicopter like the instructor assisting a first-timer on a pony-trekking trip. Even with the Captain's help, the Master lost his footing on the tussocky ground. The moment did nothing for his dignity, though as he fell he felt grateful to be the only member of the party not carrying a Kalashnikov.

They watched the helicopter disappear into the sky, and turned to face the Holy Mountain.

Its lowest slopes were a verdant meadow, bright with flowers and fast-running streams. These gave way to scree slopes – black cascades of stone, tarnished with moss and lichen. Above these rose the vast squarish bulk of the mountain itself. Its broad body was banded with distinct geological layers. Snow streaked its flanks like wounds of sacrifice. The top was obscured in mist. It was hard to imagine that it had a summit; that it didn't just reach upwards until it met the stars. Major Surikov gazed up in awe.

'The Hindus believe that climbing this mountain will wash away your sins,' said Surikov.

'What are yours, sir?' asked Tsybukin.

'Ask my ex-wife,' returned Surikov. 'She's got them written down in a big book.'

'What about you, Mikhail Afanasyevich?' pushed Tsybukin. 'Have you anything to declare?'

The Master, his eyes on the shrouded heights of the mountain, considered giving Tsybukin a serious answer to the question. But he thought better of it. The moral and intellectual distance between him and these men was a crevasse across which it would be impossible to throw a rope.

'I have many sins,' said the Master. 'Most of them highly original.'

The climb was hard. The air was thin. The combination was overpowering. The Master felt the blood shrieking in his ears. His brain seemed dull and waterlogged. His mouth felt so dry that his lips made the same involuntary movement made by someone sucking a lemon.

Time Lords are not generally susceptible to altitude sickness. The Master was puzzled by his symptoms. He had the sensation that if he looked up at the sky, it might crash down upon him. He felt a tingling on his skin, which he attributed to some force inside the mountain. He also became convinced that someone was following the expedition. Every now and then he saw a flash of red among the rocks; heard something disturb the ground behind them. He remembered that the Doctor owned a red velvet jacket.

He did not share these fears with the other members of his party. Surikov, Tsybukin and the others looked stupidly cheerful. They were in their element, sharing rations from their kit bags, singing army songs, telling jokes to each other.

'Hey,' said Tsybukin. 'Did you hear about that parrot who flew into the Kremlin and started badmouthing the Party? *The KGB is a crochet circle! Brezhnev wears a brassiere!* So our good friend old

Pletrov follows this parrot back home, and he knocks on the door and says, *Good morning, sir, do you by any chance have a parrot?* And the man says: *Yes I do, officer.* And old Pletrov says: *Could we see it?* And the man says: *Certainly, please come in.* And they enter the apartment and the man walks into the kitchen and takes the parrot out of the freezer. It isn't dead, but it's shivering and its teeth are chattering.'

'Parrots don't have teeth, Captain,' said the Kosygin the radio operator.

'It was an egg tooth, you halfwit,' said Tsybukin. 'So – old Pletrov says: *Parrot, what are your views on communism and the Soviet Union?* And the parrot answers: *Long live the Soviet Union, long live the Communist Party!* And Pletrov is puzzled, but he leaves. And once he's gone, the man turns to his parrot and says: *Now that you know what the gulag feels like, will you keep your damn mouth shut?*'

There was general laughter. The Master did not laugh. It was a joke for humans. He was tired. His thoughts refused to clarify. The cold occupied his bones and he sensed its appetite for permanent conquest. There had been moments in the past half-century when he had felt something approaching affection for the Earth people among whom he lived. There was a young mycologist on Sakhalin Island, who strongly reminded him of Josephine Grant. Surikov had been loyal, and not always because hypnotic control had drained away his will – slowly, slowly, like the proverbial frog in a pan of hot water. And Mrs Pelageya Vlasova's small acts of kindness towards him were little landmarks in his long life. Climbing the mountain, however, made him forget those moments. There was just the thin, scratchy air, the searing cold, the inane humour of the Soviet solider released from his normal routines.

He was concerned about the state of his mind. The gathering notes of the opening of Beethoven's Ninth Symphony kept playing in his head. It was not like remembering the music. It was as if his head had become a radio receiver, and he was picking up a transmission from the Bolshoi.

It took three days to reach the plateau. Tents were pitched, food concentrates dissolved in tepid water. Stimulants in glass ampoules were distributed to keep themselves conscious as they trudged onwards and upwards through the almost-vertical wilderness. The Master had little experience of climbing. The ropes confused him. Without the expertise of his companions, he would have died a hundred times. For this, he could summon no gratitude. Nor could he rid himself of his suspicions. Every few hours, he registered the movement of something fast and red, just at the limit of his field of vision. He asked Captain Tsybukin to check his eyes for a burst blood vessel, but the Captain could see nothing.

It was during this examination that the Master saw, over the Captain's shoulder, the object of their search. A monumental door set into the basalt cliff, large enough to drive a tank through. There was a carving in the stone. A face with hooded, heavy eyes, a long fluted mouth, flap-like ears and a third eye sunk in a ridged and crested forehead.

'Gentlemen,' he announced. 'This is why we are here. This is the entrance to the Holy Mountain of *Homo reptilia*.'

'That's your girlfriend,' said Kosygin.

The Master studied the carving. The man had a point. It might have been a portrait of K'vo. It even seemed to have her supercilious expression.

For such a large door, it took surprisingly little effort to open. Seven men pushing created just the right amount of kinetic energy. Its two halves swung inwards, smoothly and soundlessly.

They broke out the head-torches from their kit bags. The Master found himself unable to get the elastic over his head in the correct way. Kosygin the radio operator helped him.

'Ready?' asked Surikov. 'Then let's go inside. Maybe they left the gas on. It'd be good to feel my toes again.'

The party crossed the threshold. The space beyond was ceremonial and industrial. A mosaic on the wall showed a phalanx of reptile people working happily on the harvest. Some were scaling the cave walls on ropes and harnesses, gathering armfuls of polychromatic mushrooms and depositing them in voluminous wicker baskets. Others were depicted in the act of cleaning and processing the fruit. At the far end of the chamber, reptile families were shown tucking into the finished product, which had been prepared in a variety of elaborate ways. It reminded the Master of the mural in the lobby of the Ministry of Agriculture in Moscow, in which a group of flower-decked collective farm workers assembled in a cornfield at the magic hour.

Surikov ordered the Kosygin to remain in the first chamber. The others moved on, into the interior.

It was just as K'vo had described.

They emerged on a stone platform that spanned the vast space of the hollow mountain. In the middle was a spiral staircase that wound its way into the depths below. The Master peered over the edge, and thought of K'vo's remarks about being at the bottom of the sea. She'd chosen the right simile. Motionless shoals of phosphorescent mushrooms fanned out over the rocks. A huge slippery forest of fungi twisted up from the gloomy depths of the cave. Colour pulsed everywhere.

The men descended the staircase. Captain Tsybukin called out to the rocks and listened to the echoes ringing back at him. The Master inhaled. Spores tickled his nose. It was a wonderful feeling. The admirable Major Surikov led, as he always did. Which is why he was the first to see the horrible object that blocked their way. A human corpse in an advanced state of atrophy.

The man had been bound and gagged, presumably while he was still alive. In death, his body had become a garden. His arms and legs sprouted with thin yellow mushrooms. His skull was almost entirely encased in feathery white bioluminescent bracket fungi. Sticky threads of mould draped him like grave clothes.

'Poor devil,' said Surikov. 'How long has he been down here?'

The Master pointed to the man's feet. His boots were exactly like their own. 'I think this is Kosygin,' he said.

There was no time to express their collective horror. They were under attack. The Master looked up to see a reptile man on the stairs above. He was naked and hunched and his scales were a deep shade of scarlet. The reptile man threw his head back and gave a deranged hoot of rage and triumph, then produced a blowpipe from a pouch strapped to his thigh.

Tsybukin was the first to be killed. His hand went to his neck, and found a wooden dart embedded there. Fungi had begun to erupt from his skin before his corpse hit the ground. The reptile man shrieked and howled. The Master saw the three Yedinitza troops fall, Kalashnikovs discharging as they crashed to the ground. Major Surikov was felled by a stray bullet. As he died, he flashed an apologetic look at the Master.

The reptile man raised his blowpipe again. The Master made an instant decision. He leapt from the stone staircase and out into the void of the cavern. Fungi smashed and burst around him as he fell.

He awoke half-submerged in a dense, soft web of fungal mycelia. For a few minutes – or possibly several hours – he lay there in its wet embrace, enjoying the fact that he was alive, and that an insane reptilian hermit was not trying to revise that status. He was also relieved to find that his knapsack was still attached to his back.

He seemed to be at the very bottom of the mountain – or perhaps beneath it, in some womb-like cavern under its base. Fat limbs of fungi and shrouds of thread-like hyphae crowded about him. He struggled to his feet and tried to pick his way carefully across the cave floor, but every step seemed to break a delicate branch of fruiting matter or cause a puffball to explode beneath his feet.

He looked above, to judge how far he had fallen, but something was blocking his view. A large dark body about thirty feet above his head. He'd been staring at it for ten minutes before he realised that it was the underside of the cap of a gigantic mushroom. He could see its gills and the spores lodged within them. The Master determined to climb it, and stand on top.

In that moment, it felt like the most urgent challenge of his life; a religious mission that could not be shirked. He hurried to the foot of the mushroom, which rose above him like the trunk of a Californian Redwood. He opened his knapsack and pulled out his set of pitons and a coil of rope ladder. The mushroom was structured like any other: the volva, like an inverted cup, gave rise to the stem, then the ring-shaped annulus. Above that was the cap, with its radial spread of gills, wide as a cathedral roof. He slapped his first piton into the flesh of the volva and tested it with a foot. It felt secure. He climbed, feeling that this ascent was rather easier than the one he'd made on the other side of the great rock wall. At every stage, the mushroom accepted the blade of his piton with good grace. Traversing the underside of the cap presented more serious difficulty, but the gills offered good sticky footholds, and after a few uncertain moves, the Master was making progress for which a panel of distinguished geckos might have given him straight tens.

By the time he was dragging himself on top of the mushroom, he was hot and breathless. The gently domed expanse of the cap stretched out before him. Its surface was not smooth, but pocked with scales and areolae. The dominant colour was red. And up ahead, in the dead centre of the circle, was a man.

It was not Major Surikov. It was not Captain Tsybukin. He was dressed in a velvet frock coat the colour of a good Beaujolais. A cloak of the same colour flowed all around him, meeting the red flesh of the mushroom.

The Master knew him at once. The beaky nose, the shock of white hair, the face that suggested both great age and boyish sensitivity.

'Hello, my dear fellow,' called the Doctor.

The Master crossed the roof of the mushroom to meet him.

'They're testing experiences, aren't they, these journeys to the mountain?' said the Doctor. 'And in the last few miles, well, you don't know whether it's the exertion that makes you feel so weighed down or the heavy symbolism of it all. But you've got to face your fears, haven't you? What are yours, I wonder?'

The Master was too exhausted to register any shock. Perhaps, he reflected, he'd been expecting this encounter all along. He sat down opposite the Doctor, assuming the same cross-legged posture.

'What if they turned out to be you?' he asked.

'Then I think,' said the Doctor, 'that you'd be very disappointed in yourself.'

They looked into each other's eyes.

'We've come a long way, you and I,' said the Doctor.

'I've come further than you,' replied the Master.

The Doctor peered carefully at him. 'I'll say. Fancy some cheese and biscuits?'

The Master noted that there was now a cheeseboard in the space between them. The Doctor closed his eyes in concentration. The cheeseboard rose into the air.

'You don't need to do that, you know,' said the Master. 'They were just as easy to reach on the ground.'

'Tell me,' said the Doctor, 'what's it like to be exiled in your own past? Does it give you an opportunity to reassess old choices? Or is it just very boring and embarrassing, like re-reading your teenage poetry?'

'It makes me angry,' said the Master, helping himself to something French and deliquescent. 'And then it makes me angrier.'

'Crackers?' said the Doctor

'Totally,' said the Master.

The Doctor took a slice of Gorgonzola, then propelled the cheeseboard gently in the Master's direction. He began to eat.

'This is absolutely marvellous,' he said. 'You must try some.' But the morsel of blue cheese quickly became a source of difficulty rather than pleasure. The Doctor tried to swallow it, but it declined to be swallowed.

'*Penicillium glaucum*,' said the Master. He was concentrating hard. 'Let's see if you are who you say you are.'

The Doctor's hand went to his throat. Blue-green fungal filaments were rushing from his mouth and waving like the fronds of a sea anemone. They surged over his face, transforming it into a mask of twitching matter.

The Master reached forwards, grabbed at the skin under the Doctor's chin, and pulled. It peeled away in his hand. Beneath it was another face, one that he recognised from a solitary journey home after a night out at the cinema. The skin was crumpled and scorched, the eyes two tiny glistening specks. Without the toupee, Comrade Cap looked even worse than before.

'I tried to warn you,' said Comrade Cap. 'Tried to dissuade you. I thought you were interested in money. I suppose that was my mistake.'

'Yes,' said the Master, quietly. 'It was.'

'I couldn't let you do it. Your experiments in the dark under Sakhalin Island. That stuff with *Saliota venetatum*. I have fifth-dimensional contacts, you see. We're everywhere. Our great mutual web stretches in time and well as space. So I knew where all this was leading.' Righteous anger blazed in Comrade Cap's little raisin eyes. 'The great Soviet fungal food revolution,' he sneered. 'Fermentation tanks. Egg albumen. The mass production of mycoprotein. I couldn't let it happen. I couldn't let your utopia be constructed on the bodies of my innocent children. It would have been an atrocity.'

The Master registered the fire in those tiny eyes, and understood. Comrade Cap's comrades were not the citizens of the USSR. They were the subjects of an older kingdom, one whose cities and thrones and powers were administered in the depths of the earth. One his work had offended.

'When did this stop being real?' asked the Master. 'We had our party at the Kremlin, didn't we? I'm still a member of the Order of Lenin?'

'Oh yes,' said Comrade Cap. 'Everything after that point probably shouldn't be trusted. But we couldn't rob you of your gong.'

'We?'

'K'vo and myself,' said Comrade Cap. 'I couldn't have done it without K'vo. She laid the mushroom trail from Sakhalin to Paldiski. She's planted enough evidence to discredit your experiments. And she led you to this place. Built it, in a manner of speaking. In your mind.' Comrade Cap look pityingly at the Master. 'And what a fetid swamp of bitterness and jealousy your mind is. I haven't enjoyed sharing it with you.'

'K'vo?' stammered the Master. 'Why did she do it?'

'She hates the Earth,' explained Comrade Cap. 'Hates what those apes have done to it in her absence. So she's running away with me. I'm taking her to a world where the reptiles still rule.'

The Master was speechless with sorrow. He bowed his head. Then he felt a weight land on his shoulder. He turned his head to see Margarita, her plumage blood-red, her eyes yellow and intelligent.

'You're going to die inside the Holy Mountain,' said Comrade Cap, with measured clarity. 'The Holy Mountain inside your own head. You're going to die now. I'm ordering you to do it. And so is this very beautiful parrot.'

'You will obey me,' said Margarita.

Spring was coming to Moscow. You could feel it in the air. You could hear it as the last of the ice shifted in the trees and fell as water. But Mrs Pelageya Vlasova felt no joy. She often wept in secret, a long and bitter weeping. She wept for love, of course, and because she did not know who it was she loved: a living man or a dead one? And the longer the desperate days went on, the more often, especially at twilight, did the thought come to her that she was bound to a dead man. She had either to forget him or to die herself. It was impossible to drag on with such a life. But he would not be forgotten, that was the trouble.

She dried her eyes and thought of the last time she had seen Mikhail Afanasyevich, and had to dry them again. It was the morning he had rung her doorbell, and she had been so flustered and delighted that she forgot to worry about not wearing any make-up. She had eaten his gift of pastry with pleasure, making it last, savouring it slowly throughout the day. Its cardboard box remained on her coffee table. It had become the locus of her fears, and of one in particular – that Mikhaïl Afanasyevich was in grave trouble, or possibly the grave itself.

On that last night, she had not intercepted her neighbour as she normally did, because he returned unexpectedly early. By the time she realised that he was back, he was no longer alone. She heard the sound of a party and smelt the aroma of something good in the oven. Shortly after midnight, another guest rang the bell, and joined them. Beethoven's Ninth Symphony went on the record player, too loudly for such an hour, as if to mask some other sound. At about 2am, everything had fallen silent. Everything except Mrs Pelageya Vlasova, who let out a long and quite unstoppable moan of disappointment.

The following day, she saw nobody leave or enter the apartment. But it was not empty. She had heard low voices, then sobbing. Once, when she pressed a vodka glass to the wall, she detected the rattle of thick and troublesome breathing.

At midday she practised a speech about having more asparagus than she could cook, and would Mikhail Afanasyevich care to take the surplus? At two o'clock she rang the bell, and received no answer. At three o'clock she rang again.

'I've got the key,' said Mrs Pelageya Vlasova, turning over the copy she had cut at the heel bar the previous week. 'But I can't go in there. What am I to do, Margarita?'

Margarita shifted on her perch. She seemed at a loss for words.

Mrs Pelageya Vlasova decided to act.

'I'm not doing this on my own,' she said, coaxing Margarita onto her shoulder. Pelageya Vlasova took the key from her housecoat pocket and, heart thumping, went to the door of her neighbour's flat, inserted the key and pushed open the door. After which, she clapped her hand to her mouth in horror.

Mikhail Afanasyevich Gospodinov was sitting at his dining table. His hands were taped to the chair. The plastic floral tablecloth was in a state of disarray. Broken chunks of mushroom littered its glossy surface. Somebody, she realised, had been force-feeding him. The apartment was also in a state of disarray. Dirty washing, empty bottles and tins of food were thrown carelessly on the floor. Red wine and a bowl of salted peanuts had been spilled.

Immobile at the dining table, Mikhail Afanasyevich did not register the presence of his neighbour. His breathing was fast and shallow and his bloodshot eyes were fixed on the middle distance. He was pulling and pursing his lips, as if his mouth were painfully dry. His unshaven skin looked raw, and there was a red mark on his face where someone had scratched him.

Pelageya Vlasova knelt by the chair and tried to unpeel the tape. Margarita kept her place on her shoulder.

'What's happened to you, Mischa? Oh my Mischa!' Pelageya Vlasova ran to the kitchen and poured a glass of water, but her neighbour seemed unable to drink it. It spilled uselessly down his face.

'Who did this?' she wailed. 'Who did this?'

Margarita fluttered down to the tablecloth. The Master opened his eyes and watched the parrot pick her way across the patterned plastic. The eyes of Mrs Pelageya Vlasova, however, were fixed on her neighbour's bedroom doorway, which was occupied by the most alarming sight she had ever witnessed.

Two figures. One was a six-foot tall reptile in a tightly tailored man's suit and a platinum blonde wig. It had long painted talons and its ribbed, flute-like mouth was filled with a large Cuban cigar. Standing beside the reptile was something very like a man. It was wearing a knitted jumper, corduroy trousers and cheap black plastic shoes. For a moment Pelageya Vlasova took it be an inanimate object. A puppet or a scarecrow, something assembled from the day's unsold vegetables by the unloved son of a greengrocer.

Then it spoke. 'Got your own key, have you?' it rasped, nastily. 'Very progressive.'

Mrs Pelageya Vlasova had led a sheltered life. Her father had treated her like a baby even when she was in her teens and twenties. She felt ashamed of that selfish girl who had demanded sugar mice even when the Motherland was facing ruin and destruction. She was also doubtful about the woman who married Mr Ivan Ivanovich Vlasova, a man as boring as his name, who tried and failed to maintain the precedents established by her father.

In this moment, however, Pelageya was bright with plain and serious purpose. She reached under the dining table. There, exactly as she had left it, was the little metal device stowed by her neighbour. She tore it from its place and directed it at the two figures in the bedroom door, pressed the trigger button and fired.

The little machine screamed.

A burst of white light engulfed the room.

Margarita flapped across the dining table, scared and disorientated.

The eyes of Mikhail Afanasyevich Gospodinov darted around the room.

Pelageya Vlasova looked down to the carpet and saw what she expected to see. Two six-inch, doll-like objects; the miniaturised corpses of the monsters who had been torturing her neighbour. She put the little machine on the dining table, fetched a knife from the kitchen and cut through the cuffs of tape around his wrists.

His eyes opened, but he seemed not to know where he was. He struggled to his feet, muttering and twitching, then slumped forwards into Pelageya Vlasova's arms.

'It's all right, Mischa,' she cooed. 'I'll look after you now.'

Slowly and laboriously, Pelageya Vlasova manoeuvred her neighbour across the hallway and into her flat. By the time she was lifting his legs onto her bed, his eyes were closed again.

Pelageya Vlasova knelt by the bedside and watched him sleep until the sunlight had faded from the room. Then she returned to the flat next door. She swept up olive stones and peanut shells, tidied the empty bottles and wiped down the kitchen work surfaces. She stooped to pick up the little grey man and the shrunken lizard in its smart eveningwear and Marlene wig, and took them home to inspect. The lizard, she concluded, would look good on her mantelpiece. Its companion, however, was not quite so pleasing to the eye. She turned it over between her fingers. She tore off its little corduroy trousers and knitted sweater. Nakedness revealed its true nature. It was like a mushroom. A twisted, harmless mushroom.

She raised it to her face and inhaled. The scent of the woodland filled her nostrils. It was the smell of carefree childhood summers. Pelageya Vlasova felt invigorated. She was seized with a strange joy that she had not felt since she was six years old. That night, she collected a few handfuls of soil from the communal garden in front of the block, placed it in an old ice-cream tub, planted the mushroom and stowed it in her airing cupboard. She even wished it goodnight as she closed the door.

The Master spent two weeks convalescing in the bed of Mrs Pelageya Vlasova. He did not come down from the Holy Mountain until the end of the first. He talked heedlessly about blowpipes and cave-monsters and fungus under the skin.

Sometimes he was kind. Sometimes he was mad. He kept pressing at his cheeks and neck, and asking whether anything was pushing its way through.

His hostess obliged him to consume fruit compote and sugary drinks. She fed him chocolates and calcium tablets and slept on the hard cramped space of the sofa, and was happy.

On the eighth day, the Master suddenly remembered where he was. He held out his hand and asked Margarita to come to him. She did.

'I am the Master,' he told her, 'and you will obey me.'

On the thirteenth day, when he was strong enough to walk around the flat a little and concentrate on a news report about the Sino-Vietnamese war, Mrs Pelageya Vlasova heard someone ring the bell of her neighbour's apartment. She peered through the spyhole and saw a middle-aged man in a smart black raincoat.

She went out into the hallway and asked him what he wanted. He explained that he was looking for an employee who had failed to come into work. It was clear that he was not permitted to say more.

'I wish I could tell you where he was,' said Mrs Pelageya Vlasova. 'I didn't know him very well, of course, but he was always very polite when I met him on the stairs. I suppose he must have found a job in another town.'

Major Surikov supposed she was right, thanked her for her time, and stepped into the lift. As the doors closed, he said: 'Please don't go anywhere for the next few weeks. We may want to interview you.'

When she returned to her apartment, Pelageya Vlasova found her patient on his feet, looking in the mirror. 'I know who that was,' he said, inspecting his hair and teeth. 'Please forgive me, but I need to go next door.'

Pelageya Vlasova watched him disappear into his own apartment. She knew what was coming. She heard him opening drawers and removing books from the bookshelves; listened to the distant buzz of his electric razor; did her very best not to weep. Half an hour later he was at her door in a thick woollen overcoat, a suitcase beside him on the floor.

'Mrs Pelageya Vlasova,' he began. 'I have lived many lives. I have been a sinner. I have been cruel. I have caused pain, and delighted in it. No priest could ever absolve me of the things I have done. No psychiatrist could ever reform me.'

'I don't care,' said Mrs Pelageya Vlasova, in a small, hopeless voice.

'And neither do I,' returned the Master. 'Not one bit. And that is the point I'm trying to make.'

'But you must, Mischa,' she said. 'You must care just a little bit.'

'No,' said the Master, firmly.

'Then why are you leaving?'

The Master gave her a withering look.

'I'll tell you why. Because that man is going to come back,' said Pelageya Vlasova. 'And if he finds you here, then we'll both be sent to the gulag. And that's why you're leaving. To save me.'

The Master felt a flash of contemptuous anger. But in that moment, he realised that she was right.

He picked up his suitcase.

He smiled and bowed.

He called the lift and stepped through its doors.

Mrs Pelageya Vlasova went to the window, and watched him leave the lobby and cross the boulevard. The cherry blossom was in full bloom, and its pink and white clouds made it hard to follow his progress. That, and the tears pooling in her eyes. She let them fall. They consoled her.

She heard a sound in the room behind her, and turned, expecting to see Margarita scratching at the furniture. But Margarita was still and quiet on her perch.

The noise came again. A soft tapping on wood. It was coming from the airing cupboard. Something was pushing open from inside. A pseudopodia of fungus that poured out like miraculous porridge in a children's story and moved in her direction with a thick, insistent motion. She could now see that its foremost part possessed bundles and bumps of matter like a human face. Then two black raisin-like eyes emerged, and Mrs Pelageya Vlasova realised that she was watching the rebirth of Comrade Cap.

'I have only one thing to say to you,' spat Comrade Cap in his hoarse and charmless voice. 'Look at your mantelpiece, you sad, stupid fool.'

She looked. And saw instantly that the shrunken body of the reptile woman K'vo had been removed from its place, and packed, presumably, in her neighbour's suitcase.

'He doesn't love you,' said Comrade Cap. 'You're ridiculous.'

The mushroom gave a low chuckle, then surged over the room, smearing himself over the paintwork, the doors and the windows, until the flat was robbed of all its light.

The sun was out. Boys were playing football under the trees. An optimistic ice cream vendor had set up his stand on the grass. The Master inhaled the scent of the blossom, put down his suitcase and purchased a small vanilla cone.

'Off on your travels, comrade?' asked the ice cream man.

'Yes,' said the Master.

'I hear the Baltic coast is beautiful in the springtime.'

'I was there a few weeks ago,' said the Master. 'But it was a work thing, you know?'

The boys under the trees had lost interest in their ball and were clustering around the stand. The Master bought ice cream for everyone.

Did the Doctor, he wondered, have moments like this? Did he walk through Hyde Park, enjoying a warm spring day? Or did all his recreations involve motor oil and patronising people? Perhaps, thought the Master, the Doctor's exile to Earth, though shorter, had never been free of anger and dismay. The Doctor had tolerated UNIT and the Brigadier. His companions had been forced upon him by officialdom or circumstance. He had chosen nothing. The Master's case was different. He had followed his desires and had awoken them in others. The Major had adored him like a sheepdog loves the shepherd. Pelageya Vlasova had made him dinner every night; an office that nobody in the universe had ever performed. K'vo had betrayed him, but she had done so by forming an alliance with an alien invader. Her treachery had been an act of tribute. He could not hate her for it. Quite the opposite. Which is why she was now packed in his suitcase, among his shirts and socks and shaving equipment.

The Master bought a paper ticket from the machine at Cheryomushki station. He was just about to feed it into the barrier when he noticed a familiar figure standing by the newspaper kiosk. Old Pletrov of the KGB, buying tobacco. The Master had been relatively carefree as he walked from his flat to the metro, but the sight of Pletrov changed his mood. He registered a ripple of shame, remembering the morning he had convinced himself that the intelligence officer with the bad knees was the Doctor in disguise.

Pletrov lingered at the kiosk window, making up his pipe. When it was lit, he left the station and began walking along the boulevard in the direction of Tower Number Eight. The Master felt himself reglaciating. He thought of Mrs Pelageya Vlasova, up in her apartment, her head buzzing with sentimental feelings about him, and – much more worryingly – detailed knowledge about his recent ordeals.

Why had he allowed himself to be compromised by her tenderness? It was out of character. It was embarrassing. He felt the tissue compression eliminator purr gently in the pocket of his overcoat, and resolved to return to the apartment and kill her. Old Pletrov too. He was slow on his feet. The Master could easily overtake him and lie in wait for him on the landing. No questions would be asked, no answers received.

Neither man, however, reached the block.

At first, the Master thought he had heard the opening thunderclap of a spring thunderstorm. Then he realised that he was witnessing a catastrophe. The Cheryomushki tower that had been his home was in freefall before his eyes. He could see the concrete crumbling and fragmenting in the air; hear the squeal of steel bones bending and breaking. Debris streamed downwards like a mushroom cloud in reverse, roaring down the boulevard and tearing through the cherry trees. Grit and gravel and plaster and blossom boiled in the air. Old Pletrov was consumed by it. The Master threw himself to the ground to save his eyes, and hoped he would not choke. Screams rang out down the concrete streets, then sirens.

The Master was unused to being caught up in chaos and destruction. Generally, he liked to be the cause of it, and enjoy the results from a safe distance. But events overtook him. He allowed the medics to check him over, wrap him in a blanket, supply him with a paper cup of sweet black tea. It was while he was drinking this, perched on the pavement, that he saw Margarita the parrot, blanched by the dust, fluttering down to greet him.

The parrot settled on his shoulder. The Master was pleased to see her.

'You are real, aren't you?' he asked, as she rubbed her beak into his beard. 'You're not some mushroom dream?'

Margarita did not answer.

The Master rose to his feet, and walked, a little unsteadily, towards the broken body of the tower block. Ambulance crews were dressing wounds and applying splints to broken arms and legs. Firefighters were digging in the rubble to look for survivors, and not finding them. Could Mrs Pelageya Vlasova have survived? It seemed impossible. The rescue work was futile.

How human, thought the Master, to keep on working, when all was lost.

'Don't look,' said Margarita.

'I won't, little bird,' he said.

They went on together, into the spring afternoon.

'You're a long way from home, Margarita,' said the Master. 'Why don't I take you back there? I should like to see the Amazon.'

With a rush of red feathers, the parrot lifted herself into the air.

The Master followed.